READY
FOR YOU

BY SAMANTHA LEIGH

Valentine Bay Series
Ready For You

SAMANTHA LEIGH

Dedication

To those first readers who took a chance on my debut.
You know who you are. Thank you.

1

EMILY

"HEY, NEW GIRL."

I was on my knees on the wooden floor of Valentine Bay's one and only yoga studio, rolling up my mat and debating whether to order single-serve takeout for the third night in a row, when the woman who ran the class called out across the room.

I looked over my shoulder, then up at her. "Me?"

She chuckled and bounced towards me. "Yeah, you. Emily, right?"

I stood and shook the hand she offered. "Yes, Emily Jones. Nice to meet you."

Be cool, Emily. Don't say anything stupid. If you want a new life that includes new friends, you have to talk to someone other than yourself.

The woman was a blonde, bronzed goddess, so perfectly put together that the sheen of perspiration

1

on her forehead made her look glowing and gorgeous, while I stood there no taller than her chin feeling short and sweaty and gross.

"Abbie Ellison," she said. "You're new to Valentine Bay, aren't you? You've been in twice a week for the last six weeks, so you're not just passing through."

I tucked a piece of my hair behind my ear, still surprised it stopped short enough to leave the nape of my neck bare. "I moved into a little apartment on Cockle Street a couple of months ago."

Abbie cocked her head. "Just you?"

I flushed and scrunched up my shoulders. "Just me."

"Hm. You look like you could use a drink, Emily Jones. Feel like meeting a friend and me for margaritas later?"

"Yes! I mean, sure. That sounds like fun."

She grinned. "And you sound like my kind of girl."

And that's how three hours later at eight o'clock on a Friday night, I was hovering outside The Salty Stop wearing the second-best dress I owned, feeling like my entire future hinged on how well things went in the next two hours. The pressure to get it right was as heavy as if I were going on a blind date.

No. Given what I'd been through in the last three months, it was weightier than that. I was a twenty-six-year-old single woman trying to make friends. The stakes were much higher.

I pushed on the heavy timber door of Valentine Bay's best pub and walked into a friendly cacophony of live music, weekend conversation, and the *clink-clink* of cutlery and glasses. I stood just inside the doorway, told myself I was imagining the press of eyes on me, and scanned the place for Abbie. The venue was all polished timber, industrial metal, exposed brick, and moody lighting, and I didn't spot her straightaway, but then she jumped up and waved wildly at me from a booth towards the back. I smiled and snaked my way over.

"Here," Abbie said, pushing an empty salt-rimmed margarita glass at me as I slid into the booth, then filling it from an enormous jug that sat at the centre of the table. "Have one of these."

"Thanks." I'd never had a margarita before, so I took a tentative sip while flicking a glance at the third person in the booth. Swallowing and choking back a little cough, I set the glass down and gave Abbie a small smile. "Delicious."

"The guy who owns this place—Will—makes the best margaritas, and they're bottomless, so don't be shy."

Abbie gestured at the person sitting beside her, a woman dressed in slightly creased but neat office clothes already halfway through a margarita of her own. "This is Jessica."

I reached over and shook her hand. "Nice to meet you. I'm Emily."

"Hello. It's lovely to meet you too." Jessica slid her black-framed glasses higher up her nose as her chocolate brown eyes slid away from me before darting back again. I glanced over my shoulder to see what had distracted her.

And what I found were three men. Three *beautiful* men huddled at the bar with frothy amber beers in front of them, laughing and shoving each other with the easy humour of old friends. The bartender joined them, grinning and handing over fresh drinks, and then there were four. A quick check of the pub revealed I wasn't the only one checking them out.

"Jess, don't torture yourself." Abbie topped up Jessica's glass and put the cocktail in her hand. Jess threw it down her throat.

"Do you know them?" I asked.

Jess sniffled, and Abbie patted her hand. "We went to school together," she replied, pointing as she spoke. "Pretty boy behind the bar is Will Kidd. Owns this place. Good guy, but don't fall for the dimple. I'll introduce you later." Her finger shifted a little. "The one closest to us, with the black beard, big arms, and bigger laugh, is Isaac Greene. Cop. Another good guy. I'll introduce you later. Next to him, the brooding blond with all the shoulders, is Joshua Ford. Paramedic. Also a good guy. Probably *won't* introduce you later. And the one on the end is Luca Rossetti."

I waited a beat for more information—wondering as much about the mysterious Luca Rossetti as why I wasn't going to meet Josh—but Abbie picked up her drink, making it clear that was all I was going to get. I looked at Jess, who twisted her empty glass around by the stem and stared at the water ring it left on the table.

I was missing something. Something big, if my instincts were right. Would asking for details make me seem nosy? Would *not* asking give Abbie and Jess the impression

4

I didn't care? I followed their examples and slurped my margarita. Best to start with the less obvious question.

"So, meeting Josh … Bad idea?"

"No, not exactly," Abbie said with a sigh and a toss of her hair. "You can meet him. I'm only trying to save myself an argument. The man doesn't date, and he'll be grumpy as fuck if he thinks I'm trying to set him up."

I stole a look at the blond guy with the curls. And the shoulders. And the sweet smile. He was hot enough to be a Hemsworth, and he looked pleasant enough to me, relaxed and joking as much as everyone else. I wondered why Abbie called him brooding and why he didn't date. I was about to ask when the conversation got away from me.

"Can I tell her?" Abbie muttered, throwing me a conspiratorial wink as she refilled Jess's glass, and Jess chuckled under her breath.

"You might as well. She's bound to find out sooner or later."

"Don't I know it." Abbie crossed her arms on the table and leaned towards me. "Jess and Luca were together for —what? Seven years?" Jess nodded morosely and took a sip. "Three years ago, he got a job in Sydney and moved out of the Bay, so they broke up, not wanting to do the long-distance thing. We hardly saw him after that, until a couple of months ago, when he moved back—"

"With his *girlfriend*," Jess finished with a sigh.

A raucous laugh went up at the bar, and I turned in time to see dark-haired Isaac with his head thrown back, his mates chuckling and shaking their heads around him.

I looked back at Jess, knowing the exact brand of pain she was in. "I'm sorry, Jess. That's tough." I worried at my bottom lip, contemplating how hard to push. Snoopy versus supportive ... Ah, to hell with it. I knocked back my drink. Gossip was essential to good friendships, wasn't it?

"So," I said. "Luca's not one of the good guys?"

A self-deprecating laugh escaped Jess's lips. "No, he is. That's what makes it so hard." She gazed over at her ex. "Luca's the best."

As if he'd heard her say his name, Luca turned our way. Abbie glued a dazzling, over-the-top smile on her face and waved with her whole arm, and after Luca tipped his chin and raised a hand to say hello, he quickly turned back to his friends.

Abbie sighed. "We're still in love with him."

"We?" I asked.

"I use the royal *we*, of course. I don't do love." Abbie shimmied her shoulders in an exaggerated shudder.

"You don't do love?" I echoed, both intrigued and horrified by her confession.

"I'm a free spirit." Abbie tilted her perfect little nose up in the air. "A purveyor of good times and great lovers. I have a motto and everything. A man—"

"Is for now, not forever," Jess finished.

"Exactly."

"So, you don't date?" I asked, refilling my glass.

Abbie tilted her head and squinted up at the ceiling. "Define date." I opened my mouth, and she laughed. "No need. It doesn't matter. Here's the thing. I have no interest in love or marriage or *babies*, but I don't want to die old and alone either. So, I'm going to tell you a secret. Swear you'll never tell anyone."

I crossed my fluttering heart and raised my hand. "I don't know anyone to tell, but I promise. Not a word."

"Valentine Bay's a small town. Stick with us, and you'll have people knocking on your door swapping cups of sugar for spilled tea in no time. But I trust you, Em—can I call you Em? You have an honest face and eyes for days, but enough about you. Here's the deal. I have an arrangement with playboy Will over there. Neither of us wants the boring life of school lunches and couples' bowling, so we've made a pact to grow old together while seeing other people. Mum loves him, and as long as he and I are *a couple*"—she said the words with air quotes—"she stays out of my hair. Will's my get-out-of-marriage-free card."

I schooled my face to stillness. "That's ... clever?"

Abbie slurped her cocktail and grinned. "Isn't it?"

"You just haven't met the one yet," Jess replied, but when Abbie groaned, Jess threw up her hands. "Okay, okay. We won't get into that tonight. I can't be bothered, and after all the drama I've been through with Luca, maybe you've got it right after all."

Abbie clutched her chest. "I never thought I'd live to hear you say that."

Jess dropped her head in her hands. "Me neither."

"Anyway!" Abbie shifted her body to give me her full attention. "Your turn."

My gaze flitted to the door, and it didn't go unnoticed.

"Come on!" Abbie picked up the margarita jug and refilled all our glasses. "We're only two drinks in. The night is young, and so are you. You look twenty-five, maybe twenty-six? We want to know more about Emily Jones."

"I'm twenty-six," I mumbled, hoping they'd leave it at that.

"Cool. We're twenty-eight." Abbie put her elbows on the table and clasped her hands together. "What else?"

I stared into my glass, then took a big gulp. *You knew a fresh start wouldn't be easy.*

Taking a deep breath, I blew it out and said his name before I chickened out. "Tyler Banks."

"Who's that?" Jess asked. She looked over at Luca, then back to me, and the effort it took her to focus on the conversation was obvious.

I cleared my throat. "He is—was—my fiancé. We, uh, were supposed to get married last December, but then he, well, he said I wasn't *the one*"—I screwed up my nose as I recalled the way he'd used those exact words—"and so, three days before I was supposed to say I do, I was calling the caterer instead, and the florist, and ... I had to cancel my dress and return the engagement ring ..." I choked back a sob.

"Oh, hey now." Abbie came around to my side of the booth, sat next to me, and wrapped an arm around my shoulders. "He's obviously an idiot. Class-A jerk."

"Absolutely," Jess agreed, scooting closer on my other side and rubbing my back. "Any man who waits until three days before your wedding to cancel it … Well, what a scumbag."

I ducked my head and wiped my nose with the back of my hand, nodding my thanks as they called Tyler perfectly reasonable things, like "moronic prick" and "heartless dick".

"Oh, hey, Rossetti," Abbie said, and I sensed more than saw someone standing over us. I snatched up a napkin and blotted my eyes before glancing up.

Luca stood there, looking tall, dark, and uncomfortable. "Hey, Ellison. Hi, Jess."

"Hello," Jess murmured, tucking her shoulder-length, ash-brown waves behind her ears. She couldn't take her eyes off him, and I couldn't blame her. Luca was yummy.

"You guys leaving already?" Abbie asked.

I checked the bar, but the group of very handsome men was no more. Instead, Will served customers with a wink and a grin. The one with inky hair, Isaac, stood at the door, grinning and waving at us as he waited for Luca. Josh was nowhere to be seen.

"Yeah. Ford and Greene are working tomorrow." Then he smiled at me and offered a hand. "These girls have no manners. I'm Luca. Pleasure to meet you."

"Emily," I replied, shaking his hand. "Nice to meet you, too."

Luca glanced over his shoulder at Isaac, who yawned theatrically, covering his open mouth with a fist, and Luca ran a hand over his dark hair. "Guess I should get going. Good to see you, Jess."

"You, too," she replied in a cracking whisper.

Luca seemed to sense that Jess was about to lose it, so he backed away and headed straight for the door. As I watched Luca and Isaac leave, I glimpsed Josh waiting outside on the street. Then the door closed, and they were gone.

2

JOSH

———————

THE BELL CHIMED as I opened the coffee shop door, and Old Tony behind the counter beamed at me. "Josh! You're back!"

I felt, rather than saw, all eyes land on me, and I considered turning and making a run for it, but the aroma of fresh coffee drew me in. Scanning the place for the usual offenders and spotting only one do-gooder who might give me trouble, I dropped my eyes and headed straight for Tony. If I could get in and out of there without dealing with Dawn Linley, I'd chalk up the entire day as a success.

"Morning, Tony. Yeah, I got home yesterday. Coffee?"

Tony nodded, already prepping my regular order. He probably would have liked to chat—and I would have liked to humour him—but he knew the heat I'd get if I stayed still too long, so he kept it short.

"Fishing again?"

I nodded.

"Catch anything?"

Shrugging uncomfortably, I shook my head. "No bites."

I hadn't really gone fishing. I didn't even like fishing. I told people that's where I went because everyone seemed to think it was an acceptable reason for a twenty-eight-year-old guy to disappear for days—sometimes weeks—at a time. I didn't get it, but I was glad everybody else did because I had no intention of telling the truth.

I thought of the apartment in the city I'd been staying in on and off for the last six months. I'd been renting a room to get a feel for it—exposure therapy to acclimate myself to a life outside Valentine Bay—and I was almost ready to say goodbye for good. Almost.

I blinked the sting from my eyes, and Tony pretended not to notice as he pushed a cardboard coffee cup across the counter. "I'll add it to your tab."

Clearing my throat, I gave Tony a grateful smile. "Thanks. I owe you one."

I spun around, thankful I'd managed to avoid Dawn, and found her standing in my way. Jerking back to save her from a gush of hot coffee, I bit back a curse. Like always, she wore layers of brightly coloured clothes, so many that I wondered if she walked around town draped in everything she owned. Today, her long blonde hair had beaded braids along the front.

I liked Dawn, but in small doses, and I had to force myself to smile down at her. "Morning, Dawn. How are you?"

"Good morning, Josh. I'm great, and you? How was your trip?"

"It was fine. Relaxing. Refreshing. You know."

"You were gone a while." When I just nodded, she went on. "Off to work now, are you?"

"This afternoon, actually, so I really can't stay and talk."

"How's the job? Enjoying it?"

I frowned. I'd been a paramedic for four years, and it wasn't like Dawn to dance around like this. We were thirty seconds into a conversation, and she hadn't mentioned my love life. My hackles rose. She was up to something.

"It's going well, as always." I shrugged. "It's important work."

Dawn smiled, but her eyes were sad, and I had to swallow the lump in my throat. "Glad to hear it," she replied. "You're very good at it, and you've got such a big heart."

"Mm. Well, it was nice to talk to you, but I've got to get going." I tried to step around her, but she shadowed me, and I stopped.

"I have a little favour to ask you," she said. "I wouldn't ask if I didn't have to."

"I don't have a lot of time right now. I'm working extra hours this week. You know how it is."

"Yes, yes." Dawn pinched my elbow and dragged me to the side of the coffee shop. The other customers watched us, then bent their heads together, and I sighed.

"Really, I have to go. Could you get to the point?"

"It's about a girl."

I tensed up. "I'm not interested."

13

This was why it was time to leave Valentine Bay. No matter how many times I'd said it, people like Dawn couldn't take the hint. The only answer was to make a fresh start in a place far from here, where people would look at me without seeing my past. I relaxed my muscles with effort.

"It's not like that," Dawn soothed. "She's new in town. Been here six weeks, and I only met her last Tuesday. Can you believe it? She's renting that tiny flat on Cockle Street and keeps to herself mostly, but she was in the shop last week. Pretty thing, and nothing of her. So tiny I could have put her in my pocket. And just browsing, didn't buy anything, but she was there for, oh, at least fifteen minutes. It was hard work getting a word out of her, but it *did* come up that she was single, and I thought to myself, I know! I'll see if Josh has time to show her the sights."

I'd started to glaze over, but at the last comment, I had to grin. "The sights?" I asked. "Dawn, this is Valentine Bay. What do you want me to show her? The potholes on Main Street? The garden benches in Pearl Road Park?" She huffed, and I chuckled. "The smoky remains from last week's bonfire on the beach?" Dawn crossed her bony arms, and I sighed. "The answer's no."

"Her name is—"

"Nope, don't want to know."

She pursed her lips, then opened them again to say more, but I glared until she flung up her hands. "Fine. Fine! Forget it. And how's your dad today? Jack's been scarce while you were gone, but Maz checked in on him."

Dawn was at least fifteen years older than me, and

14

after my mother died, she became one of my half-a-dozen surrogate aunts. Maryanne "Maz" Diaz, who lived on my street, was another. They kept as close an eye on my dad as they did on me, the town's tragic bachelor duo, and it helped to know that if I left the Bay—*when* I left the Bay—he'd have plenty of well-meaning busybodies watching out for him. It didn't resolve my guilt completely—I'm not sure anything could—but it was something.

My mother died nearly fifteen years ago, and while I remembered every little thing about her, Dad didn't like to reminisce. I knew the pain memories caused him, so I never asked questions. He'd taught me a lot about grief. The way it stopped life in its tracks. The way it hung around, hiding as much in plain sight as it did in the shadows. The way shutting down and switching off were the only options for reprieve.

The way it stopped you from moving forward unless you found a way to leave it behind.

"He's fine. Thanks for asking." I gave Dawn's upper arm a quick squeeze to let her know I appreciated her concern. "Good talking to you, as always."

"If you change your mind about—"

"I won't!" I called over my shoulder, taking three long strides towards the door.

Free at last, I powered up Main Street as if Dawn were on my heels, taking a cautious sip of my coffee and finding it a little too warm to slurp. I squinted out at the surf and pulled out my phone to check the time. I had four hours to myself. Plenty of time to collect my board and—

I turned the corner and ran straight into someone, the coffee in my hand exploding on impact. Yelping as hot liquid spilled over my hand, I hopped around as my legs tangled in the leads the other person held. She squealed too and danced with me as the coffee poured down the front of her shirt. Huffing and screeching, she tried to shake the leads free from my legs without losing hold of her ... piglets?

"Ouch!" she gasped, tripping a little as the pigs pulled on their tethers. "Oh, no! I'm so sorry."

"No, no. It's my fault." I tugged my legs free and stepped back, only then seeing how badly the coffee had drenched her clothes. "Oh, shit. Look at you. Are you burned? Does it hurt?"

I stretched out a hand to check the skin beneath the stain, but she drew back, and I felt my neck burn red. First, because my medical response instincts had kicked in and I'd tried to examine her without asking. And second, because the liquid had now well and truly soaked through, turning the thin white fabric of her shirt transparent and slicking it to her chest. "Uh, I'm sorry."

I met her eyes. They were pale green, wide and uncertain. She had pretty features—creamy, sun-kissed skin over high cheekbones, and pink, pillowy lips—framed by short, dark hair that gave her an elfin look. She smelled delicious, like vanilla and sugar—and, of course, coffee.

A pretty blush rose in her cheeks, and her arm jerked as the piglets tugged. There were only three of them, and they really weren't that big, but she was so tiny I worried they might tip her over.

"Are you sure it doesn't hurt?" I asked. "I'm a paramedic. I can check it for you."

I glanced at her chest again, and she pulled at the shirt, trying to detach it from her skin. I noticed the khaki skirt then, stopping mid-thigh to reveal smooth, shapely legs, and the coordinated khaki logo on the clean side of her shirt. It read "Dr Hobbes' Veterinary Clinic".

"You work here?" I asked. The girl looked around as if she thought that by *here*, I meant *on the street*. "I mean, here in Valentine Bay," I added. "You work at Summer's clinic?" I sounded like an idiot.

"Oh! Yes."

"Are you sure? I don't think I know you."

"Yes, I'm *sure*." She drew an arm across her chest to cover the wet stain.

I smiled at her attitude. "I mean, I've lived here all my life, and I've never seen you before. That doesn't happen often around here unless someone's passing through."

She squinted up at me, a crease between her brows. "I moved here six weeks ago, and Dr Hobbes gave me a position at the front desk."

I grinned and nodded at the piglets. "Is your job title *pig whisperer*?"

She rewarded me with a small smile before looking down the street towards the clinic and back at me as though nervous about sharing a secret. "Summer's fantastic, but she asks me to do the oddest things. Walking piglets is the least of it. Last week it was cats. The week before that, a turtle. I couldn't do it! I carried the little guy to the park and waited until I was alone before spending half an hour leading him a dozen steps. The only thing I *haven't* walked since I've been here is a dog." She leaned in and whispered, "Is she having me on?"

I grinned wider. "Summer's just like that. She'd walk them herself if you weren't here. We're used to it. If anything, she's doing you a favour. Anyone who sees you walking Mrs Nasso's chickens will take you for a local, no matter that they've never seen your face before."

Though anyone who didn't notice that face had blinders on.

"Oh." She looked relieved, like I'd just solved a riddle for her, and I felt a warm thrill at pleasing her. Now, if only I could make sure I hadn't disfigured her with my coffee.

"Summer won't care where you walk the pigs, as long as they get walked," I assured her. "My place isn't far. Let me take you there and check your skin. It may need a dressing."

"It's really fine—"

"Please? I won't rest until I know it's taken care of properly."

"Um …"

She bit her lip, and for the first time in a long time, I felt … attracted. Not just turned on by a beautiful woman but *interested*. Curious. I cleared my throat and shifted a little as I waited.

"You don't recognise me, do you?" she asked.

I drew back and looked at her closely, but nothing about

her face looked familiar. "No, sorry. Should I?"

She shook her head. "No. I'm Emily Jones. I was at The Stop last night with Abbie and Jess."

"Oh." I'd avoided looking directly at the girls last night and hadn't paid attention to who was there. I'd been gone for two weeks, and Abbie was only going to give me a hard time about it. Plus, there was all the weirdness between Luca and Jess. It had been easier to keep my head down and get out of there early.

Emily pulled back on the snuffling pigs and looked up and down the street again. I followed her gaze and noticed inquisitive eyes on us, as well as the type of bent heads that accompanied whispers. Thankfully, I couldn't see Dawn anywhere, but there'd be plenty of rumours for her to hear within the hour.

"So, will you let me take a look?" I asked.

"All right," Emily said with a sigh. "But I'll need to swing past my car to get a fresh shirt."

3

EMILY

MORTIFIED. I WAS *mortified.* This man was a god—a blond, bronzed, towering *god*—and I was a bumbling mess, covered in coffee that was starting to sour.

Josh didn't say much as he followed me to the street where my car was parked, only a block away but far enough to feel like miles. I opened the rear door, and he held out a hand to take the piglets. I handed them over so I could dig around in the back seat for a clean shirt. The spare one I had wasn't part of the standard-issue uniform for the vet clinic, but it was white, so it would do.

I hadn't yet kicked the habit of keeping an extra set of clothes in my car. Extra clothes, a spare toothbrush, a travel-size hair straightener ... All those essential things a girl might need if she ended up staying overnight somewhere unexpectedly.

I'd had to be prepared with Tyler. He'd never agreed to moving in together, not until we were married, so I used to shuttle back and forth between my share house and his apartment. Tyler had insisted it kept our relationship fresh and exciting. With the benefit of distance and bitterness, I knew our arrangement kept *Tyler* feeling fresh and exciting—and single. I'd never again fall for a guy who lived a part-time life or made our relationship a part-time commitment. I felt so stupid that it had taken me three years to learn that lesson.

Armed with the clean shirt, I straightened from the car and turned to see Josh staring at me. He cleared his throat and dropped his warm amber eyes, but a red flush stained his neck. I looked into the car, where I'd been leaning into the back seat with my arse in the air, then back at Josh.

Shit. I tugged at the hem of my skirt. It wasn't short, but I hadn't checked the view at that angle either. I'd probably been flashing him my underwear. Could this get any more awkward?

"How far is your place?" I asked, taking the leads from him and starting up the street.

"Er, not far," Josh said, but he didn't follow. When I turned and waited, he pointed in the opposite direction. "It's that way."

My cheeks heated. I walked back towards him with my head down, and he fell in beside me. The pigs trotted along happily enough, but I silently begged them to play up a little. Animal misbehaviour would give me and Josh

21

something to talk about, at least. I chewed the inside of my cheek and discarded a dozen different things I could have said. This beautiful man had me feeling like a clumsy idiot.

And he *was* beautiful. That clean, strong jawline. The sun-bleached hair long enough to bend into gentle curls around his ears and neck. Those warm eyes. And the *shoulders*. Tyler hadn't been so broad or so tall. I felt tiny beside Josh, and the more I thought about the way his arms stretched the fabric of his shirt, and the more I tried to peek at his large, smooth hands, the quieter and more lost in thought I became—so much so that I jumped when he finally spoke.

"So, what brings you to Valentine Bay?"

"Oh, no reason in particular," I said, rolling out my standard lines. "I've always lived in the city, but it got boring. I wanted to try something new, and what could go wrong with a small town and sunshine?"

Josh grunted. "You'd be surprised."

"I'm sorry?"

He shook himself and smiled, but it wasn't the warm grin he'd given me earlier. This one didn't reach his eyes. "Nothing. Well, welcome to Valentine Bay."

"Thank you," I murmured, peeking up at him from the corner of my eye as I reconsidered the wisdom of following this guy to his house.

He seemed to pick up on my discomfort, grimacing as he dragged a hand through his hair. "We're generally a friendly bunch, if you can excuse the odd coffee spilled down your shirt and occasional grumpy shift worker.

I'm sorry you've had to deal with both today. I could probably do with a nap."

"Oh, if this is a bad time, I can just go back …"

"No, not a bad time at all. And anyway, we're already here." He turned into a driveway and jogged ahead a few steps to unlock the front door of the house. From this angle, I was able to check out *his* backside. Fair was fair, after all, and it really was nice. *Very* nice. And Joshua Ford clearly never skipped leg day …

Too late, I realised he'd stopped and turned, and was now watching me. Waiting. My gaze darted up and away, and I strode past him, focused on getting through the open door as quickly as possible.

"Uh, I can tie the piglets up here until we're done," he said, stopping me before I dragged the animals inside.

"Oh, right! Of course. Here you go." I thrust the leads at him. I had to get this over and done with before any more instances of total humiliation.

Josh took the leads and secured the pigs, then led me inside. The house was small and plain, like most of the houses in Valentine Bay—a modest brick home with three or four bedrooms, a neat kitchen, and a comfortable living area. Josh took me into the dining room and gestured to a chair.

"Sit down, if you like." He kept walking, moving into the kitchen. "I'll get water for the piglets, and then I'll be with you."

He disappeared, and I looked down into my wet shirt. The coffee hadn't been all that hot, and my skin wasn't even red. This examination was unnecessary, but then Josh

23

strode back in the room, his face a panty-melting mix of competence and concern.

I was there now. I should probably just go with it.

He'd retrieved a cold compress from the kitchen and now knelt in front of me, gingerly touching the collar of my shirt. He started to pull the fabric open, then paused to ask, "May I?"

I couldn't make myself speak, so I bobbed my head.

Clearing his throat, Josh undid the first button, then the second, and my pulse kicked up a gear both times. He undid the third button and then pulled open my shirt just enough to check my skin underneath. When he brushed his fingertips over the area and applied the compress, holding it still for a moment before moving it over my chest, I felt a pulse between my legs and embarrassed myself—again—with a shaky breath.

"I think it's fine," he said, abruptly standing and hurrying away. He returned with a folded blue towel. "The bathroom is just down the hall. You can clean up in there, if you like."

"Thank you," I whispered.

I took the towel and went to the bathroom, closing the door behind me with a click. I had to grip the basin with shaky hands, and I stared into the mirror for the longest moment. Who was this girl? Her colour was high, her eyes were bright, and her chest heaved with excitement.

"Emily Jones, just what the hell do you think you're doing?"

The girl in the mirror had no answer.

I gave myself a little shake and stripped off the wet shirt, rolling it into a ball and tucking it into my oversized handbag. I splashed water over the stickiness on my skin and wiped it dry. With a clean shirt on, I took time to fix my face as well, blotting away some of the glow and reapplying my lip gloss.

"Get a grip," I chastised myself.

The girl in the mirror smirked.

When I emerged from the bathroom, still feeling the awkwardness of Josh putting his hands on me, I stalled in the hallway, surprised at the sight of him sitting at the table with an older man sipping coffee and reading a newspaper. Josh and the newcomer had to be related, because this was what Josh would look like in thirty years or so, the lines on his face and the silver in his hair in no way detracting from his appeal. The older man was broad across the shoulders, like Josh, and although he was sitting, I'd have bet money he was almost as tall. The older man didn't look up when I approached, and I paused, unsure what to do.

"Emily, this is my dad, Jack Ford," Josh said, looking directly at the other man. "Dad, this is Emily. She's new in town."

Jack put down the paper and stretched out a hand. "Pleased to meet you, Emily."

I put my hand in his and shook it. "You, too, Jack."

Josh pushed up from the table. "I'm just going to grab my board from the shed and then I'll walk you and the piglets back into town. Dad, will you be all right with Emily for a few minutes?"

"Of course, I'll be all right. You think you go out of town for a couple of weeks and I lose the ability to hold a decent conversation?" He closed the paper with a smack and waved Josh from the room. "We'll be fine, won't we, Emily?"

"Absolutely," I replied, liking the twinkle in Jack's golden-brown gaze.

Josh rolled his eyes, but he left us alone. I remained standing, looking around the house with polite curiosity. It was neat and put-together but dated. Every piece of furniture, artwork, cushion, and colour looked like it had been chosen twenty years in the past.

"Your home is very nice," I commented.

Jack looked around in surprise. "Is it? Well, thank you. Josh's mother did all the decorating. I wouldn't know how to change it, even if I wanted to."

"Change it?"

Jack removed his glasses and stood, leading me to a row of framed pictures on a bureau in the living room. He pointed to a photograph of him when he was much younger, a pretty blonde woman in a veil by his side.

"That's my Kelly," he said. "Josh's mum. She's not with us anymore. Hasn't been for a long time." He gestured at the room, taking in the wall paint and the carpets and the curtains. "She did all of this. So, what's there to change?"

I swallowed the lump in my throat. "Nothing. It's lovely just like this."

Jack nodded once and returned to the table, and I took the seat Josh had vacated.

"So, what brings you to Valentine Bay?" he asked. "You setting up a home here with your family?"

Here we go. I plastered on an easy-breezy smile. "No, just me. I've always lived in the city, but it got boring. I wanted to try something new, and what could go wrong with a small town and sunshine?"

Jack's face clouded over. "You'd be surprised."

The echo of Josh's words gave me a chill.

Jack looked at me sharply then, his head tilted and his eyes shrewd. "You interested in Josh, then?"

"What? No! I mean, I've only just met him. We bumped into each other—"

"That's well, then," he interrupted. "Josh isn't the sort of man you set your heart on. I don't say this to upset you, you understand? Or to badmouth my boy. He's a good kid, the best. Reliable and hardworking, big heart, and the patience of a saint. But if you're thinking about something serious ..."

I eyed the front door and wondered if it would be more polite to excuse myself than encourage gossip about Josh, but in the end, I decided it was kinder to bite my tongue and listen.

Jack sighed and rubbed his eyes, then leaned forward. "He thinks I don't know it, but he's planning on leaving. Oh, he hasn't said it in so many words, but he's been spending more and more time in the city, and I reckon he's about set to move there. Fresh start, you know? And God knows, he deserves it. He's got two lives on the go right now, and he'll have to choose one of 'em sooner or later.

27

I don't want him to leave but ..." He shook his head. "I want what's best for him, and I don't know if that's Valentine Bay. There's too much here that hurts."

I nodded slowly, making sense of what Jack was *really* saying. Josh was a man with a part-time life. He probably had a girlfriend in the city. A wife. An entire family. Or maybe he was another Tyler, screwing anything in a skirt.

My heart stuttered, and I pressed a hand to my stomach, which was suddenly queasy. I didn't need a reminder of all the things that had gone wrong in my life, and if what Jack had said so far was true, I didn't need to know any more about Josh. And why wouldn't it be true? Nobody could know him better than his own dad. I needed to get out of there.

I looked at the clock on the wall, and then at the watch on my wrist. The times didn't match.

"I think your clock needs a new battery," I observed.

"Ah, that old thing," Jack said. "It's not the battery. It hasn't ticked over in five years or more."

"Oh." I pushed back the chair and stood. "I didn't realise how late it is, and I'm supposed to be at work. Can you tell Josh I said thank you? I really should get going."

Jack got to his feet and scratched his head. "I hope I didn't offend you, Emily."

"What? No! Of course not. I really am running late."

"Well, all right then. If you're sure? And look, if you don't mind, please don't mention this to Josh. He don't know I know about his plans. He keeps his cards close to his chest. I only said all that to you because you're new, see, and everyone around these parts knows Josh don't date. I thought you should know, too."

I smiled as best I could and patted Jack on the arm. "It's fine, really. I just need to get back to work."

I forced myself to walk slowly to the front door, but once out of sight, I tore at the leads tied to the porch and led the piglets down to the road. I looked over my shoulder more than once to be sure Josh wasn't following and was only at ease again when I made it back to Main Street and the clinic was in my sights. The squeeze in my stomach released a little, and I took in lungfuls of the moist, salty air.

If I was this flustered over *looking* at a gorgeous face, what hope did I have of choosing better men in my new life? I mean, it was a *very* gorgeous face, hardly the type I'd expect to come across every day, and it came with a set of incredible shoulders ...

No! There was one important thing to take away from this whole debacle, and I had to hold on to it with two hands. I was going to do things right this time. Tyler had been good-looking, too, but that didn't make him good on the inside. I wasn't a fool, and I resented the way Tyler had caused me to behave like one.

I had no use for men who kept parts of their lives secret from the people they were supposed to love, no matter how well they filled out a T-shirt.

4

JOSH
———————

"WHERE'S EMILY?"

I shifted my surfboard under my arm and peered down the hall. The bathroom door was open, and Emily was nowhere to be seen.

"She had to go," Dad replied, staring at his newspaper. "Said to say sorry—no, said to say thank you—but she had to get back to work."

"Right," I murmured, staring out the front door as though I might catch a glimpse of her.

Dad took a slurp of his coffee. "Pretty little thing, isn't she?"

"Yeah, I guess."

Had I made her uncomfortable with all the touching? I'd tried to keep things professional, but the way her skin had felt underneath my fingertips—the way her breath had trembled when I'd touched her—I'd had to pull away before I did something stupid, like kiss her.

I'd *wanted* to kiss her, and I hadn't wanted to kiss any woman in a very long time. The shock of it knocked the breath out of me.

"Real sweet, too," Jack added.

"Hm?"

If I left now, I still might catch up to her on the road.

"You going for a surf?" Jack asked, eyeing my board.

"What? Oh, yeah. Just a few waves before work. I'll, uh … I'll be back soon."

"Take your time. I've got nowhere else to be."

"Sure, all right. See you later."

Jack smiled and took another gulp of his drink. "I'll see you."

I was halfway down the street before I noticed I didn't have a towel. Never mind. It was hot enough that the walk home would be more pleasant if done dripping wet.

Emily must have been moving at a decent clip because I didn't pass her on the road, and when I arrived on Main Street, she was still nowhere to be seen. I crossed the road so she wouldn't catch me parading past the vet clinic window, but I turned my head as I passed to make sure she was there. And she was. She had the phone to her ear and her eyes lowered, as if writing something down. I slowed a little and took advantage of her distraction, watching her talk and laugh, but then she put the phone down and turned.

Shit. She looked right at me, and our eyes met. I debated going over there but settled for a casual wave instead. She waved back, and then another face popped out from behind the desk. Abbie Ellison. Grimacing, I ducked my head and kept on towards the beach.

Cool, Josh. Real cool.

When my feet hit the hot sand, I pulled off my T-shirt but didn't go in the water straightaway. I stood there a moment, enjoying the sun on my shoulders, watching the sets roll in, and clocking riders floating in the back as they waited for their breaks. As always, the sound of the ocean and the smell of salt soothed my nerves. I breathed in deep and closed my eyes. I'd miss this beach when I moved to the city.

The squeak of footsteps on the sand and the mingled scents of sunscreen and coconut oil alerted me to the fact someone wanted to join me. I knew who it was, but I kept my eyes shut, trying to bottle some of that calm before I had to face her.

"Hey, Ellison," I said eventually.

She moved close enough that her arm brushed up against mine. "Hey, Ford."

I cracked one eye to look down at her. Abbie faced the waves the same way I did, mirroring my posture. I sighed. "Can I help you?"

"Welcome back," she said, ignoring the question.

"Miss me?"

She elbowed my ribs. "You know I did. The Bay's not the same without you."

"Sure it is."

Abbie opened her mouth, appeared to think better of whatever she was going to say, and closed it again. A moment passed before she asked, "How's Jack?"

"He's good, but that's not what you want to ask me."

She looked up at me with narrowed eyes, but then turned back to the ocean. "How are you doing?"

I took deliberate deep breaths to slow my heart rate. "I'm okay."

"You missed Maggie's birthday."

I knew this would come up. "No, I didn't," I said, squinting at the water instead of meeting Abbie's eyes.

"You weren't here."

"But I didn't miss her birthday."

Abbie put a hand on my arm. "Okay."

We were silent for a beat, but we both knew I had to ask. "Bonfire?"

"Of course."

"Good turn out?"

"Everyone but you."

I watched an unfamiliar surfer drop into a decent wave, but his form was average, and he wiped out almost instantly.

Abbie threaded her arm through mine and took my hand, giving it a squeeze. "It was a good night, but we missed you. Everyone's noticed that you're coming and going more often and staying away longer. You've never missed her birthday before. What's going on?"

Abbie and I had gone to high school together—her, me, and Maggie. She'd been one of Maggie's best friends, and there was a bunch of us who got together every year to mark Maggie's birthday. We always lit a bonfire on the beach, got drunk, and talked about her. Well, I didn't talk, but it was the one time of year I let myself listen.

33

"Nothing's going on," I replied. "I just wanted to do my own thing this year."

"It's okay to move on, you know. Maggie loved you, but she'd want you to be happy. Imagine how pissed off she'd be if you stayed single the rest of your life because you can't stop missing her."

My cheek twitched before I could stop it. Maggie had had a short fuse, but her temper never lasted long, and nobody had bugged her more than me. She'd hated that she couldn't rile me up, and it drove her bonkers when I called her outbursts *tantrums*.

Too much thinking was never a good thing. Time to change the subject. "How do you know Emily Jones?"

Why the fuck did I say that?

Abbie dropped my arm and looked up at me, her eyes suspicious and her hands on her hips. "How do *I* know Emily Jones? How do *you* know Emily Jones?"

Crap. I'd sounded too interested. "I bumped into her this morning," I replied, feigning calm. "Literally. Spilled my coffee all over her. I took her back to the house so I could check the burn and she could clean up— What?"

Abbie's expression had gone from surprised to speculative. "I just dropped in on her at Summer's clinic to say hello, and she said nothing to me about any of that. Interesting."

So, I didn't even rate a mention. "Not interesting at all. It was so *un*interesting it's not worth talking about." I sounded petulant, and I winced.

Abbie shook her head. "That's not what I meant," she murmured, and she looked thoughtful for a second.

She was going to try to set me up. I could see the cogs moving, and I recognised that look. More women than Abbie had given me *that* look.

Strangely enough, the thought didn't fill me with the usual dread. It didn't cause my palms to sweat or my stomach to turn. It *did* have my heart racing, but not in a way that made me want to bolt.

But then Abbie shook her head. "I think you should steer clear of Emily." She raised her hands defensively, anticipating a protest at the suggestion of me dating again. "I'm not implying that you would ask her out. If anything, I'm on your side this time. Getting involved with Emily would be a terrible idea."

"What? Why?"

Calm down, moron.

Abbie cocked an eyebrow. "I ... can't tell you. No! Honestly, I can't say anything about ... anything. But maybe ..." She chewed her lip and glanced back toward Main Street where Emily was hidden inside the vet clinic. Then she looked up at me, and I almost stepped back.

This wasn't the look people gave me when they tried to set me up, the sly wink or the goofy grin. It wasn't even the sad eyes and sympathetic hug of someone who knew how much I missed Maggie. Abbie looked at me in a way only she could, as someone who shared more than twenty years of my history and the grief of loving a girl who was gone.

"You've spent years mourning Maggie, and now you've finally got one foot out of Valentine Bay. Maybe you need to leave all this behind to have a chance at happiness.

Maybe that's your best shot. Emily … well, Emily doesn't deserve to be screwed around, even if you don't mean to do it. She's not a person you can try on for size and then abandon when she doesn't fit or dump if you get scared. Don't let her be your test case. It's not fair to either of you."

"You think I'm that much of an arsehole?" I hadn't been this frank about my feelings with anyone in a long time, but somehow, I didn't care about keeping my guard up right now. Not when it meant finding out more about Emily, however cryptic Abbie wanted to be.

If Abbie thought my question was out of character, she didn't let on. "You're not an arsehole, Josh. You're the most decent man I know. But you haven't dated anyone in years! There's simply no chance that the first girl you take out after Maggie will be the last. You've got dozens of women in your future. Hundreds, even!" She waggled her eyebrows. "You've got *years* of fun ahead of you."

I snorted. "Doubt it."

She picked up my hand again. "One day, you'll think differently, and I can't tell you how happy I am at the idea of you dating again. It's way overdue, but not Emily, okay? Start with lower stakes."

I lifted one shoulder. "I'm not interested, anyway. I don't know what gave you the idea I was."

Her smile was crooked and her honey-brown eyes too knowing. The heat of embarrassment seeped into my cheeks.

"Okay, that's settled then." She checked the time on her watch. "I've got to run. Class in half an hour. Will I see you around later?"

I shook my head. "Working."

"What about Friday night? A few of us are going to The Stop to drink away our heartache and avoid the Valentine's Day festivities." Her face screwed up in disgust. "The tourism council has really gone all out this year. Have you seen the decorations they're putting up? Makes me want to vomit. Valentine's Day weekend is the worst time of year for a town called Valentine Bay."

"Can't make it," I told her. "Working again."

"Loser. Check you later, okay?"

I waved as Abbie jogged up the beach, watching her for a minute and then returning my gaze to the water. If I wanted to go in and make it to work on time, I had to start now, but I just stood there, staring out at the waves and riders.

Abbie was right. Not about the years of fun and dozens of women ahead of me—more like deluded there—but about my future being outside of Valentine Bay. And she was spot on about hurting anyone I got involved with. What did I have to offer a woman but half a damaged heart? And what did I know about love other than loss and grief? I'd learned that lesson twice over, and my father was living proof of the future I had to look forward to.

I'd accepted my lot, and if I couldn't make the best of it, well, I could at least put one foot in front of the other. I'd said the same thing for four years, given myself the same advice over and over, and I'd never been uneasy with it.

Now, for the first time in a long time, it felt like something was missing—something that wasn't Maggie.

5

EMILY

I STOPPED AGAIN as the Labrador I was walking paused to sniff at a discarded sandwich wrapper. It was a relief to finally have a canine at the end of the lead, though the task wasn't as nearly straightforward—or as pleasant—as I'd hoped it would be. The dog weighed nearly as much as I did, and he wasn't well trained. Anyone watching the tug-of-war between us would wonder if I was taking the animal for a walk or if it was the other way around.

I'd left the clinic forty-five minutes earlier, powered down Main Street, and disappeared into the park, keeping my head down while the lab got his exercise. I'd done the same thing for three days straight now, in what had become a covert ritual. First, I panicked when Summer asked me to leave the clinic. Then, I put on a cap and glasses like I was in some kind of spy novel. I scanned the street and if the coast was clear, I dragged whatever animal needed walking out the door and directly to the park, where I assumed I'd be safe from bumping into anyone.

Well, not anyone. One person.

Josh Ford.

It was ridiculous. I knew my behaviour was over the top even as I went through the motions again and again. Josh wasn't hiding around corners, waiting to douse me with hot coffee and peel off my shirt. He hadn't given me a second thought since that day—Emily Jones just wasn't that memorable—but in case he happened to be out and about, I was determined to avoid him. Valentine Bay was my new beginning, and Josh, with his suspicious disappearances and careful, capable hands, didn't fit in that picture at all.

I checked the time, then scratched the dog behind his ears. "Okay, Schnookums. Five more minutes and it's back to the clinic. Fine. Ten minutes max, and I mean it this time." Schnookums looked up at me like I was mad, and I sighed. "You have no idea."

My phone chimed and I pulled it out, expecting a message from one of two people: Abbie, who was still trying to convince me to go with her to The Salty Stop for an anti-Valentine's Day drink on Friday night; or Summer asking me to return to the clinic. I wasn't prepared for the name that flashed up on the screen. My hands trembled as I swiped to open the message.

Tyler: I made a huge mistake. I'm sorry. I need you and I want you back.

My head shook, my body saying "no" before my mind caught up, and my hand crept over my mouth to cover my shock.

Tyler was sorry and he wanted me back. He was sorry. He wanted me back.

I hobbled over to a park bench, sank onto it with distracted relief, and read the message again. Tyler was sorry, and he needed me, and he wanted me back.

What the actual fuck?

He'd spent three years stringing me along. Two months had passed without so much as a peep from him. I'd left behind my home and every memory the two of us had ever made so I could start over. And now he wanted me *back*?

I couldn't recall a time I'd felt this type of burning, violent, let-me-at-him-I'm-going-to-kill-him rage, and that included the moment Tyler had dumped me. I'd been too humiliated and too devastated to feel much more than numb at the time. I was still humiliated and still devastated, but it paled compared to the fury of staring at that message and all that it implied.

Abbie and Jess were right about Tyler. He was a jerk. A prick. A moronic, heartless dick. I couldn't wait to tell him so. My eyes stung, all my anger and pain at the way this man continued to torture me needing to escape my body the fastest way it knew how. I sobbed as quietly as I could, enjoying the release in those angry, salty tears.

My fingers were poised over the phone's screen, ready to give Tyler a piece of my mind, when a shadow fell over me. I looked up and straight into Josh's big, golden-brown eyes. My heart thudded, and my face felt red and damp from all the crying and furious thinking.

"You all right?" he asked.

I jumped to my feet. "Me? I'm great. Thanks."

He seemed to pick up on the fact I didn't want to talk about it, whatever "it" might be, so he pretended not to notice my snotty nose and blotchy skin. "Are you on your lunch break?"

"No, I'm walking ... Shit!" I looked down at my empty hands, then around the park. "Schnookums!" I shouted. "Here, boy! Schnookums!"

Josh quirked one thick eyebrow. "Schnookums?"

"Yes, he's a yellow lab. Belongs to the Cheevers over on Monday Lane. Dammit! I can't believe I've lost him. What am I supposed to tell Summer? I'll lose my job. Can this day get any worse?" I rushed away, stumbling over my own feet, wanting nothing more than to find Schnookums and get away from Josh.

Unfortunately, he followed me, reaching out and wrapping a firm, warm hand around my arm. "I'll go this way and you go that way, okay? We'll find him and everything will be fine. He can't have gone far."

I opened my mouth to protest, but my chin trembled too much to talk, so I just nodded.

"Hey, it's going to be all right." Josh leaned down to look under my cap. "We'll fix whatever's wrong, okay?"

I laughed humourlessly and shook my head. "I wish that were possible."

He frowned before taking off in the opposite direction,

and I ran up a different path, calling out for the lab. I could hear Josh yelling "Schnookums!" somewhere behind me, and I smiled a little. It really was an awful name to scream across a public park.

Five minutes passed, then ten. Fifteen minutes into the search, I was convinced we'd never find Schnookums. What if he'd been dognapped? Or hit by a car? What if I had to return to the clinic empty handed or carrying an enormous, injured pooch? My short stint in Valentine Bay wouldn't be enough to convince anyone to forgive me for messing up so badly. And the Cheevers! This would crush them.

As I ran and shouted, panicking about Schnookums and Tyler and the collapse of the new life I'd only just begun to build, I grew certain it was about to come to a sudden, scandalous end.

And then a rowdy Labrador crested the hill, dragging a determined Josh behind him. I folded forwards with relief, tempted to collapse completely.

"Found him head-first in a bin." Josh pulled the pup to a sit and patted his side. "He may or may not have downed a pizza box."

"Thank you so much," I said, crouching down to scratch the dog's ears. "I'm so mad at myself. I got distracted and dropped the lead, I guess. I mean, I don't even know how it happened."

"Distracted by someone on the phone?" Josh suggested.

I straightened and touched the phone in my pocket, Tyler's number flashing again in my head. "Yeah."

Josh waited for me to say more, and when I didn't, he handed me the lead. "Well, it's all fixed now."

"It's not," I replied without thinking. "It can't be fixed, and it's so typical. He's gone and ruined everything. Again."

Josh glanced at the dog. "Uh, I'm sure he didn't mean it." My cheeks bloomed and my hand strayed to my phone again. Understanding lit Josh's features. "You're not talking about Schnookums."

"No. Not Schnookums."

"Boyfriend?"

Josh's expression was so open and sympathetic that I answered honestly. "Fiancé. No, ex! Ex-fiancé." I cursed my brain for turning to mush. "We—he—called it off months ago and I haven't heard from him since. Until now. He just sent me a text."

Josh smiled. "Well, that's great news, isn't it? He's come to his senses."

I scowled, the anger rising again. "Tyler's *senses* are partial to disappearing for days at a time and sneaking around behind my back. Cancelling our engagement *three days* before our wedding and leaving me to clean up his mess." Tears burned my eyes and throat, and my voice cracked. Josh said nothing, and my words hung like cobwebs in the air—unwanted and unavoidable. Would there be a time I *didn't* make a fool of myself in front of this man?

"Well, I've humiliated myself enough for one day," I announced. "Thanks again for your help. Hopefully, it's the last time you'll need to rescue me."

Josh said nothing, just watched me with steady, liquid eyes. I gave him a wave—awkward because we were standing too close for a wave to make any sense—then spun and ran away. Schnookums appreciated the gallop and nearly tore my arm from the socket.

"Emily!" Josh called.

I stopped, Schnookums nearly heaving me right over, and I righted myself with effort. *Pull your shit together, Emily.* I plastered a smile on my face and turned, looking as carefree as I could manage. "Did I forget something?"

"Are you going to The Stop tomorrow night? For Valentine's Day. Abbie mentioned she'd be there with some friends."

"Um, I haven't decided yet. Valentine's Day's not my favourite time of the year."

He smiled crookedly and looked damn sexy doing it. "It's not mine either. Maybe I'll see you there."

My mouth went dry. "Maybe," I croaked. Regretting the almost-commitment to meet him at a bar on Valentine's Day, I did that silly wave again, flushed brightly, and hightailed it out of the park.

6

JOSH

I'D NEVER BEEN so disappointed in my wardrobe. I chose a white collared shirt for The Salty Stop on Valentine's Day night, the only decent option among a handful of navy paramedic uniforms, a stack of worn board shorts, and a sad selection of T-shirts that were good enough for The Stop any other time, but not tonight.

"Where you off to?" Dad asked as I stowed my phone and keys in the pockets of my dark blue jeans.

"Nowhere special. Drinks at The Stop."

"Just the usual crew?"

"It usually is." I checked myself in the hall mirror and ran my fingers through my hair. It was dry and salty from the surf. I should have washed it. "I'll be late. Don't wait up."

Dad had already returned to his newspaper, smirking at whatever he was reading. "Wouldn't dream of it."

I kept my head down as I made the fifteen-minute walk to the bar. I didn't want to have to stop and chat with anyone and, in the Bay, that was always a risk if you walked in a way that invited eye contact. Maybe I didn't need to worry because the town buzzed tonight. The night markets were packed, and Abbie had been right about the vomitous riot of pink and red decorations. The balloons and streamers and festoon lights hanging from poles and awnings and trees along Main Street were borderline offensive.

When I reached the bar, I was relieved to see there was one place, at least, that had resisted the celebrations. To either side of The Salty Stop, storefronts were garlanded with twinkling lights and bouquets of rose-coloured balloons. My best mate Will's place was the hulking, brooding brother in the middle, and I smiled at his resistance. The tourism council would have pitched a pink fit about this. Literally.

The door swung open as I approached, letting out an older couple along with the sounds of a local cover band, and I ducked inside. It was the same as it always was, layers of timber and low, moody lighting, the mouth-watering fragrances of spicy tapas wafting from the kitchen.

"Hey, handsome!" Abbie called out, standing and flailing an arm to wave me over.

She was seated at the bar, flirting with Will, as always. I didn't quite understand their relationship, even after all these years. It was more than a friendship, yet I didn't think they'd ever slept together. They each had their flings with other people, but Will had always been cagey about the rules, and I tried not to judge. If I thought for one second he was taking Abbie for a ride, I'd have said something, but it wasn't like that. Some days, I wondered if I should be worried about *him*. Will adored Abbie—possibly even loved her. His infatuation with that woman was clear to anyone who cared enough to look, and she seemed oblivious to it.

"Hey, Ellison." I reached over the bar and shook Will's hand. "Kidd."

"Hey, Ford. Beer?"

"You know it." Will poured me a glass of the local IPA. "And what's the lady drinking?" I asked, eyeing the cocktail in front of Abbie.

Abbie looked over her shoulder one way, then the other. "Lady? Where?"

Will rolled his eyes. "She's got a bottomless margarita, in case you couldn't tell."

Abbie batted her eyelashes. "You spoil me, babe."

"Keep it up, *babe*, and I'll be carrying you home in less than an hour."

Abbie winked, and Will moved along the bar to serve other customers. As soon as he was distracted, Abbie miraculously sobered up.

"You're having him on," I accused.

"He likes it that way, but enough about Will. What are you doing here? I thought you were working."

I started to scan the bar but stopped myself and took a drink of my beer. "I felt like hanging out with you instead."

"Oh, good! So, Jess said she'd come, but only if Luca doesn't, and he said he might, but it depends on Natasha. Isaac will drop in if he can be bothered, but he's working later, so he probably won't." Abbie put up her fingers one by one as she did the maths. "So, it'll probably be just you and me."

Disappointment dropped like a rock in my gut, but I raised my glass. "Sounds like a party. Cheers."

Abbie grinned and tapped her glass against mine. "Cheers, big ears." She took a gulp of her cocktail, then brightened as her eyes lit on someone over my shoulder. She stood and waved wildly. "Hey, Em! Over here!"

Emily was here. It took effort to swallow my beer without choking, and I pretended casualness, turning my head a little to get a look at her. That rock in my stomach catapulted into my throat. Holy hell, Emily was a knockout.

She was wrapped up tight in an olive dress that clung to her tiny waist and the curves of her breasts. It showed off her flat stomach and tight, high backside, skimming her legs to barely mid-thigh, so she showed off more leg than she had in her work uniform. She wore sandals—everyone did around here—but fuck, I'd have liked to see her in heels with that dress.

I forced myself to look her in the eye and smile in a way I hoped was friendly. Cool. Relaxed. I wasn't the only guy in the bar who'd looked at her longer than was polite, and perhaps she noticed because her cheeks were flushed. Tugging once at the hem of her dress and then smoothing the hair at the nape of her neck, she rushed her steps to get to Abbie. I stood as she approached and offered her my seat.

Abbie's eyes bounced back and forth between Emily and me, her expression composed. "You two know each other, or so I've been told?"

Emily glanced at me, then looked away. "Sort of, I guess."

"There was the coffee thing," I said, distracted by the smooth curve of her neck. "Then I rescued her dog."

Emily's mouth quirked into a small smile. "It was the Cheevers' dog."

"*Right*," Abbie drawled, then she gave Emily a hug. "I'm so glad you could make it."

Emily slid onto a seat, and Abbie took the stool next to her, forcing me to sit on Abbie's other side.

"Margarita?" Abbie asked her.

She looked at Abbie's glass warily. "It's pink tonight. Is it as strong as the ones we had last time?"

"Ha! Stronger. Here, have a sip and tell me what you think."

"Mm. It's good. I'll have one too."

"Excellent." Abbie stood, feet on the bottom rung of the stool, and leaned right over the bar, her arse high in the air. "Hey! Babe! Bottomless margarita for my friend here."

I leaned back so I could get a glimpse of Emily around Abbie's bottom, but Emily was especially committed to looking straight ahead.

Will came over holding a silver cocktail shaker and a fresh glass with a salted rim. "Hey. *Babe.* Stop screeching at me while I'm working." He jerked his head at Emily. "Is she giving you grief?"

Emily laughed, and I sat up straighter at the sound of it. "Not yet."

"Give me a shout when things get rowdy, okay?" Will said.

"Will do." Emily took a sip of her drink. "Yum. Thanks."

"My pleasure."

For the next hour, Will moved up and down the bar, pouring drinks for the expanding crowd and joining our conversation now and then, while I spent the better part of that time speaking to Abbie, who had taken it upon herself to act as a go-between for Emily. I took a long swallow of my third beer and smacked the glass on the bar, frustrated, just as Abbie bounced to her feet.

"I need to go to the bathroom. Coming, Em?"

Emily's eyes drifted to me, then back to Abbie. "Ah, no thanks. I'm fine."

Abbie frowned, first at Emily, then at me. "Okay. I'll be back in a minute."

Twisting around to watch Abbie as she walked away, I noticed for the first time how packed the place had become. There were a lot of broken hearts in Valentine Bay tonight—or cynical ones, at least. I waited for Abbie to disappear into the crowd and made sure Will was busy at the other end of the bar before I spoke.

"How are you doing today?"

Emily shifted a little closer, her face apologetic. "Sorry? I can't hear you."

I moved to the stool next to her and sat closer than was necessary, close enough that my arm brushed against hers. I told myself it couldn't be helped, but it was a big fat lie, and tilted my head towards hers. "How are you doing today?"

Emily rolled her eyes in embarrassment. "I'm fine. Honestly. You caught me at a bad moment yesterday. I'm not usually like that."

"We all have bad days." I paused, unsure if I wanted the answer to my next question. "So, did you sort things out with your ex?"

She nodded proudly if a little unsteadily. "Told him to go f— Well, it wasn't nice, let's put it that way."

I chuckled, appreciating the unexpected spit of fire. "And how'd he take it?"

She put her margarita to her lips, and I stared, mesmerised, as the salt stuck to her mouth, at the way she ran her tongue over it, top then bottom, corner to corner.

Jesus. My cock twitched, and I looked away, rolling my beer glass between my palms.

"He said he wouldn't give up," she said.

I cleared my throat. "I can understand that."

Her cheeks turned a pretty shade of pink, and I took another drink, hoping the ale would wash away my nerves. "So, I was thinking maybe we—"

"Hey, baby," a deep voice cut me off. "I was hoping I'd find you here."

7

EMILY

I SPUN ON my stool, flinging out an arm towards Josh, and when I found his hand, I grabbed it. Hard. It was probably a bad idea, but I needed the reassurance. Better if Abbie had been here to give it, I thought, as Josh twined his warm fingers in mine. His skin felt good, maybe too good, and his hand was so large and strong as he gave my much smaller one a gentle squeeze.

Tyler had found me. Not hard to do, I suppose. I'd told him where I was going, but only so he'd take me seriously about having moved on. What an idiot move that was, I realised now. Of course, he'd followed me. Tyler was ninety per cent ego, ten per cent cologne. I used to like that about him once upon a time. Now, it was coming back to bite me on the arse.

"Tyler," I breathed.

Tyler glanced at Josh's hand in mine, and his sharp, dark eyes twitched, but he gathered himself quickly. He looked painfully out of place at The Stop, with his slicked-back hair and tailored grey suit, and I could see the effort it took him to dismiss Josh. It felt like a win.

"Emily, I'm here to take you home."

"Valentine Bay is my home now." I hated the way my voice trembled. I looked around the bar for Abbie but couldn't see her anywhere.

"You've only been here five minutes. Come on. Let's go somewhere we can talk." Throwing Josh an irritated glance, Tyler shifted his back to him and leaned towards me, brushing my arm with the back of his fingers. "Alone."

"I don't think that's a good idea," I said.

As Tyler ran his fingers over my shoulder and up my neck, my treacherous skin pebbled. I couldn't tell if was with repulsion or desire—a bit of both, I had to admit. Dammit.

He took a lock of my hair between his fingertips. "You cut your hair. Looks ... good."

Ha! He hated it. I didn't know why that felt like another win, but I latched onto the feeling and held my tongue.

"Please?" he wheedled. "I just want to talk."

I pressed my eyes closed and wished he'd disappear, then wished I didn't feel gratified that he was willing to try to get me back. I didn't want him in my life, but there was no way around it. Closure would be easier if *I* had rejected *him* rather than having to live the rest of my life knowing he was the one who walked away. I couldn't believe I'd fallen for this guy.

Josh had been silent, and now he tried to pull his fingers free, but I didn't want to let go. I didn't feel ready to deal with Tyler alone yet, and if he wouldn't leave because I asked him to, I had no idea how to make him go. How long would he stay? He'd made his play, and that monstrous ego wasn't going to let him walk away with egg on his face. I squeezed Josh's hand and held on tight.

"Emily doesn't want to talk to you right now," Josh said.

My eyes flew open.

"I wasn't talking to you," Tyler snapped.

"Doesn't change the fact that she doesn't want to talk to you right now."

Tyler glared, then jerked his chin. "And who the hell are you?"

"Emily's fiancé."

I gasped, then desperately smoothed my features. Josh's jaw clenched, but his hand was steady, and I wondered what the hell he was thinking. This was a terrible idea … wasn't it?

"Her *fiancé*?" Tyler looked at me and laughed. "Who is this idiot?"

Was he laughing at me? This man who'd dumped me less than a week before our wedding couldn't believe someone else might want me, and he *laughed*?

"This is Josh," I said, looking away from Tyler and up at the blond hero who had come to my rescue yet again. "And he's not an idiot."

Tyler looked from Josh to me and back again, for the first time appearing uncertain. "But he's not your fiancé."

"Hello, stranger," Abbie said, bouncing into our little circle and sweeping her eyes up and down Tyler appraisingly. "Do we know you?"

Tyler stuck out his hand. "I'm Tyler Banks. Emily's fiancé."

Abbie glanced at Tyler's hand, ignored it, then met my eyes.

Yep, this is the guy. Please don't judge me.

Abbie noticed my hand, then, with Josh's fingers wrapped around it, and she looked at Josh. I had to give it to her. Not a flicker of surprise passed across her face, even though this must have been beyond confusing.

"And *I* was just telling Tyler here that things have changed," Josh said. "Me and Em—"

"He says they're getting married," Tyler scoffed.

Abbie took another look at me, her face a mask of pure composure. I smiled, but it was small and awkward, and Abbie didn't miss my free hand gripping the edge of my seat. She blinked twice, then turned to Tyler with a mega-watt grin.

"It happened *so* fast, but that's the thing about love at first sight, isn't it? And I've never seen anyone more in love than these two. Ask anyone in the Bay, and they'll tell you. Here, I'll do it for you." Abbie pushed towards the bar, forcing Tyler back a step as she flung herself over it. "Will! Babe! Come here a second." Will threw his dish towel over one shoulder and walked over. "What do you think about Em and Josh getting engaged?" Abbie asked. "Can't wait for the wedding, can we?"

Will didn't miss a beat. "More excited about the bucks' night, to be honest." He winked at me. "Don't worry, Em. We'll get him back to you in one piece."

In that moment, I could have kissed Will—his expression was so boyishly handsome, and his eyes said "we've got you"—but all I could do was grin. This was what I'd been looking for when I moved to Valentine Bay. Not just friends to share a drink with, but the kind of people who took you in and didn't let you go. Kept you on your feet when you felt like you were falling.

"When's the wedding?" Tyler demanded.

I raised my chin, pulled Josh's hand into my lap, and tried not to think about where his fingers rested, how they might feel exploring other parts of my body. I resolutely ignored the throb of warmth between my legs. "Three weeks."

As Tyler's nostrils flared, he glared first at Josh, then at me, and murmured under his breath. "Are you knocked up?"

Josh stood. That was all, and I was ridiculously pleased that he was easily a head taller than Tyler. "You should leave," Josh murmured.

Tyler sized up Josh and took note of Will behind the bar, who'd put down his dish cloth and now rested both hands on the counter. Tyler took a step to the side and tilted his forehead towards me, but I pulled back a little and dropped my eyes to the ground beside his feet.

"I'm not leaving this town without you," he said between clenched teeth. "Three years with me can't compare to what you think you have going on here. I won't give up until there's a ring on your finger, and it's going to be mine."

Josh rubbed soothing circles over the back of my hand, ran his thumb over the ridges of my knuckles, and swept it up and down my naked fingers. I hoped Tyler didn't notice the lack of an engagement ring.

"Don't stay, Tyler," I said. "We're over."

"No. I need you."

He leaned in to kiss me, and I turned my head away in time for his lips to land on my cheek. Only when I knew he'd left the bar did I let out a breath.

"I leave you two alone for five minutes, and you get engaged?" Abbie asked. She exchanged a worried look with Will across the bar, but I didn't look back to check his expression.

"It's my fault," Josh explained. "Emily told me about her ex, and she seemed uncomfortable when he got here ..."

I dropped Josh's hand as the reality of what we'd just done hit home. It was hard to breathe.

"I'm sorry," Josh said with a worried frown. "I wasn't thinking."

"No, I understand," I mumbled. "Thank you for trying to help."

"But?"

"You heard him!" I put a hand on my chest and sucked in a breath. "He's not going to leave me alone. He still wants to get married. Idiot!"

"But ..." Josh said with a sheepish look on his face. "He can't marry you if you're married to me, right?"

Will leaned towards me and ducked his head. "Josh and I could go see him with a few mates. You know, have a little chat. Explain how things are."

Just as my heart thudded at what he was suggesting, Abbie snorted. "Oh, sorry," she said. "I thought that was a joke. Be real, Will. You haven't hit anyone since high school, and Josh, you've never thrown a punch. You'd both hurt yourselves before you hurt anyone else."

Will straightened and crossed his arms. "I didn't say we were going to *hit* him. Just …"

"What?" Abbie's eyes sparkled. "What were you going to do?"

I interrupted, eager to put an end to this twist in the conversation. "I appreciate the thought, but Tyler works for the department of public prosecutions, and as you might have guessed, he's used to getting what he wants. He's used to winning. You should probably steer clear of him."

"He's a lawyer?" Josh grunted. "Why am I not surprised?"

Will smiled grimly and shrugged. "If you change your mind—"

"I won't." I gave him a grateful smile. "But thank you."

"Why do men behave like such Neanderthals?" Abbie huffed, taking me by the shoulders. "Emily, sweetie, what do you want to do? You and I can find Tyler tomorrow, tell him the truth and convince him to leave you alone. Clear this whole thing up like it never happened."

Abbie dropped her hands and I swung around to the bar, picking up my margarita. What was the smart thing to do?

Josh and Abbie exchanged loaded looks, and I let myself swoon a little over the serious expression on his face. There was that competence and concern again. I couldn't think straight.

"Tyler's not going to leave me alone that easily," I reasoned. "Why do you think I left the city in the first place? Among other things, he's arrogant and stubborn, and I had really hoped he'd just forgotten me these last couple of months. Out of sight, out of mind. That always worked for him when it was convenient." I downed my cocktail. For three years, Tyler made me feel *less than*. Not anymore. I smacked my hand on the bar. "Let's do this. How hard can it be to fake a wedding, right?"

Abbie scrunched her nose. "Outsmart a lawyer? You think Tyler's going to fall for it?"

"If we see it through to the end," Josh said quietly, "I don't see how he wouldn't."

I couldn't meet Josh's eyes, and he avoided looking at me, too, so we sat there like a couple of kids who'd been caught kissing on the playground. Abbie and Josh swapped a look again, and a brief flare of envy burned across my skin. Not because I believed there was anything romantic between them, but because what they had was special enough that they could pass an entire conversation with a glance alone.

Abbie gave Josh's hand a quick squeeze, then reached over the bar. "Babe, hand me my phone. I've got to call Dawn."

Will tossed a phone into Abbie's outstretched palm, then dug his own phone out of his pocket and began tapping on the screen.

"What … What are you doing?" I asked.

Abbie had the phone to her ear. "Hello? Dawn, hold on a minute. I need to talk to you." Abbie moved the phone away from her ear and spoke to me. "If we're going to convince Tyler that you and Josh are a thing, we're going to need to get the whole Bay on board. The fastest way to do that is through Dawn."

I blanched. For the first time, I thought about what a fake engagement was going to involve. How I'd just gone through the heartache of planning a wedding that never happened, and now I was going to do it again. I wanted to throw up.

"And you, Will?" I whispered. "What are you doing?"

"Texting the crew." He looked up at Josh and grinned. "They're going to want to know that our terminal bachelor here has gone and got himself a missus."

8

EMILY

I SWALLOWED MY nerves and knocked on the door of Josh's house. I'd thought about things overnight, and while Sensible Emily knew Josh's plan was a terrible idea, Fresh Start Emily had shut down the entire debate with one little question: how else was I going to get Tyler Banks out of my life?

I cleared my throat and smoothed my hair, tucking it behind my ears and skimming over where it stopped on the back of my neck. I loved the pixie cut, though I still wasn't used to it. I'd done the predictable thing and chopped it all off after Tyler called off the wedding, even though I'd been growing it out for a full twelve months so it would look a certain way with my veil attached. It had almost reached the small of my back, and the hot thrill of rebellious freedom when the hairdresser had run her scissors over it had been euphoric. I'd donated the ponytail, got in my new, second-hand car, and driven straight to Valentine Bay.

I knocked on the door again and was about to leave when it opened. Jack stood on the other side, not Josh, and I looked over the older man's shoulder, expecting to see Josh somewhere inside. When he didn't appear, I suddenly recalled the conversation I'd had with Jack earlier in the week, and I smiled uncomfortably.

"Hi. Is Josh home?"

Jack pushed open the screen door and moved aside. Taking that as confirmation that Josh was inside somewhere, I walked in and looked around.

"Sorry, Emily. Josh isn't here right now. Can I get you a drink?"

"Oh. No, thanks. I don't want to bother you."

Jack gestured at the package I had in my hands. "Is that for Josh?"

"No. Well, yes. Sort of." I flushed. "It's for both of you." I extended the wrapped item to Jack, and he looked at it for a moment as though unsure what to do with it. Finally, he took it and tore away the brown paper.

Inside was a clock with a black frame and white face, a series of grey dots for the numbers and silver hands marking the time. I'd already inserted a battery and set it correctly, so all Josh or Jack had to do was hang it on the wall in place of the one that had been broken for five years.

Jack stared at it as if dumbfounded, for long enough that I started to think I'd done something wrong.

"I just wanted to do something nice for Josh. He ... helped me out with something last night, and I couldn't think of a way to say thank you. If you're worried about the money, please don't. It wasn't expensive. It's a token, really. And if you don't like it, that's fine too. I can take it back. No, I've opened it. Um, I can put it on a wall at my place. It would look great in the bathroom. Actually, now that I think about it, it probably would look better there. Black and white isn't really the right fit for this room, now that I see it again. Here, let me take that for you." I put my hand out.

Please, please give me the clock, so I can get out of here before Josh gets back. I couldn't take looking like an idiot in front of him. Again.

"Emily," Jack said, raising his hand to quiet me. "It's a lovely thought. If you'll move to the side a little, I'll hang it right now."

I shifted away from the dining table, and Jack pulled out a chair to stand on. He removed the old, broken clock from the wall, set it on the table, and replaced it with the new one. When he'd climbed down again, we stood shoulder to shoulder for a moment, looking up at it. It was a little momentous for something as simple as a clock, and I snuck a peek at Jack from the corner of my eye. He looked thoughtful. Oh, no. Was he crying?

"So," I said, desperate for some small talk. "Is Josh at work today?"

Jack coughed. "Josh? No, not working today."

"Oh. Surfing, then?"

"Don't think so. His board's still here."

"Right." I ran out of things to say, and I didn't know if Jack was aware of the "engagement" yet, so I took a step back, planning to leave, when Jack looked at me sideways.

"Ah, Emily," he said with a sigh. "You seem like a decent girl, which is the only reason I'm saying this again, but don't set your heart on him."

"Why not?" I asked, surprising both myself and Jack. "Is he seeing someone? A lot of someones? Is he a playboy? Selfish? Heartless? Cruel? The type of man who'll tell you he loves you, then sleep with a stranger and leave you three days before your wedding?"

"No, no. He's none of those things." Jack lifted a hand as though to touch my arm but let it drop. "He's just not … available. His heart is broken."

"His isn't the only one," I murmured.

Without warning, the front door banged open, and Josh walked in. He wore sneakers and shorts but no shirt, and he was covered in sweat. He must have been out for a run.

Yes, I ogled him. I couldn't stop myself. I ran my eyes over his shoulders and arms, across his smooth chest and down his sculpted abs. His V-lines dragged my gaze—kicking and screaming, I promise—to his groin. I blushed when I reached the bulge in his pants and coolly returned my attention to his face, but I was warm all over. Really warm.

His eyes met mine, and I swear they lit up. His grin stretched wider, and he came closer, but then he saw the old clock on the table, and a new one on the wall, and his expression darkened.

"What's that?"

"Emily came by with a gift," Jack explained. "Last time she was here, she noticed the clock was broken, so she went and bought us a new one."

Josh frowned, then reached up to pull the clock off the wall. "We don't want it."

I didn't know if I'd heard him right. "If it's not the right colour, I can take it back."

He didn't look at me, just thrust the clock in my direction. I was too stunned to make my hands do what they were supposed to, so Josh dropped the clock on the table and returned the old one to the hook. I looked uncertainly at Jack, but he just watched Josh with a flat mouth. I tried again. "I just thought—"

"We don't *want* it," Josh barked.

I concentrated on the old clock, back up there on the wall. It wasn't just broken—it was ancient. It had a geometric wooden frame, a brown face and gold-plated hands—a relic straight out of the 1980s. "But ... that one is broken. It doesn't work."

"What do you think you're doing?" Josh clenched his fists, and his eyes flashed. "Who are you to say what works in this house and what doesn't?"

I licked my lips and tried to swallow, but my throat was all sharp and dry.

"Just because we're in this fake engagement right now to help you dump your creepy ex-fiancé, don't think you can come in here and change things," Josh growled, the muscles in his jaw feathering. "Dad and I are fine on our own. Have been for a long time and will be long after you're gone."

"Okay, Josh, that's enough," Jack said firmly. "More than enough."

"It's fine," I whispered, trying to smile and failing. "He's right. I don't know either of you. I'm sorry about the clock."

I ran out the door and kept running until I fell and scraped my knees and hands on the bitumen road. The pain was the last straw, or the perfect excuse perhaps, to finally let myself cry. I let a few tears escape, keeping it together as best I could until I got home, where I really lost it. The last twenty-four hours tumbled down on me. Tyler showing up out of nowhere. Josh's proposal. Allowing myself to believe—even for a minute—that Josh might be one of the good guys.

Tomorrow, when I was done with my tears, I was going to find Josh and tell him I didn't want to continue with the engagement. I still didn't know how I was going to convince Tyler to leave town, but I was a smart girl. I'd figure it out.

In the meantime, I had a wedding to cancel. Again. Dawn had already called me that morning to discuss the details, and she'd wasted no time getting things started.

I grabbed my phone and dialled her number. She needed to know that the faux engagement was off.

9

JOSH

———————

DAWN WAS ON the phone when I walked into her shop. Double Take was a high-end thrift store filled with designer dresses and vintage jewellery, first-edition books and autographed headshots of Hollywood stars. Tourists loved the place, and busses of city dwellers visited year-round to check it out. Dawn was stubborn about keeping the business offline, and the exclusive nature of the things she sold only added to their astronomical price tags.

Her expression shifted when she saw me, and she quickly ended her call. "What can I do for you, Josh?" she asked a little brusquely.

"I need a ring. For Emily."

I ducked my head and wandered over to the jewellery case holding dozens of pieces in gold and platinum and silver, diamonds and rubies and emeralds. I pretended to know what I was doing, but the truth was, I was lost. Jesus Christ, was I lost.

Dawn met me on the other side of the counter. "I don't mean to pry, but I've just been on the phone with Emily, and she tells a different story. It's her opinion that we need to cancel this wedding. Immediately."

I wasn't surprised. I kept staring at the rings, not seeing them anymore, and nodded. Dawn allowed the silence.

"I always thought when I chose a ring, it'd be for Maggie, you know?" I heard the words and wondered what had possessed me to say them. I didn't speak without thinking first, and now I'd gone and done it twice in two days.

"I do," Dawn replied softly. "She was a beautiful girl."

"She was. But I have to look at pictures of her now if I want to remember the details. Like the tiny freckle on her lip or her tan lines, even in the winter."

"That makes sense. Time does that to us. It's natural, Josh."

"I'd have bought her a diamond, of course, and she might have liked it, but if I think about it now—now that I'm older—I don't think she'd have wanted a diamond at all. A black sapphire maybe, or a pearl. Something unexpected."

Dawn smiled fondly, and her eyes were glassy. "She was certainly one of a kind."

"She's why I became a paramedic." I didn't know why I kept talking, but it felt … not good but inescapable. Something inside had loosened where before it was only ever screwed up tight. "But going to car accidents is still tough."

"I'm sure it is."

"I always go, and I'm always the last one to give up." I moved up the jewellery case, scrutinising the rings without noticing any of them.

Dawn shadowed me, but I didn't look up. "Emily came by the house this morning," I said.

"She told me."

"She brought a clock with her to replace the one over the dining table. The thing hasn't ticked over in five years or more, but Dad hasn't touched it."

"That doesn't surprise me."

"He hasn't replaced anything in that house. Not the leaky tap in the bathroom, or the chipped glass in the laundry window, or the flaking paint on the kitchen cupboards."

"I know."

"So, when I got home this morning and saw Mum's clock on the table, and Dad and Emily staring up at the new one like they'd decided to move on behind my back … I snapped."

"I can understand that."

I laughed, though nothing about this was funny. "Do you want to explain it to me?"

Dawn sighed and shook her head. "You're not *ready*, Josh, and it's okay. You can't rush these things. Losing Maggie when we did, the way we did … And losing your mother when you were just fourteen …" She sighed again. "Jack has shown you the way to grieve, and it's the only way you know. Moving on doesn't come easily to either of you."

"Is this what it feels like, moving on? It's shit."

"Is it?" She put a hand on my arm. "Well, I'm sorry to hear that. Change is never easy, but sometimes it's unavoidable. Even necessary, some might say."

I frowned. "Maggie was too good for me. I didn't know it until it was too late, and it makes no sense that she's gone and I'm still here. It's my duty to honour her. Loving anyone else wouldn't be right or fair to either one of them."

It was Dawn's turn to frown. "If I'm honest, Josh, I think you're saying all these things to the wrong person. Right now, Emily thinks you're walking proof that all men are unreliable, unpredictable narcissists, and I think she's wondering what's so wrong with her that she keeps attracting that particular type of man. She deserves more than just a small part of your story. If she knew the truth, perhaps there'd be a way to save this engagement plan of yours and help her with her ex-fiancé problem—and, maybe, restore her faith in love. In *herself*."

My first response to the idea of confessing my history to Emily was horror, like snakes writhing in my stomach and twisting up my throat. But then I thought about how she'd grabbed my hand as she stood up to Tyler at the bar. I didn't like the idea of her thinking for a minute that I was anything like that jerk, and I couldn't abide the thought of Emily believing she was only deserving of men like that.

"That's not the worst idea you've had," I muttered. "If I can get the words out before she slams the door in my face."

"Well, a pretty piece of jewellery should help with that." Dawn pulled out a fabric tray and set it on the glass counter. "See anything you like?"

I examined the rings, not seeing anything good enough for Emily until the third row.

"That one," I said, pointing. The pale green stone was oval and on the large side, set in white gold and haloed with tiny sparkling diamonds. I hoped it wouldn't dwarf her finger, but that didn't change my mind. It was the one.

"Oh, that's stunning," Dawn gushed. "I had it appraised when it came in, of course, and would you believe it's aquamarine? Rare for it to have that colour, apparently. I've only seen them in blue, myself. It's expensive, though. Did you want to spend that much?"

I looked at the price tag. I had twenty times as much saved for when I left Valentine Bay. The cost didn't bother me, and perhaps it should have, but all I could think was that Emily deserved it.

Dawn popped the ring in a lined box, then a cardboard one, then a tiny little bag. It was overkill, but my head was already past the ring part of this plan and thinking about what I had to do next.

"So, you'll see Emily tonight, give her the ring, and explain everything? I'm sure she'll understand, and the two of you can work this all out." Dawn handed me the bag but didn't let go right away. "This'll be good for you, Josh. You'll see."

It was a long walk home. Emily was the first woman in four years I'd even looked at twice. Admitting that, even to myself, sent guilt shooting through my chest. Guilt and shame. I wasn't blind—I could appreciate an attractive woman when I saw one—but none had tempted me enough that I'd ever considered breaking my vow to Maggie that I'd never want anyone else. The life I had belonged to both of us, only she wasn't here anymore to share it.

By the time I got home, I had a plan. I didn't know if it was a good one, but it was the one that made the most sense. I wasn't ready enough, or whole enough, to be in a relationship. All I could do now was follow through with the so-far disastrous fake engagement plan that was, after all, my idea and keep my misery to myself. And when the wedding was done, and Emily was free to get that fresh start she so badly wanted, I was going to pack up my life, move into that apartment in the city, and make a fresh start of my own.

Dawn was right. Change was inevitable, even necessary. It was time for me to stop fighting it and leave Valentine Bay with all its memories behind.

10

EMILY

WHEN THE DOORBELL rang at eight o'clock, I assumed it was my dinner delivery. I'd already started on a jumbo tub of double-chocolate ice-cream, but who cared if dessert came first on a day like this? I'd spent the afternoon crying and dozing, and now I wanted to wallow, and the only proper way to do that was with spicy Thai food, a truckload of ice-cream, and a so-bad-it's-good romcom for one. This was the best way to deal with emotional distress. I'd had a lot of experience in this area, so I knew all about it.

I opened the door and froze. Tyler was on the other side, standing there with a cocky look I'd once thought was so sexy. Now, it gave me the impression he wanted to sell me something—something faulty and overpriced. Oh, he was still hot, and I had to swat away a flutter of the adoration I used to feel for him, but I couldn't muster up a shred of attraction. I was more interested in the large brown paper bag he held in one hand, stained with oil and giving off the mouth-watering aromas of red curry and jasmine rice.

"How'd you get that?" I demanded, trying to take it from him, but he was too fast and too tall. I refused to jump for my dinner, so I crossed my arms and glared.

"Bumped into the driver outside, saw your name on the ticket, and offered to bring it up for him. Good timing, yeah?"

"How did you know where I live?"

"It's a small town. I asked around."

I narrowed my eyes. "Stop asking questions about me."

"Okay. Let me in, and you can tell me what I need to know."

He offered me the bag, and I snatched it. "No need to come in. This won't take long. It's over, Tyler. You called off our wedding, and you know the worst part about that? It should have been *me* who dumped *you*. That's the part that kills me."

"I'm sorry, Em. I got—"

"Scared? Don't say it. Just … don't. What does that even mean? Why do men say they're scared when what they really should say is they're selfish? Or immature? Or an arsehole who can't keep it in his pants?"

He grabbed my free hand. "I didn't know if I was ready to settle down yet. I wasn't sure it was the right time or if we were doing the right thing, but things are different now. There's a … *hole* … in my life."

"And none of the other girls you've been screwing could fill that hole for you?"

He scowled. "I've never cheated on you. I've never slept with anyone else."

"You're a liar. Now get lost." I yanked my hand back and slammed the door in his face.

"I'm not giving up, Emily!" he yelled from the other side. "And I'm not leaving this stupid town until I've convinced you to go with me."

"Shut up!" shouted one of the neighbours.

I held my breath and strained my ears for the sounds of Tyler leaving. When a minute had passed, then two, then three, I exhaled and relaxed. That wouldn't be the last of him, and I still had to work out how to convince him to give up on his misguided and deluded belief that I'd take him back.

Blergh. The thought of his hands on me again, his skin pressing against mine, his lips moving over me ... It made me sick enough to want to skip dinner.

Now, if it were Josh's hands, Josh's skin, Josh's lips ... I groaned. Why did my mind run away in hopeless directions? The man was divine but obviously damaged, and I'd drawn him to me like a moth to a flame. There must have been a sign on my head that read "Wanted: man-child with intimacy issues. Must be well-versed in half-truths and shitty moods".

No, this was my own fault. It was too soon after Tyler to be taking an interest in anyone else, and that's exactly what I'd been doing when I'd agreed to go along with Josh's crack-brained fake-engagement plan. Hell, I couldn't even classify my involvement with Tyler as *over* yet, not until he got the message and left Valentine Bay. And when he was gone for good, I'd have to smooth things over with Josh. I'd let myself get carried away and assumed too much, and now I had to learn to live with him at a distance. Without any of that touching business.

The doorbell rang again. For crying out loud! Did Tyler think stalking was romantic? I wondered, very briefly, if my response to this type of behaviour would have been different if it had happened a week after the wedding when I was more heartbroken and less angry. I shuddered and thanked my luck that Tyler was too self-involved to have wanted me back right away.

"I told you to get lost!" I shouted.

He knocked again, and I huffed, thinking about my next move. Dawn was going to get back to me about the best way to cancel the wedding—I couldn't believe it had only taken one morning for her to call half the town and get things started—so until Tyler knew differently, the fiancé story was still the best weapon I had. I may as well use it while it lasted.

"Don't make me call my fiancé!" I screeched.

There was a promising pause before Tyler knocked again.

"You've got to be joking!" I stormed to the door and heaved it open. "Just how stupid are you?"

Josh stood on the other side, smiling that sexy crooked smile and looking at me with amusement. Holy heck, he was adorable.

"Pretty damn stupid," he replied.

"Oh. I thought you were Tyler."

My heart thumped at the sight of him, the way his navy T-shirt tightened around his biceps, the faint shadow darkening his jawline, the dampness that darkened his sun-bleached curls.

"No, just me."

"Oh."

I was acutely aware at that minute I was wearing my comfiest, rattiest pyjamas—a pair of pink shorts barely long enough to warrant the name and an over-sized grey tee that had lost its shape and now fell off one shoulder. I casually collected one side of the fabric, knotted it tightly at my hip, and hoped that made me more presentable.

There was an awkward pause before Josh cleared his throat. "Can I come in?"

"Um, sure." I stepped out of his way and closed the door behind him. He smelled like ocean and cedar and *man*, and he was holding a little bag, which he put on the coffee table.

"Take a seat," I said, gesturing to the sofa. "Can I get you anything? A drink?"

"No, thanks," he replied, sinking into the couch. "I just wanted to apologise for my behaviour this morning."

I moved into the kitchen. "I just ordered food. Are you hungry?"

"No, thanks," he said again. "Could you sit with me for a minute?"

I looked up at him then. For the first time since he'd surprised me on the other side of the door, I noticed how nervous he looked. Butterflies took flight in my stomach. Now wasn't the time to wonder how he could get better looking every time I saw him.

I sat on the far end of the couch and put my hands in my lap, which gave me something to look at aside from him.

"So, uh … I'm sorry for snapping at you today. It wasn't cool. The thing is, you surprised me. You and Dad, actually. We don't replace things in our house. We don't fix things or throw them away or upgrade them when they get old."

"Because of your mum," I whispered.

The muscles in his neck tightened, and his voice was carefully neutral. "Can't escape the gossip in this town."

I shook my head. "It wasn't gossip. When I was at your place so you could check the coffee burn"—I flushed as I recalled the way my body had responded to his touch—"you stepped out for a few minutes, and your dad showed me a picture of her. He explained that you've kept the house the way she liked it. I just didn't realise how literally he meant it."

Josh rubbed his palms over the tops of his thighs. "I'm sorry again, then, for assuming you'd listen to rumours."

"I didn't mean to offend you with the clock."

"I know. I overreacted like a complete idiot. But the thing is, it's not just about the house or my parents. There's something else you need to know."

Here it was. The big secret. The double life. The reason Josh was all kinds of wrong.

"If you did listen to gossip, you would have heard that I don't date, and there's a reason for that. I've already been in love. A long time ago." He paused and blinked a few times. "Her name was Maggie, and we'd been together since we were sixteen. When we were twenty-four, she died in a car accident."

"Oh, Josh." I reached out a hand and put it over his. "I'm so sorry."

"Thanks," he said roughly, pulling his hand out from under mine and hiding it between his knees.

"Is that why you're leaving the Bay?" He frowned, and I rushed to assure him. "Not rumour, I promise. Your dad told me, actually."

"I've never known him to say as much in a week as he said to you in fifteen minutes," Josh muttered. "But yeah. I'm leaving. I have to." He looked uncomfortable. "There's too much history here. I need to start fresh somewhere else."

Oh, that made so much sense, and it made me ache for him. "Okay," I whispered.

"That's it? No big speech about loss and love and hope and … and moving on?"

"Nope," I said with a shake of my head. "Look at me. I'm not exactly a success story. I understand the need to start over, though I'm beginning to think I'm a lost cause."

Josh smiled a little, and he reached over to pick up the little bag he'd brought with him. "I doubt that. You've just had a dose of bad luck with Tyler, and we're going to fix that."

"We?"

He pulled a box from the bag but didn't open it. "Now we've cleared up any misunderstandings, let's look at this fake engagement from an objective perspective, shall we? You need Tyler out of your life, and I'd like to convince you that not all men are dickheads. I got you into this mess, and I want to get you out of it. Let's go through with the plan as friends. I've got your back."

I smirked. "You've got my back?"

He flushed a little and rolled his eyes. "Whatever you want to call it. I'm here to help, okay?"

I squirmed, feeling a rush of pleasure. "What's in the box?"

"Well, on the off-chance you agreed with me, I picked up an engagement ring."

"You *what*?"

He took a black velvet box from the white cardboard one and handed it to me, but I didn't open it.

"Let's call it a promise ring instead. I promise you, I'm a good guy. And I promise you, I won't fall in love with you. When this is all over, I'll be gone, and you'll get the new beginning you came here for."

It shouldn't have been the right thing to say, but it was. Neither of us was ready or willing to get involved in something long-lasting, and this was us putting all our cards on the table.

I cracked open the box and gasped.

"It reminded me of your eyes," he said. "Do you like it?"

"Yes," I replied breathily. It was exquisite, and I *loved* it.

"So, is that a yes?"

"Yes," I murmured, staring at the ring, twisting it this way and that to set off the sparkles in the light.

Josh carefully took the box from me, pulled out the ring, and extended it. When I offered him my hand, he slipped the ring on my finger. His hand shook a little as he did, and where his fingertips grazed my skin, fire burned.

"I want to promise you something too," I whispered, resting my hand in his.

"Yeah?" His voice cracked a little, and it was the sexiest thing I'd ever heard. "What's that?"

The flutters in my body built to a hot buzz. "I promise not to fall in love with you, either."

11

JOSH

———————

I DIDN'T LET go of her hand. Her eyes were translucent, like green sea glass, and this close, her scent was overwhelming. The vanilla and the sugar, the warmth of her skin. I breathed her in, and her teeth caught her bottom lip.

"Josh?" she whispered, and the vulnerability in her voice tripped a wire somewhere in my chest.

I slid a hand behind her neck, pulled her in, and pressed my lips to hers. Her mouth was warm, and it opened without protest, her tongue hesitant at first, then insistent. Her hands twisted in my hair, and she moaned. At the sound, something primal stirred in my middle, my pants tightened, and before I could throw her down and pin her to the sofa, I pulled away, dropping my hands, and groaning at the effort it took.

"I'm sorry," I mumbled. "I shouldn't have done that."

She put a hand to her mouth, feeling at her lips as her breath came in quick pants. "I'm sorry, too. I didn't mean to—"

I stood, breathing heavily, but Emily sat there for a moment, her eyes far away as her fingertips played with her bottom lip. Jesus, she was beautiful. With a start, her eyes came into focus, but now that I was standing, the thing she had to focus on was the bulge in my pants.

Emily shot to her feet. "So, uh, thank you for the ring. Of course, I'll give it back when this is all over. I appreciate your help with Tyler."

"Happy to do it."

I ran a hand through my hair. I needed to get out of there before I did something stupid. Like kiss her again. Or run my hands over her bare shoulder and along her neck. Reach under that over-sized shirt and cup her breasts. Take her nipples into my mouth. Dig my fingers into her hips. Run my hands up her thighs. Slip my fingers into those tiny shorts ... *Fuck.*

I got to the door in record time, but she followed.

"Are you busy tomorrow?" she asked.

"Uh." My brain wouldn't work the way it needed to if I wanted to answer questions about my plans for the next day. It was too busy torturing me with suggestions of what might happen if I kissed Emily again. "Tomorrow? Um, working the morning shift from six."

"Can I take you to dinner? Please let me. It's the least I can do."

The right answer was no, but with those eyes, and the way she looked up at me as though it was just a small favour she wanted, I'd be a prick to deny her. I dropped my gaze, but it fell on her chest, and I recalled how she'd gathered the fabric of her shirt to the side and knotted it when I'd first arrived, pulling it tight and revealing the shape of her nipples as she'd done it.

"Sure. Fine." I took a step out the door.

"Is about eight o'clock okay?"

"Yeah, okay." Another step down the hallway.

"I'll text you the details after I've made a reservation."

"Sounds good," I called over my shoulder.

I wouldn't prove Emily right and be another man in her life that let her down. This was business, and we both knew it, but holy hell. I needed to get away because another second in Emily's apartment, and I was going to do things to her I hadn't done to any woman in a very long time.

———————

Emily was sitting at a table when I arrived at Coconut Joe's. The restaurant wasn't as casual as The Salty Stop, but it wasn't what anyone would call fancy either. Those kinds of places in the Bay—Valentine House, Honeysuckle Pavilion—were generally reserved for anniversary dinners, wedding receptions, and tourists with too much cash. Still, Co-Joe's was nice enough that I considered driving ten minutes out of my way after work to visit the coast's only department store and pick up a new shirt. But that would have meant I was trying to impress Emily, so I settled for the old white shirt I'd worn to The Stop on Valentine's Day. I showered quickly and skipped a shave, and barely looked in the mirror before leaving the house. I could keep things casual.

She smiled when she saw me and then stood to say hello. I wished she hadn't because it just brought her legs to my attention again, and this time, she *was* in heels. Black ones that added three inches to her height, and she still didn't clear my shoulders. She wore a dress, black this time, strapless except for thin cords that tied together at the back of her neck and shorter than the olive one she'd worn to The Stop. On closer inspection, I realised it wasn't a skirt but tiny shorts, and that just made the whole thing hotter.

There was a pause when I got to the table. Should I kiss her hello? It was awkward, and I felt like an idiot when Emily finally gave me a wave.

"Hey, thanks for coming." She dropped into her seat, and her cheeks coloured as she fussed with her napkin and took a sip of her water.

I sat, and we both spoke at the same time.

"Listen, that thing last night—"

"I'm really sorry about—"

She laughed a little and took another sip of water. "Can we just forget about it?"

I raised my palms towards her. "Yes. Absolutely. It's forgotten."

"Good. Great." She picked up the menu and flipped straight to the wine list. "Do you want a drink?"

The waiter arrived at that moment, and I ordered without checking the list.

"I'll have the local IPA on tap, and Emily will have …?"

"The same," she finished, closing the menu.

"Really?" I said as the waiter moved away. I thought back to the night at The Stop when Emily had ordered Abbie's bottomless margarita. "Isn't there something else you'd like? Something you always drink?"

She grimaced. "Actually, I'm not a big drinker. I just do it to be social."

"Well, you don't need to on my account. Here, I'll call the waiter back and cancel our beers."

"No, please. It's fine."

"Okay. If you're sure."

Clearing my throat, I looked around the room and decided I couldn't wait any longer to ask Emily some questions. That was my plan to get through the night. Keep the talk all about her. She knew more than enough about me already, and if I gave away any more of myself, there'd be nothing to take with me when I left.

I put my elbows on the table and leaned in. "So, Emily Jones, tell me about yourself. Have you always been a pig whisperer?"

The surprised, almost frightened look on her face faded as she laughed at my pathetic joke, and I relaxed almost instantly. Her face was just so telling, and I knew she was the kind of girl who trusted people, who couldn't keep a secret even if she wanted to. Those eyes would give her away. No wonder she was so vulnerable to arseholes like Tyler.

"No, not exactly. I'm a photographer, actually. Or I was, I should say. I don't do it anymore."

"That sounds cool," I said, meaning it. "Why'd you stop?"

She took a deep breath and shrugged, which did interesting things to her cleavage. I shifted a little, trying to make room in my pants.

"I was a wedding photographer, which you might not think is so *cool* after all, but I loved it. Now, I can't imagine taking pictures of happy brides and grooms on their big day." She shuddered, and it took all my willpower not to glance at her chest. "Actually, I couldn't think of anything worse."

"Yeah, that makes sense. Did you always want to be a photographer?"

She smiled a little, and I fantasised for a moment about those lips. Kissing them again, her kissing me, or her wrapping them around my ...

Focus, you animal.

"No, not really. I never thought much about what I wanted to be when I was growing up. I never knew my dad, my mum was only around enough to make sure I was fed and clothed and not much else, and my older sister bailed as soon as I turned sixteen. I can't blame her, really. She stuck around as long as she could, but as soon as I was old enough to take care of myself, she needed a fresh start." Emily's lips turned up at the corners. "And it worked for her. Why not for me too?"

"It can. It will. And the photography? How did that come about?" I hoped there'd be a happy twist to her story soon.

"It was an accident. A friend of a friend handed me her old Canon and asked me to take pictures on her wedding day—she couldn't afford the real thing—and I enjoyed it so much I saved for ages to get a camera of my own, and saved again to do a course in editing, and saved again for all the equipment I needed to do the job right. It took years to reach a point that I thought of myself as a real professional, you know?"

"Sure, but it sounds like you earned it."

"Yeah, I suppose I did."

The waiter arrived then with the drinks and to take our food orders. When he'd left, Emily was quiet. She took a sip of her beer but was careful not to reveal whether she liked it.

"So, you don't take photos anymore?" I asked, and she shook her head. "Did you get tired of it?"

"No, not at all. I don't think I could ever get bored with it."

"So, why did you stop?"

She started to shrug, but then she looked at me with a frown, and I knew she was thinking about my story. My revelations about Maggie and loss and love. I should have said she didn't owe me anything—not an explanation or an exchange of secrets—but I didn't because I wanted to know.

"I loved weddings. Oh my God, so much. Seeing all those happy brides and smitten grooms promising themselves to each other for the rest of their lives." She laughed a little, and her cheeks bloomed. "I couldn't wait for that to be me. To

have a man who loved me and a proper family all my own."
Emily looked down at her hands. "I met Tyler at a wedding.
He was a guest, and he said hello, and he was so charming.
Told me he loved weddings for all the same reasons I did,
and he wanted to find *the one* and ... You know, blah, blah,
blah." She waved a hand dismissively. "Turns out he was a
philandering arsehole, and it took me three years to realise
it. No. It took me three years to *admit* it. I didn't want to
believe. He was my hope for a happily ever after."

Tyler's smug face and infuriating sneer floated in front
of my eyes, and my biceps tensed with the desire to pound
the guy senseless.

"So anyway, I've given up all the dreaming and the
planning and the weddings. I don't take pictures of other
people's happiness anymore." Emily nodded firmly. "It's
time to forget all those things I used to want and start again.
And that's what brought me to Valentine Bay. Who knows
what I'll do next?" Her smile was glum. "I guess you're right.
Pig whisperer is as good as anything for the moment."

I thought for a second about reaching out and taking
her hand, but I didn't trust myself to touch her, so I fiddled
with my cutlery and napkin instead.

The waiter brought over our meals, and we murmured
our thankyous and ordered another round of drinks. Emily
had finished her beer and didn't object to another one, so
I assumed she found it palatable.

"Enough about me," she said, picking up her knife and
fork and starting on her grilled chicken. "Did you always
want to be a paramedic?"

The steak in my mouth turned to ashes, and I chewed slowly before swallowing. I took a swig of beer and returned it to the table while Emily waited with curious eyes.

Those fucking eyes.

"No, not really," I said. "I was a bit of a lost cause when I was young. Well, no, that's not entirely true. I always planned to do something, but I didn't perform particularly well at school, and I was never what you'd call ambitious." I paused to consider how much I should share about my life with Maggie at that age, then surprised myself by offering up the truth, ignoring the sting it set off in my chest. "Maggie used to say she felt the same way, but she was so smart and switched on that she could have done anything she set her mind to. In the end, we bummed around for years after high school, trading dreams about our future without making any real plans. She worked at The Stop with Will, and I did some landscaping and labour work with her dad. I enjoyed that—working with my hands and getting dirty."

"So, how did you go from landscaping to paramedics? They're so different."

I played for time, taking a few more mouthfuls of dinner. Emily didn't know how excruciating the answer to her question would be for me, but now that I'd started talking about Maggie, I wasn't sure I could stop. It was different telling this story to someone who never knew her.

"After the accident, I needed to do something meaningful. If I was alive and she wasn't, I had to do something really fucking important. I knew if I didn't make my life worth something, I'd probably end up dead."

Emily tucked her hair behind her ears and stared at her half-eaten meal. "Because you missed her so much?"

"Yeah. I went to a dark place. We were all in our early twenties when it happened, and so bloody close—me and Maggie, Will and Abbie, a bunch of us from high school—that losing her was like losing a limb. But their darkness wasn't like my darkness, you know? They didn't lose their *person*. They could move on."

"And you couldn't?"

"No. I don't know if I want to."

"Oh." She took another bite, and I could see her thinking about whether she should ask the next question. I wished she wouldn't, but it was there on her lips, I could tell. "Why not?"

"Because then she'll be gone," I snapped, then shook my head. "I'm sorry."

"No, I'm sorry. I didn't mean to push."

Emily did reach out a hand then, but mine were back under the table, clenched on my lap. I looked at her slim fingers, the second-last sparkling with the aquamarine engagement ring I'd given her the night before, and my stomach tightened as the kiss replayed in my head. My mind was a mess, and the emotional whiplash wasn't helping.

I picked up my cutlery. "Let's just talk about something else, okay?"

"All right." She began eating again as well. "I suppose we *should* talk about the wedding."

I smiled despite myself. "Yeah, we probably should." But then I recalled what she'd said about weddings, remembered she'd been practically left at the altar less than three months ago, and I felt like a total jerk. "Shit, this is probably torturing you. I didn't even think about that when I got you into this."

She giggled. "Actually, the possibility that it's torturing *Tyler* is more than enough to make up for it." She put her knife and fork down with a clink and assumed a dour expression. "I shouldn't have said that. This is serious business."

I grinned, a little confused, and then checked her drink. She hadn't even started her second beer, but I suspected she'd already had more than enough.

"Are you drunk?"

"No." She sighed and pushed the glass away. "Just a little buzzed. That happens when you're my size and drink so rarely. I probably need to go into training."

I took her beer and placed her water glass in front of her. "Have this, and I'll get the cheque."

Emily pulled out her purse and rummaged around for a credit card. "Absolutely not. This is my treat."

My pants protested as I ran my gaze over her mouth, her lip plumped out in a pretty, petulant pout. "Fine," I said, "but I get the next one."

"So, my sad story hasn't sent you running for the hills?"

"Hardly."

We made our way over to the counter, where Emily fixed up the bill, every second feeling longer than the last. When she had her card and receipt clutched in her hand, she looked up at me as if to say, *what next?*

My heart thundered at what I was about to say. "Now, let's get you home."

12

EMILY

———————

THE BEER I'D had with dinner had given me a good buzz, but I'd also had a full meal and two glasses of water, so I wasn't drunk, no matter what Josh thought. But the way he insisted on walking me home twisted my stomach into knots.

My apartment wasn't far from the restaurant, and our small talk dwindled to silence the closer we got to my door. I fished my key out of my bag and turned to put it in the lock, concentrating more than I needed to on the simple task. I heard Josh behind me, taking a step closer, and I swear I could feel the heat of his body, hear the breath on his lips, and smell the fragrance that was just him.

I couldn't keep talking myself around the truth that I'd never wanted anyone as badly as I wanted Josh. I'd never had such explicit thoughts about a man, not even Tyler. Josh was delectable, all soft hands and hard muscle and irresistible heat and … Last night, when I'd come face to face with his cock, the need that pulsed through me had felt like possession by a horny poltergeist. I'd had to jump away before I unzipped him and took him into my hands. Or my mouth. I very nearly moaned at the memory as the key slid into the lock.

I knew why I'd never fantasised like this before. I'd always been too busy worrying about marriage. No matter who I dated, I fell asleep asking the universe, *could I marry him?* When it came to Josh, I knew the answer already. No way in hell was he interested in marriage, and he wasn't sticking around Valentine Bay anyway. Normally, that'd make him a hard pass, but tonight, it was throwing out all kinds of possibilities.

I wanted to walk a new path, didn't I? Create a better life? Maybe part of my healing included hot, no-strings-attached sex with a gorgeous man. It was out of character, sure, but it'd put an indelible full stop on my chapter with Tyler.

"Do you want to come in?" I asked, cursing the crack in my voice. I shifted my shoulders and lifted my chin, hoping I came across as confident.

"I shouldn't," Josh murmured.

I tried to hide my disappointment. "Why not?" I pushed the door open a little further but didn't go in.

"Because if I come in, I'll want to kiss you. And if I kiss you, I'll want to touch you. And if I touch you …" He stood there, hands curled into fists, his eyes hot as they travelled over my face, my mouth, my neck, my breasts.

I glanced inside my empty apartment, gave it about three seconds of thought, and then said again, "Do you want to come in?"

His tongue brushed his bottom lip, consideration passed across his brow, then he nodded.

As soon as we were inside, Josh kicked the door closed, and the apartment plunged into darkness. I spun to face him, and he pulled me towards him, crushing his lips against mine.

Wet warmth soaked my panties as I opened my mouth and welcomed the touch of his tongue. He was so tall that I had to stretch up on my toes to reach him, and I squealed against his mouth when he set his hands on my arse and hoisted me up. I wrapped my legs around his waist and kissed him so hard I worried my lips would bruise. His cock was firm between us, pushing against me where I needed to feel it. Groaning against his mouth and circling my hips, I wished there was no fabric between us.

He lifted me onto the dining table, and as I frantically unbuttoned his shirt and ran my hands over his hard chest, he tore at the strings at my neck, yanking down the top of my playsuit and plunging his face into my cleavage. It was so fast and frenzied that I gasped as his hot mouth closed over one hard, aching nipple, then the next, his tongue lapping in greedy circles. His hand cupped my other breast, his fingers tweaking and teasing. Pleasure dropped my head back with a sigh, and I twisted my fingers in his hair.

His lips travelled up to my neck and over my collarbone, tongue swirling in glorious circles, as his hands tried and failed to remove my shorts. "It's a playsuit," I panted. "It zips up at the back."

Josh drew back, his adorable puzzlement making something bloom in my chest, and I pushed on his shoulders so I could set my feet on the floor, heels still on, and turn my back to him. I leaned on the table. "Unzip me."

He growled and tore at the zipper, then tugged my suit down. It dropped to the floor, and I giggled when he mumbled "fuck" at the sight of my black lace knickers. His soft, gentle hands closed over my shoulders, ran down the length of my back, then curled around my arse and dug into my hips. One hand snaked around my stomach, then explored lower. He touched me, a single fingertip edging into my underwear, circling my clit once, twice, and then caressing the seam.

"You're so wet," he groaned, resting his forehead on my back and moving his finger up and down again. One slow stroke, then another, and another, and my body sang. I put my hand over his and pushed, and he plunged two fingers inside me.

Folding further forward, I flattened myself on the table while he unzipped his pants, and I moaned louder as the tip of his cock brushed against me. Reaching around behind me, I wrapped a hand around his thick sex. He was hot and hard, and I wanted all of him.

"Just a second," he whispered, and I heard him rip open a condom. It was taking too long, so I pumped my fist up and down his length, then ran my thumb over the tip.

"Want me to come right now?" he growled.

"No," I said with a laugh. "Absolutely not."

"Then please stop doing that."

Spinning me around and lifting me onto the table, Josh pushed my panties down and over my ankles. He positioned himself over me, the weight of him just right, then the tip of him was against my centre, and I sucked in a surprised breath.

"Is this okay?"

I grabbed his arse and pulled the first inch of him into me. "Yes."

"Fuck." He pushed a little deeper, stretching me slowly and filling me up, testing my tolerance inch by inch until he was buried all the way. He thrust his hips faster and faster, slamming his body against my clit and sending jolts of excruciating pleasure through my core.

It was urgent and *animal*, and I bucked my hips, crying out with each thrust, feeling the pressure build deep within until I was flying towards a release that made me scream. Seconds later, Josh's cock pulsed inside me, his body rippling as he balanced over me.

Breathing hard, he dropped his head forward. "Wow."

"Yeah," I sighed, running my fingers through my hair and staring up at the ceiling. *Wow.*

We stayed that way for a minute or two, catching our breaths. I couldn't believe I'd just done that. I kind of wanted to do it again.

"I'm sorry," he said suddenly, easing away from me. "I'm just going to …" He straightened, collected his clothes from the floor, and walked to the bathroom.

I propped myself up on my elbows, finding myself aroused again at the sight of his bare arse. "Why are you sorry?"

He disappeared into the bathroom without answering.

Ignoring a flutter of anxiety at the change in him, I found my underwear and playsuit and got dressed, poured two glasses of water and put them on the table, and then sat to wait. I ran my hands over the timber top and, despite my unease, I smiled. I didn't think I'd ever be able to eat dinner here again and not think about this.

Josh emerged from the bathroom, leaving the light on and the door open to give the apartment a little illumination. His shirt was unbuttoned, his hair dishevelled—and ridiculously sexy—but the way he rubbed the back of his neck told me he was embarrassed. "Uh, I can go. If you want."

I jumped to my feet as he moved towards the door. "Wait. Why are you sorry? Why would I want you to go?"

He slumped and rubbed at his face. "I didn't plan this, you know? Or maybe I did. I feel like an arsehole."

"But why?" When he said nothing, I whispered, "You're not an arsehole."

He turned to me with a tortured face. "I hate myself. I'm supposed to be proving to you not all men are sex-crazed, selfish jerks, and here I am, acting like a sex-crazed, selfish jerk."

"Oh."

"I'll understand if you want to cancel this whole arrangement."

I bit my lip. Old Emily would have gone along with Josh's stupid guilt trip, taken the blame and accepted the outcome, even though her heart would have screamed at her to say what she really thought. Old Emily wasn't good at following her instincts. She'd been so busy keeping Tyler happy enough to marry her that she'd bitten her tongue and averted her eyes anytime things got uncomfortable. Come to think about it, she was a lot like that in life, too.

Not anymore, and not with Josh. She had nothing to lose with him. He'd be gone in a few weeks. If she were ever going to be strong enough to face the world again, she had to learn to speak up.

"You know, that was pretty great."

He opened his mouth, then closed it again with a snap.

"You're not a sex-crazed, selfish jerk," I said. "You're not leading me on or promising me something you can't give. I knew what this was when I invited you in."

His eyebrows rose with disbelief. "Yeah?"

"I could use a little fun in my life," I went on. "I've never just enjoyed a man's ... company ... without worrying about where it was going to go."

Josh looked at me like I was speaking another language. "So, you mean ... What do you mean, exactly?"

"That this was ..." I fumbled for an appropriate word and couldn't think of one. "Nice."

"Nice? It was *nice*?" He started buttoning up his shirt, grumbling under his breath.

I blushed but secretly felt relieved. "What would you call it, then?"

It was his turn to redden. "Yeah, *nice* works."

"Okay. So, maybe …" Speaking my truth was one thing. Being forward was another. "We just write this off as a fringe benefit of our little arrangement and start again tomorrow."

"A fringe benefit, huh?" He smirked, fastening the last button, and I didn't know how it was possible, but he looked even hotter fully dressed. "I can live with that."

"Good, because we have an appointment at Raelene's bakery at ten to choose a wedding cake."

"Are you serious?"

"Unfortunately, yes. Dawn has roped the entire town into our charade, and everyone's weirdly eager to help."

He snorted. "Bet they love the idea of me pretending to be your fiancé." Then his face softened. "I didn't know it'd come to this. I didn't think about the wedding part at all. Is it too much?"

"Honestly, no. It's sort of comforting. I've never had a family or friends to look out for me. This feels nice, in a twisted way."

"There's that word again."

I flushed. "And what about you? Is it too much?"

"Surprisingly, no. It's not real, right? And everyone knows it, thank God. Plus, it was my boneheaded idea." He shook his head. "It's just a few weeks. I can handle it."

"Dawn's organised a cake, and flowers, and food. I don't know how I'm going to pay for all this. I can't expect everyone to give us all this for free. It's too much."

"I can—"

I flung up a hand. "Absolutely not." I flipped my hand around and waved it in front of his face, reminding him of the ring he'd given me. "This is more than enough."

"Well, you're not alone in this, so we'll think of something, all right?"

I smiled, knowing he meant it and feeling that cuddly sensation I'd experienced in the bar with Abbie and Will. "Thanks, I appreciate that."

"Well, uh …"

It was awkward, knowing the night was over, and both of us were clearly unsure about how to say goodbye. Finally, I stood on my tiptoes and pecked him on the cheek. "Thank you for dinner."

"You paid."

"Well, thank you for everything else."

He flushed again, and I rather liked making this man blush.

"So, tomorrow at ten?" he asked.

"Yes, at *Le Gâteaux D'Amour* on Main."

"I'll see you there."

I closed the door behind him, leaned against it, and sank to the floor. The best sex I'd ever had, with the most beautiful man I'd ever known, a ring on my finger, and no emotional stakes to ruin the high. Nothing waiting in the shadows to tear my heart to pieces. I was beyond all my fairytale garbage, and it felt pretty darn fantastic.

13

JOSH

———

HOLY SHIT. I'D just had sex with Emily.

I might have said I was in shock if shock could be defined as an out-of-body sensation that made you feel freaking fantastic and freaking awful at the same time. I was furious with myself. And pretty pleased with myself. I didn't know what I felt, and I didn't know where I was going until I walked past The Salty Stop and saw the lights were off. Will lived upstairs, so I let myself into the building by the residential side entrance, climbed the stairs to his apartment, and banged on the door with my fist. Light cut in and out under the door, the muffled sound of the television paused, and I heard him moving around inside. He opened the door.

"What the fuck happened to you?"

I pushed past him and dropped onto his old sofa. "I had sex."

"Hallelujah. I'll get the whiskey."

I glanced up at the loft that was Will's bedroom. It was dark, and I couldn't see anyone up there, but Will noticed me looking.

"Abbie's been asleep for an hour. She's had a big night." He shook his head. "Nothing's waking her before morning." He handed me a tumbler with two fingers of whiskey and sat down. "Cheers."

I clinked my glass and threw it back.

"All right, then." Will got up, collected the whiskey bottle from the kitchen, and brought it back to the living room. He refilled my glass, but I held on to it this time.

"Emily?" he asked.

"Yeah."

"Well." He leaned back and ran a hand through his hair. "I hate to sound like a crass arsehole, but it's about time."

I snorted and leaned back as well, tilting my head up. "I didn't mean for it to happen."

His expression was disbelieving. "I saw you two at the bar on Friday night. She was into you."

"You think?" I blew out a tense breath, and Will waited, so I said what I'd been thinking. "That was the first time in three years."

He choked on his whiskey and then swallowed, wiping his mouth. "Sorry, but that's ... I knew it had been a while, but ... Fuck, that's painful."

I tipped up my glass. "You're telling me."

I'd only been with one woman since Maggie, and I hadn't known her well. It happened a year after Maggie died, and I thought sex with someone—anyone—might help me move on. It didn't. It felt like cheating, and I'd never been able to bring myself to do that to her again. But I couldn't explain that to Will because then I'd have to admit that sex with Emily had been different. Will would want to know why and what it meant, and I didn't know the answers. I didn't want to know.

Will stared into his drink, then looked at me sideways. "So, how was it?"

I remembered the way Emily had looked underneath me, the satiny smoothness of her skin, the way she'd wrapped her fingers around my dick, and it perked up at the memory. "Incredible."

But fast. Too fast. I should have taken my time. Touched every inch of her. I hadn't even tasted her. The thought of my tongue between her legs sent regret shooting through my middle and desire to my crotch.

"Oh, yeah?" Will replied. "Good for you."

I put my glass on the table with a dull clink and dropped my head into my hands.

"What's the problem here, exactly?" Will asked. "You were with a gorgeous girl, and you got laid for the first time in a long time. I fail to see the issue."

"It wasn't part of the plan," I muttered.

"The fake engagement plan?"

I sighed. "Yeah, that one."

He lifted an ankle onto the opposite knee and took another sip of his whiskey. "And what is the plan, exactly?"

Yes, this was what I needed. Someone to remind me

104

what was real and what was not. Go over the rules. Make me accountable. Obviously, I couldn't be trusted to keep myself in line.

"Over the next three weeks, I'm Emily's fake fiancé. My jobs—my *only* jobs—are to one, help her get rid of her dickhead ex, and two, convince her that not all men are selfish sex-crazed jerks. Then, when the wedding's done and the slimeball's gone, and she's ready to get on with her life, I'm taking off. For good."

Will shifted forward on the sofa. "Hang on a sec. We'll get to the selfish sex-crazed jerk thing in a minute— because you've seriously failed her on that count—but what's this shit about leaving? Going where? Why?"

Even though we'd been best friends since kindergarten, I hadn't told Will about my plans to leave the Bay. I'd assumed Abbie would have said something—she had to suspect after I was gone so long the last time—but he seemed clueless.

"The city." I cleared my throat. "I've been renting a place down there, getting used to it, seeing how it fits. And it fits well enough. It's time for me to go."

Will ran a hand through his short, sandy hair. "I never did buy your crap about going fishing, but I thought you were driving further up the coast, surfing and bumming around. I never asked because you never wanted to talk about it. I feel lousy now. Sorry."

I laughed, though what I felt was stupid. "That would have been an easier cover to keep. Fuck, I've been *fishing* on and off for a year now and never caught a thing.

No wonder Abbie knew I was lying." Will chuckled a little, and then I shrugged. "Starting over someplace new seems the right thing to do."

"I guess you're the best judge of that." He puffed out a breath. "The Bay won't be the same without you." Will looked into his glass and swirled the amber liquid around. "So, does Emily know you're bailing?"

"She does."

"And she still slept with you?"

My mouth quirked as I recalled the way her eyes had sparkled when she'd explained how we could move past our indiscretion. "Fringe benefit, she called it."

"Was it a one-time thing?"

"I don't know. I think so."

"Shame." Will shook his head. "Three weeks of sex with a girl like that, no commitment required? Sweet deal, if you ask me."

"She deserves more than that." I downed the last of my drink. "She deserves more than me."

Will's eyes flicked up to the loft. "Women have a funny way of deciding what they do and don't deserve. Doesn't always make sense."

I followed Will's gaze upwards. The loft was lost in shadow, but I knew Will was talking about Abbie as much as he was Emily.

"Thanks for the drink," I said, getting to my feet. "Sorry to crash your night. Hope I didn't interrupt anything."

Will followed me to the door. "Never too late to be the first to hear about your incredible sex with the knockout new girl." He latched onto my shoulder and turned me around. "Seriously, Ford. I'm happy for you."

I ran a hand through my hair. "Yeah, thanks."

I thought about Emily the entire way home. I imagined going back to her place and doing it all again—less frantic this time, more patient. Devouring her slowly and making her moan. The impulse was so intense, I wondered how I was going to stop myself from kissing her over the next three weeks. It'd take superhuman self-control to keep my mouth off her, and I didn't have it in me.

But then I turned the corner onto Bellamy Road and passed number twelve, where Maggie used to live, and I wondered if it would be better to get out of Valentine Bay tonight before walking away from Emily became impossible.

———

When I arrived at *Le Gâteaux D'Amour* on Main the next morning, Emily was waiting on the footpath outside. She looked incredible in cut-off denim shorts and a loose, cropped white tee that revealed a tiny strip of her smooth stomach. I lengthened my stride and grinned.

Le Gâteaux was one of two bakeries in Valentine Bay. It was a fancier, patisserie-style store that made French-inspired creations that locals used for weddings, anniversaries, birthdays, and parties. It was framed with black-and-white striped awnings over floor-to-ceiling windows that revealed tiny iron café tables and glass cases filled with brightly coloured delicacies that melted the minute you put them in your mouth. The sight of them reminded me of Emily's skin under my tongue, like vanilla-infused velvet, and I had to blink away the picture of my head between her thighs as my pants strained across my crotch.

Emily smiled brightly as I approached. Spots coloured her cheeks, and she bit her bottom lip at the sight of me. I almost lost it then and there.

"Morning, schnookums," she called with a wave.

I tripped over my own feet but kept walking. *Schnookums?* When I reached her, she stretched up on tiptoes and flung her arms around my neck. She was acting weird, but I didn't knock back the chance to wrap my arms around her tiny waist, lift her off the ground, and turn my nose to her neck, taking in her delicious scent.

"I'm sorry," she whispered into my ear, and the heat of her breath sent goosebumps rippling across my skin. "Tyler followed me, and he's around the corner, watching."

I put her down on the ground and lifted my head.

"Don't look! Just be cool."

Her eyes were round and pleading and tightened a little at the corners—with worry or anger, I couldn't tell—so I took her hand. "Okay, honeybun. Let go get ourselves a wedding cake."

Her shoulders loosened, and she chuckled. "Honeybun?"

"Anything's better than *schnookums*."

"Sorry. It's the first thing I thought of."

"Oh, great. So now I remind you of a dog."

She laughed, louder this time, and bumped me with

one shoulder. "Okay, it wasn't the *first* thing I thought of, but I didn't think the other names were PG enough to yell down the street."

"Interesting. I might want to hear them later," I murmured, then immediately wanted the words back.

She was quiet for a moment, but then she looked up at me with those eyes, her lips parted a little. "Maybe that could be arranged."

I lost myself so deeply in the green of her irises, the pink suffusing her cheeks, the slender, cool fingers wrapped in my large, warm ones, that the pastry chef, Raelene Perrin, had to clear her throat to get our attention.

"Okay, you two," she said with a curve to her lips and a sparkle in her eye. "Get in here and we'll go through the book."

Raelene wasn't one of the mother hens who clucked with worry about my bachelor status, but I'd gone to school with her younger brother, and she was old enough to feel entitled to her *I know better* look. I put on the glower I used whenever some do-gooder tried to interfere with my life, but Emily took one look at me and poked at the crease between my brows, then rubbed her thumb over the back of my hand. I tried to relax. This was for her, after all. And Tyler was outside, watching.

We took a seat at a table while Raelene poured coffees and put slices of raspberry clafoutis on plates. She set them down and disappeared out the back.

Emily scooped a piece of the dessert into her mouth and moaned. "Oh, this is incredible."

I watched her mouth and smiled at her delight just as Raelene returned and dropped a ratty old binder on the table. "This is my catalogue, if you can call it that. The pictures aren't great, or even recent."

"This cake is heaven," Emily said as she opened the folder and began thumbing through the sleeves. She lapsed into silent concentration as she examined every page.

Raelene looked at me with an apologetic grimace. "I take a couple of snaps in the bakery before the cakes go out, and I ask customers to send me any they take at the wedding or the party or whatever, but as you can see, they don't always do the cake justice."

Emily ran her fingers over each picture, and Raelene watched with her hands clasped in her lap and her toe tapping on the floor.

"Em's a photographer," I explained.

"What?" Emily's head jerked up, and at the anxious look on Raelene's face, she reached out and squeezed her fingers. "Oh! Yes, I'm sorry. The cakes themselves look incredible—I have no idea which to choose—but the images … You're right. They don't do your work justice. It's a shame, that's all."

I had an idea, one I was pretty sure Emily would like, and I felt a rush of excitement. "We were talking earlier, Rae, about how we're going to pay for this fake wedding—"

"Josh, stop it." Raelene smacked my arm playfully. "We've all told Dawn we'll do it for nothing. You're family."

"I appreciate that. I really do," Emily replied, "but I can't accept." Turning another page, her face suddenly lit up, and I leaned over to see what she was looking at.

The cake in the picture had two tiers covered in pale pink icing, with a tower of tiny pastel pastries forming a type of crown on top. A silver ribbon wrapped around the base of the cake, and light pink flowers were strategically placed from top to bottom. "I can't imagine the work that goes into something like this."

Raelene smiled. "You like that one? I can make the cake any flavour you like, and the macarons as well. The one you see there is a mixture of white chocolate and rose, lavender, and vanilla macarons with a white chocolate pistachio cake."

"That sounds amazing—and tricky!"

"If you want it, it's yours."

"I insist on paying you."

"I won't hear of it."

Taking that as my cue, I cleared my throat. "What would you say to a trade instead? If you make this cake for us, Emily can take professional photos of it for your catalogue." Hoping I hadn't said the wrong thing, I watched Emily's reaction from the corner of my eye.

"I couldn't …" she stammered, her eyes wide. "I mean, I don't know …"

Shit. I'd stuffed up. I should have spoken to her about this before opening my big fat mouth. But before I could figure out how to undo what I'd just done, Emily surprised me. She clasped her hands together, set them on the table in front of her, and straightened her spine.

"I'd be happy to do it, but truthfully, you'd be getting the raw end of the deal. A few photos from me are nowhere near enough to make up for this cake."

111

Damn, I was proud of her.

Raelene tilted her head to one side. "Would you be up to taking photographs of other cakes, too? I have ten orders in the next month, and it'd be fantastic to have proper pictures of them all." She chuckled a little, then sighed. "Valentine Bay is popular enough for destination weddings that I really should have done this years ago, but so many couples have their cakes delivered from the city that I didn't know how to compete. If you help me out, it'll really improve business. Makes giving you this wedding cake in return well worth the trade from my point of view."

Emily frowned, flipping the pages over and over and then back again until she was again looking at the pastel-coloured cake in question. I held my breath until she nodded tightly, as though to herself rather than me or Raelene, and she stuck out her hand. "It's a deal."

Raelene shook her hand and then laughed, clapping her hands together just under her chin. "A professional catalogue! I'm so excited. But enough about me, let's talk about you. Have you got colours in mind? If we start there, we can pick flavours to match."

Half an hour later, Emily and I were out on the street again, our wedding cake order done and dusted: coffee, vanilla, and dark chocolate macarons on a raspberry and hazelnut cake.

"I hope I didn't overstep the mark in there," I said, crossing my arms and rubbing my shoe over the cracks in the footpath. "I know you said you don't take wedding pictures, but you also said you never stopped loving the job, and this isn't *technically* wedding photography ..."

Emily was ignoring me, staring off into the distance, but then she spun around and grabbed my hands.

"Tyler's across the road," she mumbled. "Don't look!"

I glanced over the road, where her ex was sipping a coffee and watching us over the rim of his cup. Emily's smile looked glued on, and she had that deadly grip on my hands again.

"If the photography idea is too much," I said, "I'll talk to Rae about other arrangements. She'll understand."

"What? No! It's a great idea. I wish I'd thought of it." Emily's grin morphed into something more genuine, and she bounced up on her toes. "I'm kind of excited to get my gear out again."

She was fucking adorable. Pulse pounding in my ears, I leaned in. "What do you say we give Tyler something to think about?"

Before she had a chance to answer, I pulled my hands free from hers so I could cradle her head in my hands, then I tipped her mouth up and touched my lips to hers. I kissed her softly, the top lip and then the bottom, brushing her cheekbones with my thumbs and running my tongue lightly over hers. I lost myself for a moment, absorbing the heat between us.

When I drew back, her eyes were still closed, and it was a few seconds before they fluttered open. Her hands came up to circle my wrists, and when she gazed up at me, I had to remind myself it was all for show.

"Where to next, honeybun?" I asked, my voice gravelly.

"Flowers," she said with an exhaled breath. "Florist. Flowers."

I smirked and dropped my hands, then took one of hers in mine as we started up the street and away from Tyler— but not before I'd made sure there was steam coming from the jerk's ears. And there was. A fuck ton of it.

Not all men are arseholes, Emily. I'm going to prove that to you.

And when her heart is whole, and she's ready for that new beginning she wants so badly, I'm getting out of Valentine Bay and as far away from her as possible to give her a fighting chance at a happily ever after.

14

EMILY

———

CLAD IN MY work uniform and perched on one of the bar stools at The Stop, I crossed my legs and took a sip of my bottomless margarita. Next to me, Abbie had her head over her phone and was laughing at a text. When my own phone chimed, I debated whether to acknowledge it. Tyler had resorted to texting me every day, many times a day, and some of them were graphic enough to turn my stomach. If he wasn't trying to wheedle me, he was having a go at sexy, and as tempted as I was to shoot back something scathing about his "hard, hot cock", I'd decided that would only add fuel to the fire when what I really needed to do was douse him with a bucket of ice-cold water.

Abbie giggled, and her thumbs flew across her screen. Whoever she texted was more interesting than I was at that moment, so I fished my phone out of my bag and tapped on the screen, which lit up with Josh's name, and it lit something deep in my belly, too.

Josh: I'm a lousy fiancé! Sorry about my schedule this week, but I'd like to see you tonight if you're up for it. Just need to go home and shower. Should be ready by eight. Got plans?

My pulse quickened, and my fingers flew over the keyboard.

Me: Just having after-work drinks with Abbie at The Stop. Want to join?

The three dots indicating the tapping of his reply faded in and out, dragging my heart up and down, and when the text finally came through, it set it to beating a million miles per hour.

Josh: Don't think I can face the crew tonight. Drinks at your place instead?

My hands trembled, and I had to override autocorrect three times.

Me: Sounds good. See you there at eight.

His next reply was instant.

Josh: Meet me out front of The Stop, and I'll walk you home.

I bit back a smile and typed back.

Me: Okay.

"Yuck," Abbie said, nodding at the phone in my hand. "Is Tyler sending you dick pics?"

"Ha! No, but he's more than happy to describe it to me in unnecessary detail."

She snorted. "As if you haven't seen it before." Abbie laid her phone on the bar, face down. "Let's change the subject before I say something I'll regret, because you know I will. Tell me, are we going to do a hens' night?"

I tucked my phone away as well. "No! God, no. That seems overkill."

"No fair." Abbie pouted. "I wanted to order a naked man to dance for you."

I laughed. "You're going to have to wait for a real wedding, I'm afraid."

"What was your hens' do like for your wedding with Tyler?" she asked, sipping her cocktail.

"I didn't have one." Abbie's face was such a comical mix of shock and pity that I laughed. "I'm sorry to devastate you, but here's the embarrassing truth about me. I didn't have a lot of friends in the city. My friends were all Tyler's friends, and there weren't many couples among them. A week before the wedding date, I went for brunch with a woman who'd hired me to photograph her wedding. I had two mimosas and pancakes as well as eggs, and I was happy with that."

Abbie looked me square in the eye. "That may be the saddest thing I've ever heard." As I took a sip to cover the flush in my cheeks, Abbie added, "As if giving up all other men forever and ever isn't depressing enough, you didn't even get yourself flipped and folded over Magic Mike's face." Her hand shot out and grabbed mine. "Promise me, Em. If I'm ever dumb enough to get married, you'll get me a stripper. A good one. Oh, I know!" She pulled out her phone and flashed the screen at me. "I follow this guy on TikTok. Try to get him, okay?"

I laughed. "I'll do my best."

"I'm counting on it. Hey, what about a quiet girls' night instead? I'll ask Jess to join us. She could use the distraction." Abbie stood, leaned over the bar, and shouted at Will, who was serving people at the other end. "Hey! Babe! We're taking the booth in the corner. Send us out something yummy, will you?"

Will smiled at his customers, handed over their drinks, then stalked towards us. He put his elbows on the bar and leaned towards Abbie. "Hey. *Babe*. What have I said about terrorising me while I'm working?"

She grinned and leaned in so close the tips of their noses almost touched. "You love it."

He rolled his eyes and straightened, then flicked his dish towel at the bar. "You both right for drinks?" After eyeing her glass, Abbie downed the last mouthful and held it out for more. Will topped her up. "And you, Em?" he asked.

My glass was still two-thirds full. "I'm good. Thanks, Will."

"Too easy. I'll send over a plate of tapas in about twenty minutes. Now get lost. There are actual paying customers in here waiting for their drinks."

Abbie hopped off her bar stool, and I followed her to the row of dark, cosy booths on the other side of the bar. As we walked away, I glanced over my shoulder to see two girls slipping onto the stools we'd just vacated. Will poured them drinks and gave them sexy eyes while they laughed and tossed their hair. The man wasn't as broad as Josh, nor as tall, but every line of his lean body was cut to perfection. His hair was a light, earthy brown, and he had a dimple in one cheek that gave him a roguish, boy-next-door vibe. I don't know how he did it, but right in front of my eyes, he dialled up his smile from "friendly" to "dazzling," and he was, quite frankly, stupidly hot.

Abbie slid into the corner booth, and I followed her.

"I still can't believe you're a photographer," she said. "It's maybe the best news ever. Think you can take some shots of me doing yoga on the beach? It'll be great for Insta. Might even help me advertise for new clients at the studio."

"I'd love to," I said, setting my glass on a cardboard coaster. "But before we talk about that, tell me more about the deal with Will. Why aren't you guys together for real? He's beautiful."

Abbie squinted at the bar, spotted the girls falling over themselves to touch Will's arms, and pointed. "*That's* why."

Will chose that second to look over at us, and Abbie plastered a mocking smile on her face while flipping him the bird. He laughed and shook his head.

"Will and I are the same," Abbie went on. "In it for a good time, not a long time. We're friends with a relationship of convenience." As her eyes narrowed and her mouth curved upwards, she took a sip of her drink. "Speaking of which, I need to know more about what's happening with Josh. I'm doing my best to keep my nose out of your business, but say the word, and I'll jump right in. I haven't seen either of you all week, so spill. What have I missed?"

I played with the stem of my glass, then wedged my hands under my legs to stop them from fidgeting. "There's nothing much to tell. He's still on board with the wedding thing. I haven't seen him much this week, but on Monday we picked a cake and chose the flowers. Will's giving us a function room upstairs for a small reception to thank everyone who's helped us out, and we'll just use my playlist for the music. Dawn has a dress at the shop I can borrow— What? Why are you looking at me like that?"

"You slept with him," Abbie declared. She watched me over the rim of her glass as she took a long, noisy slurp.

I tried to laugh, but it sounded like a hiccup followed by choking on air. "What? Why would you say that?"

"Oh my God, you did." Abbie shuffled closer. "Tell me everything."

It didn't take much to recall the memories because I'd been replaying them over and over all week. His hands unbuttoning my shirt after he'd spilled his coffee down my chest. The way he'd kissed me, pinned me to the dining table, and sank inside me. The tenderness of his lips on mine when we'd been standing outside the bakery. My core clenched and I crossed my legs, squeezing them tight. "It was so good."

"It was? Holy crap. Holy *crap*! I can't believe it." She covered her mouth with two hands, her eyes wide over the top of them, but then they dropped. "It's not like I don't want all the horny details because believe me, I do. And I do *not* want to rain on your sex parade because believe me, I don't, but I have to ask. Is this smart?"

"He told me about Maggie. I know this thing between us isn't real and isn't going to last."

"He talked to you about that stuff? That's … surprising." Abbie swirled the liquid in her glass for a moment, then looked at me and cocked her head. "And it doesn't change things?"

"No. If anything, it makes it easier. I've decided to enjoy being with a man without wondering if he'd make a good husband. I'm not losing sleep over making Josh love me enough to marry me. I want to not care about that stuff for a while and just *be*."

Abbie crossed her arms on the table. "And Josh? What about what he wants?"

I tried not to feel offended at the protective snap in Abbie's voice. It was a fair question, given how close everyone was in the Bay, plus Josh and Abbie had shared the loss of a girl they both loved.

"I know you want what's best for him. I do, too. I promise. I'd never do anything to hurt him. We both know this is temporary. In fact, when the wedding is over, and the charade is up, he plans to leave Valentine Bay for good."

"He *what*?"

"Shit." My palms were already sweaty, and now Abbie looked ready to get up and run straight to Josh—to shake sense into him, no doubt. I rubbed my hands over my skirt. "I didn't know it was a secret. Please, don't repeat that. I wanted to reassure you that Josh knows what this is, and I know what this is, and it doesn't change the outcome. When it's over, we're both moving on."

Abbie sank into the seat, took a deep breath, and let it out with a sigh. "I didn't mean to get all dramatic like that. It's not a secret exactly—we all know he's been thinking about leaving for a while; he's a shitty liar—but we didn't think it would be so soon."

"So, you think moving away is the right thing for him to do?"

Her forehead wrinkled, and she stared into her near-empty glass. "He's held onto Maggie so tightly for so long that sometimes I think he *should* get out of here and start over somewhere new. Somewhere he's not reminded of her every day."

I didn't expect to get the sinking sensation that followed Abbie's approval of Josh's plans to bail, but I did.

I would miss him a little, that's all. There was nothing wrong with that.

"But then," Abbie continued, "he's been different lately. More *there*. When I look him in the eyes, I see Josh again. It's been nice and makes me think he doesn't need to leave the Bay in order to let her go."

It took me a minute to figure out that by *her*, Abbie meant Maggie. "He doesn't want to let her go," I murmured, recalling our conversation over dinner.

"He didn't want to before, but now, I'm not sure. Maybe he's found a reason to finally say goodbye."

I didn't know if Abbie was right, and I wasn't going to waste time worrying about it. All I wanted was two thrilling, no-strings-attached weeks of fun with a sexy paramedic who had healing hands and heart-stopping eyes and a body designed to make me think bad thoughts. And those two weeks started tonight.

It was easy to give Abbie the slip an hour later. I told her I had an early morning with wedding planning chores and left her flirting with a tall, dark stranger at the bar. Will watched her in a way that struck me as protective, his glances registering where she was and who she was with no matter how busy he was, and with a pang, I envied the way Will, Abbie, and Josh took care of each other. What would it be like to feel safe like that? Maybe I wouldn't have spent ten years desperate for a husband—and three of those years with a man like Tyler—if I'd had friends like Abbie and Will.

I leaned into the heavy bar door to open it, then stepped out into the dark street. And there was Josh, leaning against the wall with his arms crossed over his chest. The streetlight overhead cast shadows over his face—cheekbones, jawline, brow—and I was caught off-guard by how exquisite he was. And just when I thought he couldn't get any sexier, he pushed off the wall, his small smile turning to a smoulder as he glared at something over my shoulder.

I looked around to find Tyler on the corner, chatting with a girl who tucked her long, dark hair behind her ear, dipped her chin, and giggled at whatever he'd just said. I felt sick at the picture and turned back to Josh, but he looked furious, not nauseous, so I put a soothing hand on his arm. "Let's go before he sees us," I whispered.

Josh nodded tightly, grasped my hand, and pulled me up the street, only slowing when we cleared the next corner.

I was about to say something about Tyler, apologise for his being there at all, but Josh spoke first. "I'm sorry I haven't been here much this week. Work's been busy."

"Please, don't apologise. I don't expect you to drop everything for me."

"I wish I was around to keep Tyler at a distance. I didn't realise he was still following you."

The restrained hostility in Josh's voice sent a rush of desire to my lady parts. "I appreciate it, but I can take care of Tyler. And he's not following me exactly. He just pops up for a chat when I'm walking to and from work or the yoga studio."

"I don't trust him," Josh said, kicking at the ground as we walked.

"Neither do I, but he doesn't frighten me."

124

Josh barked a laugh. "That really says a lot about the guy."

We reached my building, and Josh followed me up the stairs. When I opened the door to my apartment and flicked on the light, Josh stepped inside behind me. "What the hell?"

I tossed my purse on the dining table and crossed my arms over my chest while looking around. The place was filled with flowers in all sorts of arrangements, bouquets and posies in explosions of colours and fragrances that overwhelmed the tiny space. Tyler had sent me four bunches a day for the last four days, and there'd be more tomorrow, I was sure.

"Well," Josh said, running a hand through his hair in a way that drove me wild. "If I felt like a lousy fiancé before, I feel worse now."

"Please, don't even worry about it. The only reason I've kept them is I hate the idea of waste."

"Do you usually like flowers?"

I paused to think. "Yes, and no. I love the *idea* of flowers, and I buy them for myself from time to time, but I've only ever been given them when the guy sending them has something to apologise for. I guess I associate flowers with feeling bad about something. Usually myself."

"That's tough."

"It is what it is."

I looked down at my white and khaki work uniform. I'd gone straight from my desk to The Stop, and now, with Josh here, alone with me in my apartment, smelling so good and with his hair still damp from his shower, I was desperate to freshen up.

"Listen, I really need to wash the day off. Do you mind helping yourself to a drink while I take a quick shower?"

His eyes darted to the bathroom door and back. "Uh, sure. Go right ahead."

"Thanks. I won't be long."

Taking a clean towel from the linen cupboard, I slipped first into my bedroom to collect a change of clothes. Pyjamas? No. A pair of little linen shorts and a black tank would do. But pretty knickers? Hell, yes.

I crossed the living room again, and he was standing where I left him, staring into nothing. "There's beer in the fridge," I said, and he startled. "Just give me fifteen minutes, okay?"

I closed the bathroom door behind me, scrubbed my teeth, and turned on the water. As the heat loosened my muscles, I got tingles knowing that I was naked, lathering my body while imagining Josh's hands on my skin, and he was right there waiting on the other side of the door.

15

JOSH

SHE WANTED TO take a shower? *Now?* I adjusted my pants and cursed her interpretation of water torture.

As I sat on the sofa and tried to relax, the water switched on in the bathroom, and I couldn't look away from the adjoining wall, wondering what I'd see if I had the power to look through it. Steam billowing. Emily dripping wet, rubbing herself with sweet-smelling soaps. Rivulets of water crawling down her shoulders, over her breasts, across her stomach, and between her legs.

Groaning, I stood and tugged at my pants again before going to the fridge, snatching a beer and cracking it open. I took a gulp and glared at all the flowers. Every single one made me hate the man who sent them more than I already did. I hated that he didn't deserve a woman like Emily, and yet he'd been allowed to touch her, put his mouth on her, sink into her, hear her moan, and make her scream.

With perfect timing, Emily's phone started pinging with text after text after text. The shower was still running, so I moved around the kitchen to get a look at the screen and almost threw the thing out the window.

Tyler. Tyler. Tyler. Tyler.

The water cut off, so I dropped onto the sofa and tried to look casual, which really did go out the window the second Emily stepped back into the room. She was in tiny white shorts that teased a glimpse at the crease of her arse, and a tight black tank that hugged her breasts. Her smooth arms and legs looked flushed and soft from the heat of the shower, and her eyes were downcast, almost shy, as she tucked a lock of wet hair behind an ear.

I forced myself to ease back into the sofa and take a slow sip of my drink, then I nodded at her phone. "That thing's been pinging like mad."

"Oh. Thanks." She scooped it up, looked at the screen and huffed out a breath, but she still swiped to read the texts. Colour bloomed in little spots on her cheeks, and I tried not to care what the messages said. I wasn't jealous. Just curious.

"Anything important?"

"What? Oh, no." Emily collapsed on the other end of the sofa, facing me. "It's Tyler. On top of the flowers and the following, he's been sending me texts. It's as if he Googled "how to win back a woman" and he's checking items off a list. Nothing feels real, you know?"

"What kind of texts?"

The colour in her cheeks deepened. "It's so embarrassing. He's been sending me sexts. He must think it's a turn-on."

"And it's not?"

She wrinkled her nose. Jesus, she was gorgeous. "No. At least, not from him, because either he was holding out on me for three years, or he was much more generous with his other girlfriends than he ever was with me."

"What? The sex wasn't good?"

She tucked her feet underneath her. "The sex was … adequate."

I don't know why her description gave me so much satisfaction, but it did. "And what, exactly, made it adequate?"

"It was functional, you know, fast, and when he was done, it was done."

I cleared my throat, thinking again about the ways I wanted to make this girl moan. "That sounds rough."

"I wish." Her hands flew to her cheeks as her jaw dropped. "I can't believe I just said that."

Neither could I. "Forget it," I said with a laugh, but her words would be branded on my brain forever.

"It's just … He's sending me these dirty texts, and I don't know whether to laugh or cry. I want to tell him, 'if you could pull off even half this stuff, you'd have done it a long time ago'."

"Do it."

"No, I'm ignoring everything he sends. I don't want to encourage him."

"Fair enough."

And before I knew what I was doing, I'd pulled my phone from my pocket and tapped out a text of my own.

Me: So, sexting. Not your thing, huh?

Emily's phone pinged, and she gave me a curious look, then picked it up. She swiped and opened my message, and I watched as her eyes flicked over the screen. I might have held my breath. She looked up at me with those pretty, green eyes, wide and surprised, and then down again.

I couldn't believe I'd just done that, and I was going to find out very soon if I'd live to regret it. As tension coiled in my middle, I waited, too scared to blink.

Finally, she tapped the screen. I heard the whoosh of a sent text, and my phone lit up.

Emily: I suppose it *could* be my thing if it were done right. I'd need to be convinced.

Fuck. She was into it. I put my beer on the table and held my phone with both hands.

Me: Is that a challenge?

Again, I watched her read the message and met her eyes when they darted up to mine.

Emily: It might be. What you got?

Was there such a thing as sexting performance anxiety? There was now.

Me: First, I want to apologise for the other night …

Me: If I had my time again, I'd go much, much slower.

At the first text, she frowned. At the second, one corner of her rosebud mouth curved up.

Emily: Nothing to be sorry about, believe me. But, say you had your time again, hypothetically, of course. How might that go?

Don't screw this up, you lucky bastard.

Me: I can't stop thinking about that night and how I didn't take the time to taste you, so (hypothetically, of course), I'd start there.

She bit her lip, and I got harder. Not waiting for her reply, I sent another text.

Me: I'd hold you against the wall and kiss you from ankles to thighs. I'd pull down your panties and bury my head between your legs. Lick you up and down, again and again, until I found the spot that made you scream. I'd put my fingers on you right there and fuck you with my tongue.

Emily read the message, and when she finished, her eyes fluttered closed like she couldn't bear to look at me, but then she moaned and began typing.

Emily: Where's your other hand?

Me: On you. Teasing your nipples. Pulling your hair. Stroking your throat. Thrusting inside and making you come.

I shifted on the sofa. I couldn't ignore my dick anymore, and Emily noticed. She took one look at my crotch, and her fingers flew across her phone.

Emily: Take off your pants.

Were we still sexting? Or did shit just get real?

Me: You first.

With her eyes never leaving mine, Emily set aside her phone, hooked her thumbs into the waist of her shorts, and leaned back as she shimmied them off. Underneath, she wore sheer white panties with lace trim, and as I worried I might come just looking at her, she pulled off her top, too. We'd been in the dark before, but not this time, and I could make out the pale caramel colour of her nipples, which had hardened into pebbled peaks on her perfect breasts.

"Oh, Jesus." I stood and reached to the back of my neck to pull off my shirt. I thought I heard her moan softly as I unbuttoned and unzipped my jeans, pushing them off and taking my briefs with them.

Emily picked up her phone, got to her feet, and stood across from me. Her fingers zipped over the screen.

Emily: But after I come, I still want more, so I drop to my knees, wrap my hands around your cock and kiss the tip. Gently.

Fuck.

Me: I twist my hands in your hair and beg for more.

Her fingers stayed poised over her screen, ready with her reply.

Emily: I wrap my lips around you and lick you just the way you like it. I take you all the way in, so deep you hit the back of my throat.

Then the back and forth began.

Me: I fuck your hot little mouth, but it's not enough.

Emily: I need you inside me, so I push you down and climb on top.

Me: I grab your hips and suck your nipples, one then the other. I put my fingers on you, and you're so fucking wet.

Emily: I sink down on you, inch by inch. You're so big it hurts, and I still want more.

"I can't …" I said, my voice husky. "You're going to make me come."

"No chance." She pushed me back down onto the sofa and straddled me. "Got a condom?"

I reached for my wallet and pulled one out, but Emily plucked it from my hand and tore it open. Watching her roll it over my dick, feeling her hands on me, nearly ended me, but then she pulled her panties to one side and lined me up against her entrance.

Damn, she was wet, but she went slow, so slow it was torture—tight, wet inch by tight, wet inch until I was balls deep. The sight of her impaled on my dick set off a growl deep in my chest, and I dug my fingers into her hips as she worked me in tight circles, cutting her nails into my shoulders and arching her back so that her smooth, soft throat gave me the perfect place to put my mouth.

Emily ground her hips into me, the glorious friction of the base of my cock on her clit driving both of us crazy until her core muscles contracted around me.

"Yes, yes! Josh! *Yes!*"

Hearing my name on her lips pushed me over the edge, and I came in an explosion that tore through my body and darkened the room. I clung to her for a while afterwards, my face against her neck, the smell of her hair in my nostrils, panting and waiting for the world to come into focus again.

And then I groaned.

"What it is?" she mumbled into my neck.

"Too fast. Again." She giggled against my throat, and I smiled, running my fingertips along her spine. "I can do better, I swear."

"Next time."

I turned my face and buried my nose in her hair. "Will there be a next time?" I murmured.

She pulled back and regarded me with those eyes. "I'm a reasonable woman. I'm willing to give you as many chances as you need to get it right."

I kissed her shoulder. "That's very generous of you."

"I like to think so." Then she carefully stood and turned to collect her clothes off the floor.

"I'll be right back," I told her, snatching up my pants and disappearing into the bathroom.

I cleaned up, splashed my face with cold water, and put on my jeans, and then, bracing two hands on the vanity, I stared at my reflection.

Wipe that grin off your face, you dork. It was just sex. Fucking hot sex with a beautiful woman. Fucking hot sex with a beautiful woman who was sweet and made me smile. But it didn't change anything. Nothing could make me rethink leaving the Bay. My grin turned into a glower. If anything, hot sex with Emily was one more good reason to go.

16

JOSH

I COULDN'T REMEMBER when I'd last felt so relaxed. I suspected the sex had a lot to do with it, but so did Emily. She didn't look at me with the stomach-wrenching mix of sadness and sympathy I'd become used to. She didn't see my past when she looked at me, and she didn't offer unsolicited suggestions about the way I could move forward.

Come to think of it, I'd been getting less of that type of thing in general. Since I'd been wrapped up in this fake relationship with Emily, nobody had stopped me in the street to ask how I was. Nobody had tried to set me up with their niece or granddaughter, and there'd been fewer sympathetic stares. For the first time in a long time, I wasn't shackled by where I'd been or where people wanted me to go. Valentine Bay behaved as though they had me figured out.

All that would end when Tyler was gone, only I wouldn't be able to use my "I don't date" excuse to fend off all the matchmakers. Emily was going to move on with her life here in the Bay, and I had to look for my new beginning in Sydney.

I ignored the niggle in the back of my mind that something about the thought wasn't right.

I took a drink of my beer and stretched my bare arm along the back of the sofa, reaching out and stroking Emily's neck with a featherlight touch. "So, you've already organised the flowers and the reception?"

She looked up at me, but her eyes stopped short at my bare chest. They roamed over my shoulders and arms in a way that made me warm, and when she licked her lips, she almost looked hungry, and I definitely liked that. But then she returned her attention to her phone and read from the notes she had saved.

"I made some executive decisions while you were working. I hope you don't mind. At first, I insisted on keeping everything simple and inexpensive, but whenever I offered to trade photography services for donations, everyone wanted to take full advantage and go all out with the best." She smiled apologetically, but her eyes danced. "I blame you. It was all your idea. A good one, but it's taken away our negotiating power."

I held my hands up, palms out. "Guilty as charged. But I'm off for the next three days, so how can I help?"

"Could you drop into Kate's boutique on Sunday for a suit fitting?" She concentrated on her phone, fingers

137

swiping this way and that as she checked lists and calendars and emails. "And have you given any thought to a best man? Kate bullied me into having a bridesmaid so she could show off her bridal range *and* her formalwear. Abbie's going to do it."

Great. I'd managed to dodge Abbie since Valentine's Day. I knew she'd have *thoughts* about the fake wedding, and I didn't want to hear them.

"I'll ask Will," I said, taking a slug of beer.

Emily looked up, put her phone down, and tilted her head. "It's too much, isn't it? I have a hard time saying no to people. It's something I plan to work on in my new life."

Her words hit me like a punch to the gut. The same way I wanted to start over somewhere outside the Bay, Emily was trying to do the same thing here, and she was relying on me to get a good start.

"No, don't feel bad. I mean, it's spiralling a little, but it's not your fault. I'm good with it." I rubbed my jaw. "I haven't heard what Abbie thinks about all this, and I'm sure she has plenty to say. I'm not looking forward to that conversation."

Emily bit her lip and looked away, and I was distracted by thoughts of her mouth on me. "Actually, Abbie *does* have thoughts, and I may have said something to her tonight that I shouldn't have."

Emily looked so guilty that my pulse sped up as I anticipated the worst.

She took a deep breath. "Abbie's protective of you—and that's sweet. Appropriate, even. I'm practically a stranger, after all—so when I was trying to reassure her that we both know none of this is real, I accidentally told her you were leaving Valentine Bay as soon as the wedding was done."

Shit. Abbie was definitely going to have *thoughts*. And *words*. Lots of them.

But also, none of this was real.

Emily took one look at my face and began babbling again.

"Oh, I'm sorry. I'm so sorry. I didn't know it was a secret until Abbie reacted the way she did."

"And how did she react?"

"Surprised. A little sad. But also, like she didn't know what was right or wrong or for the best. She wants you to be happy, even if it means you need to leave."

"Abbie's known for a long time that I've been thinking of going."

"From the impression I got, I'm not sure she believed you'd actually go through with it."

I stared into the distance for a bit, then took another gulp of my drink. Was I capable of leaving town? Yes, I had to be. Emily didn't know it, but she'd given me the push I needed: a public deadline. Now I had no choice. I had to go.

"Hey," she whispered, poking my shoulder. "I'm sorry. I didn't mean to say the wrong thing. It's been a week."

I tried to smile. "It's okay. In fact, it's great. I've been dreading telling Abbie about leaving, and you've done it for me. Huge favour. I owe you one."

"Well, if you're sure," she said, but she frowned.

I ran my thumb over her mouth, hoping to smooth away discomfort, and her lips parted. "I'm sure," I said. "The question is, how can I repay you?"

Her mouth turned up at the corners. "I don't know," she said, dropping her eyes. "While we think on it, do you want a tour of the place?"

She got up, and I followed, unable to take my eyes from the back of her neck, the smooth slide down her shoulders, the hourglass of her waist. She was irresistible from behind, and I noticed nothing but her as she took me to the kitchen, back through the living area, past the spare room she used for storage, onto the little balcony, and finally into her bedroom. Before she could turn to flick on the light, I bent down and kissed her, mouthing the nape of her neck. I pulled away long enough to take the hem of her top and pull it up over her head, then I turned her around and fell on her throat.

She snaked a hand into my hair. "Mm, that's a good start."

"Wait until you see the finish."

I backed her over to the bed, sat her down, and knelt on the floor in front of her, running my hands up over her calves, along the insides of her thighs, over her centre, growling with frustration at the fabric between her and my fingers. She inhaled sharply as I removed her pants, pushed her knees open, and kissed my way up.

When she leaned back on her elbows, I took hold of her hips and finally tasted her. She gasped as I teased open her velvety folds. How could she be so wet for me again? But she was, and my cock got harder as I ran my tongue in firm circles over her clit. She began to buck, and I couldn't get enough, dragging the flat of my tongue up her centre, teasing her with little flicks at the swollen top, and then starting again. When I couldn't wait anymore, I thrust my tongue inside her, fucking her like that until she cried out. She tasted incredible, and I wanted more.

"Oh, Jesus. I'm going to come," she groaned, twisting her fists into my hair.

I pressed my mouth to her clit and sucked a little, thrusting two fingers into her, stroking and pushing to find the spot that'd send her wild. I got what I came for as she tightened around me. She cried out, and I pulled her closer while she shuddered, then waited until she was still before I kissed my way up her stomach, over her breasts, to her throat again. Her pulse was flying under my tongue, and I smiled against her skin.

"Full marks for effort," she murmured, closing her eyes and smiling in the dark.

"I see that smile. Have I redeemed myself?"

"Almost. Practice makes perfect, and I'm sure you'll be even better next time."

"Ah, the elusive *next time*."

I lay down beside her as she stretched her arms over her head, pointed her toes, and sighed as she released the tension in her muscles. When she turned her head to face me, it felt like an invitation to brush my fingertips over her neck, her collarbone, the curve of her breast. Her skin pebbled, and her nipples grew stiff, and I took one into my mouth, tonguing it gently.

"Yes, next time," she purred. "I told you before. I'm a generous woman."

17

EMILY

———————

I HAD NO idea sex could be like this, and though the
first time I laid eyes on Josh, I'd referred to him as a god,
I didn't know then how right I was.

An hour after the stellar performance with his tongue,
Josh said he should get going and went in search of his
missing shirt. I wasn't sure what I was going to miss
more: the sight of his smooth chest stretched out in my
bed as though it belonged there, the orgasms he was
so eager to give me, or the contentedness I felt simply
having him near. I hadn't thought for a minute he might
stay—sleepovers were off the table in an arrangement
like ours—but I could admit to a flare of disappointment
behind my ribs as I walked him to the door.

In the hallway, he kissed me on the mouth the way
he had in front of the bakery, and even though I'd just
climaxed multiple time, the way his lips met mine, all

softness and light, the way he cradled my face, the way he brushed my tongue with the tip of his, turned my legs to water. He pulled away, and when I stumbled forward, he smirked as though he knew the effect he had on me.

"I was planning on going for a surf in the morning, but did you want to meet me afterwards at The Stop? We can have a bite to eat and put together a playlist for the party."

"That sounds great. I have a few things to take care of anyway, so I'll see you there. About two o'clock?"

Moments later, I was curled up in my sheets, inhaling the smell of him and trying hard not to giggle like a schoolgirl with a crush. I slept better that night than I had in months, waking up late in the morning with a smile on my face at the memory of his head between my legs.

I surprised myself by forgetting all about Tyler until there was a knock at the door and a delivery of calla lilies. Throwing the card in the bin without bothering to read it, I found a vase with room enough to take another bunch of flowers and squeezed them in beside a dozen pink roses. My irritation today at yet another waste of good flowers was less about Tyler not taking no for an answer and more about his intrusion on my good mood.

After I washed my face and brushed my teeth, I dressed in tights and a tank, grabbed my mat and water bottle, and headed over to Abbie's studio. It was a divine space on Ocean Parade she called Love, Yoga, and it was all smooth timber floors, clean white walls, wild green hanging plants with strings of twinkle lights between them, and floor-to-ceiling glass that showed off an indescribable view of Valentine Bay beach. Abbie was set up at the front of the room when I got there, legs crossed in easy pose, eyes closed.

Gentle music drifted from the speakers, so I rolled out my mat, settled into savasana, and tried not to think about Josh. It was a losing battle. My deep, measured breathing devolved into something just short of panting, and try as hard as I could, the rest of the lesson did nothing to focus my thoughts, centre my spirit, or settle my heart rate.

I lingered after the hour so I could check in with Abbie.

"Hey, you," she said when we were finally alone. "One of us looks like she got some last night, and sadly, it wasn't me."

I gasped. "How could you tell?"

"Your hips looked a little looser in butterfly pose today. Ha! Just kidding. I have a sixth sense when it comes to sex. It's a gift."

"What happened to the hottie you were chatting with at the bar last night?"

"Didn't pan out."

I tucked my mat under my arm as Abbie took a long drink of water from her bottle. "I had a good night," I said at last. "A great night, actually."

Abbie swallowed and wiped her mouth. "You know, with all this wedding talk and the added complication of casual nookie, I've been stressed about Josh getting out of it unscathed. Now I wonder if I need to worry about you, too."

"Me? Why?"

"Not everyone can separate sex and love, and you're acting a little too warm-and-fuzzy for my liking. Are you sure you can keep your emotions out of this?"

"Of course!" My pulse sped up again, and I didn't want to think about what it meant. "This is one friend helping another. That's all."

"*Right*," she drawled, taking another drink of water and watching me from the corner of her eye. "So, what are you and your *friend* up to this weekend?"

"Lunch later at The Stop."

"Sounds cosy."

"Hardly. We're putting together a playlist for the after-party. You should join us!"

The words were out before I'd considered whether inviting Abbie to lunch was something Josh would be okay with, but I was anxious to convince Abbie she had nothing to worry about. Anyone who saw us together would know just by looking at us there was nothing remotely approaching love going on. I needed to prove that to Abbie as much as I did to myself.

"Oh, will you let me choose your first dance song?"

I nudged her with an elbow. "It's not like that. There's not going to be a first dance. Once the ceremony's done and Tyler's limping away with his tail between his legs, we're going to have drinks and canapés to thank everyone for their help. No first dances or bouquet tosses or garter flicks or best man toasts."

"You got a cake, right? You'll have to cut it, and you'll need a song for that."

"I'm sure Will can get the kitchen staff at The Stop to take care of it."

"Boo, you. Okay, okay. Whatever you say. As your maid of honour, I'm duty bound to obey your every command."

I laughed. "Thank you. I appreciate your dedication."

"Though I do believe somewhere in my job description, there's a clause for pre-wedding celebrations. Hens' nights and that sort of thing."

"Abbie, don't you dare."

"Oh, no. You can't have your wedding cake and eat it too. If everything *after* the ceremony is strictly off-limits, then all bets are off before the big day. It's got to look like the real deal or Tyler might catch on, right?"

"Where are you going with this?"

She smiled like a discount movie villain. "Somewhere beautiful men gyrate to bad music while peeling off their pants."

Back at home, I showered again and pulled on a floaty, green summer dress that gathered at the neck and left my back and shoulders bare. There were still two hours until I had to meet Josh, which gave me just enough time to get my errands done. Well, just one errand, really.

I went straight to the town's smallest, most affordable jewellery store and tried not to pay attention to my nerves as I looked at the wedding bands, wondering which one Josh might like, then scolding myself for thinking it mattered. A ring was for show, nothing more. But there was a small chance he'd want to keep it as a memento, so I had to at least try to find something he wouldn't hate.

The retail assistant behind the counter was an older lady with an enormous bust, brightly dyed auburn hair, and a pearl chain attached to thick, old-fashioned glasses. "Can I help you, dear?"

"I need a ring for a friend," I said, twisting my fingers together and debating how much to say about why I needed it. Did—I squinted at the woman's faded name tag—*Judy* know who I was? Was she part of Dawn's bridal brigade?

"Special occasion?" Judy asked. "For a man or woman?"

I cleared my throat. "Man, and yes, something special." She started to pull out a fabric tray of gaudy yellow gold pieces. "Nothing flashy. It's symbolic more than anything. He might not even wear it."

She let go of the yellow gold and picked up a selection of white gold and platinum, placing it on the counter where I could get a closer look. None of them were right, and I felt silly about getting him a ring at all. Maybe he already had one we could use on the day.

Then I spotted it, under the glass counter, among a collection of vintage pieces. When Judy saw my eyes light up, she transferred the tray to the top of the counter. "Which one do you like?"

The one I touched was white gold, flat and thick, with a brushed finish all over but for the edges, which glinted smoothly under the lights. I picked it up, turned it over, and discovered an inscription inside. *Day One, One Day.*

"Day one, one day," I read. "What do you think it means?"

Judy took off her glasses. "That's what I like about second-chance jewellery. It's already been loved and had a life before making its way here, but when it's picked up by someone new, it gets to start again. And lucky for you, that means the inscription can mean whatever you want it to." She cocked her head. "Something tells me you already know what that might be."

"Yeah, I think I do. Thanks, Judy. I'll take it."

———————

When I finally arrived at The Stop, it was a quarter past the hour, and Josh was already settled into a booth at the back. And he wasn't alone. Abbie was with him, and so was Will. The fake lovers were laughing over something on Will's phone, but Josh's head lifted the minute I walked in, as if he could sense me there. His face was still, so I smoothed my dress over my hips and walked over, hoping I didn't look guilty.

"Sorry I'm late. I got caught up and lost track of time." I hesitated at the table, not sure whether to slide in on the left and take a seat next to Abbie or join them on the right, next to Josh. He answered my question by taking my hand and pulling me in beside him.

"Wow," I said, taking in the drinks all over the table. "Are we expecting more people?"

"Nope." Abbie pushed a margarita towards me. "I got you this."

Will shifted a tumbler with a half-inch of auburn-coloured liquid towards me. "This is a Japanese whiskey." Then he handed me a glass of chilled white wine. "And this is an Adelaide Hills pinot grigio."

Josh pointed at a beer glass, then a red wine. "Will's own IPA. Yarra Valley shiraz."

"I can't drink all this!"

"You're not supposed to." Josh tapped his glass on the one I held in my hand. "Consider it a tasting experience. We need to work out what you like. Cheers."

"Oh," I said, taken aback that they cared, and Abbie winked at me over her drink. "Thanks?"

Will chuckled. "So, what's this about Josh needing a best man for this wedding? What am I going to have to do?"

Abbie opened her mouth, and when I glared at her, she snapped her jaw closed. "Nothing much," I said to Will. "Wear a suit. Stand around. Nothing strenuous."

"A suit? Fine, but only because I like you."

His throwaway comment lit me up inside. "Thank you! Are you free tomorrow to go with us to Kate's boutique on Ocean Parade to try some things on?"

"Absolutely. Sounds like a brilliant way to spend my weekend. Nothing else I'd rather do."

Abbie rolled her eyes. "You can help me pick out a dress, too, so it won't be a total waste. And Em, what are you wearing on the big day?"

"Dawn has something vintage for me. I'll pop into her place to try it on tomorrow after your fittings."

"Excellent! Now, music." Abbie handed me her phone, opened to a playlist with a ton of songs queued up. "We made a start using my account. What do you think of these?"

I scrolled up and down, sipping the white wine and nodding in approval at its tart, fruity flavours, as well as at the combination of tracks for mood music and dancing. "I like your style."

I set down the wine, and Abbie took back her phone. "What's not to like? Now, all we need to do is decide on the song you want to play when you're walking down the aisle."

Josh's eyes widened, and I cringed. Why did Abbie insist on treating this like it was real? "It's not important," I said, flapping a hand. "Just pick something. Anything. Pachelbel's *Canon in D* will do." Avoiding Josh's gaze, I picked up another glass, took a gulp of whiskey, and regretted it immediately.

"We're going to have a killer hens' night, aren't we, Em?" Abbie said, rubbing her hands together. "Oiled pecs and arseless chaps for days." She leaned over to me with a serious look. "Are you good with cowboys, or would you like someone else to tickle your fancy?"

I covered my face with my hands. "Abbie, no," I said, the words muffled. "No hens' night." I lifted my hands just enough so that I could look at Josh behind the screen of my fingers. "I'm sorry," I mouthed at him.

He gave his head a tiny shake as if to say, *don't worry about it*. "How about we do drinks with the crew instead?" he suggested. "Wedding's in two weeks. We can do something on the beach on Friday night."

"No naked men?" Abbie pouted.

"You never know. You might get lucky," Will said with a wink.

"Not with you hanging off me, I won't. All right, be boring. A *co-ed* beach party."

As Will and Abbie began arguing about the music, Josh reached over and took my hand. I mouthed a silent *thank you* his way.

"You're welcome," he murmured, then pointedly eyed the drinks on the table. "Which one's the winner?"

I put on a dramatic thinking face. "The pinot grigio, hands down."

"Glad to hear it."

Then he surprised all of us by lifting the back of my hand to his mouth and kissing it.

18

JOSH

ABBIE TWEAKED MY narrow black tie, then flattened the collar of my white shirt over the top of it. "You're a hottie, Josh. Shame there aren't reasons to see you in a suit more often."

I looked at myself in the mirror and tried not to glare. I was not the kind of man who got around in starched shirts and pressed trousers, but it was for Emily, and I had to remind myself of that, again and again, to get through the torture that was this fitting.

Click, click, click.

There it was again. I hadn't thought far enough ahead to realise my genius plan to volunteer Emily's photography skills would drop me right in the middle of them. As I preened self-consciously in the three-way mirrors, Emily shifted the angle of her camera and took a dozen more pictures.

Snap, snap, snap.
Breathe. Smile. Be nice.

"You look good, too," I said to Abbie, who was in her fourth dress of the day. This one was a slinky thing in pink so bright I needed sunglasses to look directly at her. Everything she'd tried on was loud enough to demand attention, and I'm not sure why, but I was grumpy about it. "Don't you think something more subtle would be better? I don't know much about this stuff, but I'm pretty sure everyone's supposed to be looking at the bride, not the bridesmaid."

"I can't think of anything worse," Emily interrupted. "Abbie's doing me a favour in that dress."

Abbie twirled and placed her hands on her hips, pouting at the camera. "Is this the one, then?"

Kate, the owner of the boutique and an old friend of my mother's, hovered nearby. She had a rack full of clothes next to her, and she was swapping one dress or suit for another as soon as Emily said she had enough shots to move on to the next outfit. Kate had something in electric blue to throw at Abbie next, but she looked at Emily first for the go-ahead.

"It's gorgeous, but let's try one more."

Will stepped out of the other fitting room and whistled at Abbie. "That one's a winner," he said, going straight to his reflection and playing with his cuffs. "It goes great with my suit."

Will was in a slim-fitting navy suit with a white shirt and navy tie, and next to Abbie, they looked like something out of a fashion magazine. Will put a hand on Abbie's waist, pulled her towards him, and spun her round as if they were dancing. She giggled into his shoulder, and Emily's camera fired up.

Click, click, click, click, click.

"Oh, you two." *Click, click.* "You're so photogenic." *Click, click.* "Come stand here. I'll take some close-up shots, then we'll head out to the sand. You'll look even better in that light."

"You want us to go outside looking like this?" I asked, pointing at myself.

Emily grinned and exchanged a good-humoured look with Kate. "You bet. I'm going for a two-guys-and-a-girl vibe. Now get your shoes on, grumpy guts. Save that smoulder for the camera."

Smoulder? She thought I *smouldered*? The more I thought about that, the more I didn't hate it, so I slipped on a pair of black leather shoes and stood exactly where she pointed.

Three hours and three wardrobe changes later, Will and I had suits picked out, and Abbie had settled on a bronze dress that was much more subdued than the twenty she'd tried on before it, even counting the drop at the back that bared her skin to the waist. We'd walked along the beach while Emily buzzed around us like a persistent little bee, and I'd tried not to think about my smoulder. Too often, I'd forgotten what we were doing altogether as I watched Emily in her element. She was confident and natural with a camera, losing the self-consciousness she'd carried around since the day I met her. She bossed us about and directed our movements, checked her shots and came up with new ideas on the spot, and I was impressed. We all were, and when she showed Kate some of the frames, Kate squealed and dragged Emily into a hug that pulled her off her feet.

Half the day had disappeared by the time we stood on the street outside the boutique, outfits in garment bags, and the afternoon stretching on ahead of us.

"What's next, boss?" I asked.

Emily shifted her camera bag and ran a hand through her hair. It was all mussed up, sticking out in every direction, and I just wanted to scoop her up and bury my face in it, breathe in the smell of her shampoo, and feel the heat of her body against mine. My dick liked the idea, too.

"I have to get to Dawn's before five to try on my dress, then … nothing!" She flicked up her fingers, one by one. "Cake, flowers, party, food and drinks, music. Now the clothes. I think most of the wedding plans are done. This has been a million times easier than planning the real thing."

Emily flushed, and there was an awkward pause.

"Anyone got dinner plans?" I asked to break the silence.

"I've got to get back to the bar," Will said.

"I'll go with you," Abbie said. "Might pick myself up a date for Saturday."

Will flicked her earlobe. "Your mum will be there. I'm your date to this one, *babe*."

She swatted at him and missed. "Oh, yeah. I forgot. Well, I may as well keep you company tonight. Build up my tolerance and all that."

"I've got no dinner plans," Emily said to me, "but if Abbie wants to head over to Dawn's with me now so I can get her opinion on the dress, I can meet you afterwards?" Emily gave Abbie adorable puppy eyes. "Please?"

"Yes, I'm there. I love Dawn, but I'm not convinced she knows how to pick a wedding dress."

As they walked away, Will came to stand beside me. "I like her," he said as we watched them leave.

I couldn't keep my eyes off Emily's arse in her denim shorts. "Emily?"

"No, Rita Ora. Yes, Emily."

"I like her too."

"Like her, or *like*-like her?"

I couldn't speak until Emily disappeared around a corner, but then I shoved Will so hard he stumbled and laughed. "What are we, nine years old?" I asked.

"No, thank God. But she's a cool chick. Abbie's fallen in love with her, even if you haven't."

"Who the fuck said anything about love?"

Will raised his hands in surrender. "Not me, I promise. I'll see you later?"

I waved him off and started up the street, one arm holding my suit, the other hand in my pockets, and my head down in the way I usually walked when I was out alone around the Bay. I did it to avoid people's eyes and uncomfortable conversations as much as glimpses of the things that reminded me of Maggie.

I hadn't thought of her much in the past two weeks. She was always in the back of my mind, but my mind

157

had been fuller than usual, and I'd been able to distract myself from thoughts of her face. The guilt of that hit me like a sledgehammer. I had at least an hour to fill before Emily would be done, so I lifted my head, set my jaw, and started walking.

I went past Maggie's old house first. Her family had moved about a year after the accident, and a young couple lived there now, but—except for the gardens, which Maggie's dad had always kept immaculate and now ran riot—the house looked much the same. I'd had a hundred dinners in that kitchen. Kissed Maggie a thousand times on that porch. Touched her body and heard her sigh on the other side of that window, in her bed, when nobody was home.

I walked past Billy Goat's Hill, a wide stretch of grass wedged out of sight that inclined first up and then away from the road, creating a secret nook for the local kids. Maggie and I would go there with the crew, all of us hiding from our parents, smoking their stolen cigarettes and sipping cheap booze. I'd kissed her under that tree over there, and she'd tasted like passionfruit.

I passed the old movie theatre, one of our favourite places to go on Sunday nights. She'd always order popcorn and ice-cream but forget the napkins. I'd always slip back out to get them for her.

I passed the lookout, where we'd stared out over the ocean and dreamed about chasing the horizon on a sailboat we'd buy with money we'd save working jobs that weren't forever.

I looked down the beach to the circle of rocks where kids sat around bonfires, the same place we had ours. She loved those nights, and I had, too. I still did. Though her absence caused us all some measure of pain, I'd always been there on fire night, even after she was gone. My friends might not have felt her loss the way I did, but they were the only ones who came close.

It was nearly five o'clock by then and time to end the grief tour. I tried to ignore the fact that it didn't hurt as much as it usually did and refused to think about why. Maggie deserved better, and I'd have to do better. If the pain was gone, then she'd be gone, and that was unacceptable.

I didn't want to keep Emily waiting, so I hurried back to Dawn's shop. Emily wasn't waiting for me outside, but I heard Abbie's voice floating out of the open doorway, so I took a seat on a bench to wait. The store was faced with expanses of glass, displays perfectly presented inside as irresistible lures for window shoppers and passers-by. I stared through the glass, not seeing anything in particular, marvelling absent-mindedly that Dawn could charge the exorbitant prices she did, until Emily twirled into view. And then, I couldn't see anything else.

The dress she wore was icy white, in a fabric that looked like it would slide away under my touch, like satin. It tied at the neck, plunged at the front, left her back bare, and clung to every curve. She wore a narrow, netted veil over her eyes, attached to a tiny cap of pearls in her short dark hair. It left her mouth bare, inviting me to kiss it.

I didn't even realise I'd stood up until I was up against the glass, staring in, soaking up every detail. Then she turned around and saw me, and time stood still.

Time started up again with a screech from Abbie, who noticed me there, spun Emily around by her shoulders, and hustled her deeper into the store. I watched her go, then stumbled backwards onto the bench. I wasn't ready for this. I wasn't okay with feeling like this.

A minute later, Abbie stormed out, planting herself in front of me and parking her fists on her hips. "It's bad luck to see the bride before the wedding," she snapped.

I laughed under my breath and shook my head, overwhelmed at how unreal this situation had become. "It's not a real wedding. It doesn't matter."

Abbie crossed her arms. I waited for her to say something snarky, but when I squinted up at her, she was staring at me with a funny look on her face.

"You're right," she said. "I overreacted." She gestured back at the shop. "Emily's getting dressed, and she'll be out in a minute."

"Great." I pressed my hands together and stared down at my fingertips.

"So, I'm going to head off."

"Sure. Have a good night."

She leaned over and kissed the top of my head. "You, too. I'll talk to you soon, Ford."

I had to clear my throat to talk. "See you later, Ellison."

She was clear of the street by the time Emily reappeared. Her cheeks were rosy with a gentle flush, and she refused to meet my eye. I wanted to wrap my arms around her and never let her go, so I stood up and clutched the garment bag with two hands.

"Hungry?" I asked.

Her shoulders dropped, and she smiled up at me. "Yes. I'm starving."

19

EMILY

———————

JOSH SUGGESTED WE pick up a pizza and go back to my place, and that sounded good to me. I was exhausted from the long day behind a camera, but more than that, I was overwhelmed by what had happened at my dress fitting. Turning to find Josh in the window, looking at me as though there were no barriers between us … No glass. No ghosts. I'd frozen on the spot, and nothing had existed but him for the longest fraction of a second, but then Abbie swooped in, scooped me up, and the moment passed. Hidden in the changing room, I'd had to press a hand to my stomach to settle the butterflies before panic set in. The look on Josh's face made it feel as if this was no longer pretend.

The dress itself was a masterpiece, but nothing like what I'd have picked if I'd been shopping without Dawn or Abbie. For my wedding to Tyler, I'd chosen a strapless bodice with a cloud for a skirt because, you know, *fairytale*. But Dawn's choice, a slinky, vintage piece by a defunct New York label, fit like it was made for me, and the moment I saw myself in it, the differences between my real wedding and my fake one came into focus.

This time, I hadn't made a single decision based on what someone else might like. Vanilla and coffee macarons instead of raspberry and coconut. White dahlias instead of red roses. A playlist and a low-key party instead of a sit-down reception with a minute-by-minute run sheet. In the last couple of weeks, I'd learned a hundred things about myself that I didn't know before, and it gave me the confidence to say yes to a dress New Emily loved but Old Emily wouldn't have looked at twice.

Perhaps Josh had been surprised by the style of it, the same as me. As we walked home from the pizza shop, I chewed the inside of my cheek, obsessing in silence over the wisdom of wearing the dress for the ceremony. By the time we got to my door, I'd twisted myself into a knot and decided the best way to unravel it was to call Dawn and ask her to find me something less flashy. I didn't want to make a fool of myself in what was, after all, a fake wedding.

"You look upset," Josh said, balancing the pizza box on one arm as I opened the door to my apartment and let him in.

"Do I?"

"Yeah." He put the box down on the coffee table and his garment bag over the back of the sofa as I switched on the light. He glared around at the flowers but said nothing.

I pulled a couple of plates and a stack of napkins from the cupboards and two bottles of water from the fridge. I put them out next to the pizza, tucked my feet underneath me on the sofa, and shrugged. "I'm not upset. I've just been thinking."

"I don't mind listening if you want to talk about it."

I sighed and ran my hands through my hair. It was starting to grow out and probably looked like a bird's nest. "This experience has been so different for me. The wedding I was supposed to have with Tyler was like completing one of those numbered dot-to-dot drawings. I found a checklist on the internet, ticked every box, and did it all on my own. I couldn't find my mother to invite her, and my sister couldn't get off work or afford the flights to be there. Tyler let me make all the decisions, but I chose everything based on what I knew he would like. I never stopped to think if it was the wedding I'd have chosen for myself."

"All right. I'm following so far. You've always been a people pleaser, but I knew that about you already."

"I'm starting to wonder why it never bothered me before. And maybe I'm a little embarrassed that I didn't know enough about myself to realise it *should* bother me, but I've had a million times more fun planning this wedding with you and Abbie than I ever had with Tyler. It's helping me find myself."

"I'm glad to hear it." Josh stared at me, and I could see something working behind his eyes. I didn't know what I wanted him to say. Something that would confirm the moment that had passed between us earlier, or something

164

that would stop me from hoping that what we had was the seed of something real. "It's been fun for me, too."

I laughed. "You mean all the sex is fun."

The corner of his mouth turned up. "I won't lie. It has been nice."

"*Nice*. There's that word again."

"You know what? You're right." He put his bottle of water down. "It might be time to do something about that."

My heart rate went from resting to rioting in three seconds flat, and I leaned back into the sofa as Josh stood with a predatory look in his eyes. He scooped me up, tossed me over one shoulder, and lightly spanked my arse as he took me to the bedroom. Then he laid me down on the bed and stood over me, staring down with hungry eyes, and I lost the ability to speak. When he reached behind his neck and yanked off his shirt, I lost the ability to *think*.

"I'm going to undress you," he said, his voice gravelly. "I'm going to touch you. I'm going to kiss you, and I'm going to fuck you. And you're going to keep your hands to yourself. Understand?"

Oh my God. Oh my God. Oh my God.

I nodded, shamelessly devouring the sight of his sculpted chest and towering cock. When he was naked, he undid the button of my shorts, pulled them down, and tossed them aside. Next to go was my shirt, then my bra. He ran a single finger around the waist of my panties, and I shivered.

"Put your hands over your head," he commanded, and I did. "Good girl. Now close your eyes." I did that too.

His mouth descended onto my stomach, his tongue swirling around my navel, and my hips lifted to meet him. His lips moved north, closing over first one nipple, then the other, licking and nibbling them to aching buds. I moaned and twirled my fingers in his hair, and he lifted his head. When I realised the kissing had stopped, I opened my eyes to find him staring at me, those amber eyes burning.

"I said no touching. Don't make me remind you again."

I whimpered and put my hands over my head, begging with my eyes for him to keep going.

"But you can keep your eyes open," he whispered.

Josh knew what to do with his hands. Oh God, his hands. He grazed my ribs with the lightest touch, sending goosebumps rippling over my skin. He squeezed my breasts, brushing his thumbs over my stiff nipples. He ran his palms over my hips, then tucked his fingertips into my underwear and dragged them down my legs.

After opening my knees and brushing his lips along my centre, he closed his mouth over my clit, and I shuddered when he groaned at the wetness. I almost latched onto his head again but forced myself to grab fistfuls of the sheets instead. I rocked underneath him, desperate for penetration. Damn, this was torture!

"Did you want something?" he asked.

"Yes," I gasped.

"You're going to have to ask for it." He straightened and circled my swollen nub with the pad of one thumb while watching me writhe beneath him. His eyes on me, so fevered and desperate, were such a turn-on.

"I want … I want you inside me," I panted.

He slipped two fingers into me, stroking and rubbing against that spot only he could find, coiling my insides tighter and tighter.

"Yes. Yes. Just like that," I cried, and his fingers grew more insistent, releasing the tension in an explosion that arched my back and sent pulses of agonised ecstasy rolling through my body.

"Did you like that?" he murmured, kneeling over me.

"God, yes," I groaned. "But I need more." I eyed the stiff length of him, thick and throbbing, and then propped myself up on my elbows. "Can I touch you now?"

"It's against the rules."

He dragged his teeth over his bottom lip, and I nearly launched myself at him, but instead, I sat up and wrapped my hand around his cock. "Then you're just going to have to punish me."

I parted my lips and rubbed the smooth tip of him over the top, then the bottom. He moaned and ran his fingers through my hair, and I let go and pulled back, looking up at him with wide, innocent eyes.

"*Tsk, tsk*. Bad manners, Mr Ford. No touching, remember?"

He groaned and hooked his hands behind his neck, looking up at the ceiling.

"That's better." I wrapped one fist around the base of his dick and circled my tongue over the crown, tasting the drop of arousal that had beaded on the tip. Opening my mouth wider and taking him in a little at a time, I sucked gently at first, then harder as I moved my fist up and down, pulling him in deeper. His hips started to thrust, and he breathed heavily above me, and I felt all kinds of powerful. In control. In charge. I opened my mouth wider and took him deep enough to hit the back of my throat, moaning and gasping at the sensation, which only drove Josh wilder.

"Jesus," he rasped. "This feels so fucking good."

I sucked harder, wanting more of him than I could take. His hips grew more frantic, and when he curled his fists in my hair, I let him. I looked up then and met his eyes. They were still burning, and it sent a fresh rush of desire through me. When his cock throbbed, I knew he was almost there, and I was ready to take him all, but then he pulled out and pushed me down on the bed, scrambling in his pants for a condom, which he tore open and put on in record time. Stretched out over me, he kissed my mouth desperately, stroking my tongue with his in fierce, greedy thrusts.

"I need to be inside you. I need to fuck you. Hard."

I widened my knees, feeling the same way, and he slid into me, slowly at first, the size of him stretching and filling me with pleasure that bordered on pain.

"Deeper," I moaned.

He hooked one of my legs over his arm, leaned in, and powered into me, filling me all the way with his hard, slippery drives, then pulling out and doing it again, harder and faster each time. I held on and circled my hips, bucking like a starved woman, my inner walls contracting as I milked his cock and flew towards another orgasm.

"Come for me," he growled in my ear, sensing I was close.

His voice, rough and hot, pressed buttons I'd already thought activated, and my core tightened around him as the rest of me flew apart. Josh tensed, and his cock pulsed inside me as he groaned before his head dropped onto my forehead.

"Emily," he whispered between breaths. "That was … Fuck. You've ruined me for life."

I froze, then forced myself to relax again almost immediately. More to soothe myself than anything else, I dragged my fingertips up and down the dip of his spine.

Please stop giving me reasons to hope this thing between us is real.

"I think you've got that the other way around."

Afterwards, we lay together in the tangled sheets, our limbs intertwined, my head on his chest and his arm around my shoulders, empty pizza boxes on the floor. I never wanted to move again.

"I have to tell you something," I murmured.

He kissed the top of my head. "Sounds ominous."

I chuckled quietly. "I've never had sex like this before. It's … epic."

His fingers brushed the curve of my hip, and I felt his cock stir against my thigh. "That may be the highest praise you could give a man. I feel like the king of the world."

I smacked his chest, and he chuckled, squeezing me closer.

"There's something I can't understand," he said, inhaling the scent of my hair, and the gesture turned my insides to mush. "Tyler treated you badly, right? He cheated on you, and he didn't even care enough to make you come. Why did you stay with him as long as you did? And why did you agree to marry him?"

I tried not to take offence at the hint of judgement in his voice because these were the kinds of questions I'd asked myself more than once with no good answers.

"I've thought about this a lot," I said. "And the best answer I can come up with is that I needed to know I belonged." I circled his nipple with a finger. He breathed in sharply, and I smiled, but I didn't stop. "I needed an anchor in my life. I've never had a real home, and Tyler was the first man to offer me that. I couldn't risk saying no and having him be the last."

Josh was silent, but his fingers still brushed my arm. I refused to look up at him. I could ignore the judgement in his voice but not in his eyes. "Even if that meant pretending not to know about his cheating? And never having great sex?"

I tried to shrug, which was impossible with Josh's heavy arm wrapped around me. "Fidelity and foreplay seemed like small sacrifices to make for my chance at a real family."

"Is that still what you want?"

"A family?" This was something I knew the answer to, and I wasn't about to hide it. "Yes. A home? Absolutely. I can't wait to have those things." I hesitated, then added, "With the right person, of course."

His fingers on my arm froze, and the tension in his biceps was hard to ignore. I needed to reassure him that I didn't expect the right person to be him.

"So, you haven't said much about when you're moving," I said, making my tone light. "Do you need any help? I'm a great packer. It's the least I can do. Favour for a favour and all that."

Josh cleared his throat and pulled his arm out from under me, sitting up and reaching for his pants. "I haven't set a date yet, but you're right. I should, and I will, but I want to give it time to make sure Tyler's well and truly gone."

I sat up, pulling the sheet up over my bare breasts, and stared at the muscles rippling across his back. I ignored the twinge in my stomach when I said, "That sounds like a plan. Have you signed a lease yet?

"Not yet." He pushed his arms into his T-shirt and pulled it over his head. "I've got a shortlist of places. Just have to get the applications in."

"I can help with those, too."

"That'd be great."

"I know the area well. Let me know if you need advice on where's best."

"Will do."

He was acting cagey, and I didn't like the way it made my chest tighten. "You promise you'll let me help when you're ready to start looking?"

He looked over his shoulder at me, then leaned in and kissed my forehead. "You'll be the first to know, but don't worry about me. Wedding first, then the move. One thing at a time, okay?"

I let out a relieved breath. "Good thinking. One thing at a time."

We said goodbye with a quick kiss at the door, and he walked away with his shoulders hunched and his hands buried in his pockets. For a guy who was easily six foot tall and more, he looked a lot like a little boy.

It had to be done. Great sex and easy conversation were blurring the lines, and the lines had been drawn at the beginning. Old Emily might have ignored the warning signs and pinned her hopes on a man with one foot out the door, but New Emily was too smart for that.

Josh and I were both looking for a fresh start. Mine was here in Valentine Bay, and Josh's was not. The sooner he remembered that, the safer my heart would be.

20

JOSH

FIRST THING THE next day, I spoke to my boss about transferring to a station in Sydney. It wasn't the first time I'd raised the subject, but any conversations we'd had in the past had only ever been in the abstract. I'd used phrases like "If I …" and "I might …" and "I was thinking about …" so that I never had to commit to anything. I'd filled out the transfer forms but not submitted them. This time was different. I went into work half an hour early to review the paperwork and handed it in before starting my shift, throwing myself into my work to keep me from dwelling on the fact I'd taken my first real step out of the Bay. Away from Maggie and away from Emily.

When I finished work in the afternoon, I called the landlord who'd been renting out a room to me for the past six months and let him know I'd pay for the next four weeks, but then I'd be moving on. As soon as

I ended that call, I dialled the numbers of six leasing agents for properties that looked promising, asking them for inspection times and copies of the application forms.

None of it made me feel the way I'd imagined it would—lighter, freer, and more like my old self than I'd been in four years. Instead, my stomach was in knots, and I had to resist the urge to call everyone back and tell them I'd changed my mind. It was a bit like staring down a heavy wave, knowing it had the potential to pound you senseless as much as to take you higher than you'd ever been before. There was a fine line between nauseated and liberated whenever you got to the edge of something that made jumping worth the risk, and I refused to give in to the panic of cold feet.

By the time I got home, I'd put the wheels in motion, and they'd continue moving forward without any interference from me. I was free to focus on more important things, the things that were only going to last another two weeks and then would be gone forever. Emily had reminded me I was going to lose her, and as much as it stung, she'd done me a favour. She wouldn't be mine forever, and I couldn't afford to forget that.

When I lost Maggie, it came out of nowhere. I hadn't known to treasure every minute we had together because soon she'd be gone. I'd been young and stupid and not at all suspicious of how happy I'd been the day, the week, the month that she died. If I'd only known to brace, I could have prepared myself for the grief. It was a soul-destroying lesson to have to learn. When you knew the end was coming—and the end always came—you knew to keep a piece of your heart for yourself, so it wouldn't hurt as much when it broke. You could make plans for *after*—when the darkness closed in on you. The key, I'd discovered, was to move.

My dad was the perfect example of sitting still while sadness gnawed at you. I understood why he'd never opened himself up to love again after losing my mother, and my future was destined to be the same. A loop of nothingness. That was why I needed to leave the Bay. It wasn't because I thought I'd find love again, no matter what anyone else believed. I was too smart for that. All I wanted was to escape my story and everyone who knew it. The problem was that my story now included Emily. I was going to lose her too, but I was determined to do things differently this time around. Emily wanted to make Valentine Bay her future, and I was about to make it my past. If this overlap in our futures was all the last burst of joy I was going to get in life, I was going to make the most of it while it lasted.

———

That night, I met the boys at the North End Hotel for a bite to eat and a game of pool. Ten years ago, this was something we did every week, but with Isaac and me working shifts, Logan living overseas, Will buying and building up The Stop, and Luca leaving town then returning three months ago with a new girlfriend, we were lucky to do it once a month.

Isaac chalked his cue, leaned over the table, and took the break shot. I watched the balls roll around the table, noted the two that disappeared into one side and one corner pocket, then crossed my arms to wait my turn. Will leaned against a table along the wall, his head bent over his phone, but he put it down when Luca made his way back from the bar with a tray of drinks.

Will chose a glass and took a sip. "You haven't told us much about what happened with Jess when you got back," he said to Luca. "Just how fucked up are things these days?"

Luca grunted. "It's not good, and it's about to get worse."

Jessica and Luca first got together when we were all eighteen years old. I'd been with Maggie for two years by then, and the four of us had spent a lot of time together. Three years ago, Luca decided to get out of the Bay and see how city life fit. I didn't know why Jess didn't go with him, but they broke up before he left. I never thought he'd come back, but he did—and not alone. His new girlfriend, Natasha, was nice enough, but she wasn't Jess, and we were still a tight-knit crew.

The awkwardness of Luca moving back with a girlfriend had seeped its way into all our friendships with Jess, and the idea that it might get worse did not appeal to me at all. As Isaac straightened and forgot about taking his shot, and Will's drink stalled halfway to his mouth, I guessed none of us had a good feeling about what was coming next.

"What's that supposed to mean?" I asked.

Luca ran a hand over his darkly stubbled jaw. "I'm going to ask Tash to marry me."

The silence went a beat too long before I stuck out my hand. "Wow. That's massive news. Congratulations."

Isaac and Will said much the same thing, clapping Luca on the back and muttering their approvals, but we were poor actors.

"Jess is going to be devastated," Isaac said, then he grimaced and rubbed at his face. "Not the right thing to say. Sorry. I don't mean to shit on a happy moment. I just—"

"Don't think I haven't thought about it," Luca cut in. "I care about Jess a lot. I always will, but Tash is the one."

"Then we're happy for you, man." Will raised his glass, and we all followed. "To Luca and Natasha. We wish you a long life of shit-hot sex and a shit ton of kids."

Luca choked on his beer. "Slow down. I'll take the hot sex, but the rug rats can wait."

I stared into my drink for a moment, comparing Luca's real engagement to my fake one with Emily, and I recalled the vision of her in that wedding dress. From there, I pictured her with a blond-haired toddler on her hip, and something hitched inside my chest.

"I've called Logan and told him," Luca continued. "I wanted to give him plenty of notice to get here for the wedding."

Logan was the fifth and final member of our crew. Six years ago, he'd left the Bay to go backpacking through Europe, but he'd found a wife in London and stayed there. He'd only been back once since—four years ago, when Maggie died.

Will whistled. "Way to rub salt in the wound. You're going to tell Jess you're marrying someone else, *and* you're going to throw Logan into the mix? You'll be lucky if you get through the wedding with your scrotum still attached." He chuckled under his breath. "That goes for Logan, too."

Isaac picked up his cue again. The stick looked miniature in his enormous hands. "Let's give Jess the benefit of the doubt. Distance makes the heart grow fonder or some crap like that. She might have outgrown her grudge by now."

"No chance," I said. "Jess loves to hate Logan and tormenting her was always his favourite hobby."

"It's been years since all that shit," Isaac replied. "Plus, the guy's married! We've all grown up."

Luca groaned. "I don't want to talk about it anymore. Just keep it to yourselves for now, all right? I don't want word to get around to Tash. Will, no slipping it to Abbie—"

"He wishes," Isaac said, choking with laughter at the murder on Will's face.

Luca rolled his eyes, then looked at me. "And no pillow talk with Emily, got it?"

I was momentarily stunned, then I glared at Will. "You've got a big fucking mouth."

Will raised his hands. "It wasn't me. You've been walking around the Bay with a near-constant post-coital glow. Doesn't take a genius to put two and two together."

I stared at the ceiling, wondering what I'd done to deserve friends like this. "I won't say anything to Emily. Don't worry about it."

The crack of billiard balls sounded, and we studied the results of Isaac's last shot. None were sunk, so I grabbed the chalk and rubbed it over my cue stick.

"How's it going, anyway?" Luca asked. "Not sure I'd be able to take all the wedding talk if it wasn't for real. Doesn't it make your skin crawl?"

I lined up my shot, hit the ball, and missed. "It hasn't been that bad."

"Of course not," Will said. "You're getting laid."

"Jesus, Will." I felt a surge of irritation. "It's not always about sex."

He quirked an eyebrow, a small smile playing on his mouth. "That right?"

I stalked around the table, making room for Isaac to take a shot. From the corner of my eye, I saw Luca and Will exchange a glance, and Will shrug his shoulders.

I took deliberate, calming breaths. "Emily's talented and smart, and she's taken a chance moving to the Bay on her own, building a new beginning. She's got guts."

"She sounds cool," Isaac said. "Why haven't I met her yet?"

I snatched up my bottle and took a long drink. "We're having a bonfire on the beach on Friday, sort of a hens-bucks thing. You'll see her then."

Luca picked at the label on his drink. "I suppose Jess will be there?"

"Yes," I said, dredging up my last shred of patience, "but this sort of thing is going to happen if you want to live here. You and Jess and Tash are going to have to learn how to be in the same room or on the same sand with each other. Tough shit."

Luca took a drink. "You're right. I'll talk to Tash."

Isaac sunk another ball, then paced around the table, analysing possible shots. "So, what you're saying is, you like her?"

I stared at the green of the table, imagining Emily's face. "Yeah. I like her."

"Then why all the make-believe? Why not be with the girl for real?"

I shook myself out of the daydream, which had slipped south of Emily's eyes, to her mouth, then the hollow at her throat, to her incredible breasts with their pale caramel nipples … My dick jumped, and I walked to the other side of the table. "It's not what she wants, or what I want. I'm just doing her a favour."

Luca crossed his arms. "Getting rid of the ex?"

"Yep. And then, I'm gone."

Luca's head jerked to Will, then Isaac, but Isaac looked as poleaxed as Luca.

"I told you I hadn't said anything," Will said.

"What do you mean, you're gone?" Luca asked.

"I'm moving to Sydney. Leaving the Bay and all my baggage behind." I clenched my fists and looked at each of my friends. We'd been in each other's lives since we were five years old. I didn't often believe that the Bay had more good memories than bad, but watching their faces, I had to admit it was true of them. "Everywhere I go in this place, there's another thing that reminds me of Maggie. People look at me with pity, and every time I have to grin and bear it, I think of her. I can't take the do-gooders trying to fix me. I just want to start again in a place where nobody knows who I am."

Isaac frowned. "You want to forget about Maggie?"

"Fuck, no. Never. But I'm stuck in a loop here."

Luca rubbed the back of his neck. "So, you want to find someone new?"

"Yes. No." All the reasons I had to leave made so much sense in my head, but now they were coming out all garbled. "I don't see that happening for me again. I don't even want it to. There are other things I want to do with my life."

Isaac walked over and leaned on the table next to Luca. "Like what?"

"Work," I snapped.

Isaac frowned, and there was silence.

Will straightened and took Isaac's cue from him. "Like I said to Ford, he's the best one to judge what he needs to do. You've got our support, whatever you decide."

His words knocked Isaac out of his contemplation. "Shit. Yeah, of course you do. I'm being a big fucking baby about it. The Bay won't be the same without you."

My throat tightened. "You'll survive."

"What does Emily think about you leaving?" Luca asked.

I picked up my drink and took a long swallow. "She's all for it. Can't wait to see the back of me."

I turned my back on them to line up my next shot.

It didn't matter what my mates had to say. Emily and I had an expiration date. Still, the end was weeks away, and if memories were all I'd ever have, I was going to make the kind that'd keep me warm every night for the rest of my life.

21

EMILY

———

DR HOBBES WAS on the phone when it was time for me to leave work for the day, so I waved at her on my way to the staff room, and she smiled and nodded in return.

I felt a twinge of guilt as I washed my hands and collected my things. Summer had taken a chance on me when I'd shown up at her clinic, a stranger with red-rimmed eyes and no experience working with animals, and if it wasn't for this job at her veterinary clinic, I don't know if I'd have had the courage to give things a real go in Valentine Bay. I certainly wouldn't have had the funds. But now that I was behind a camera again, I couldn't give it up, and if things kept going as well as they had been, I'd soon have to quit my day job.

Kate and Raelene had shown a few of my pictures to the president of the tourism council, and he'd called me earlier in the day to hire me for a proper online marketing campaign for the Bay. On top of that, two people in the last three days had stopped me in the street to ask if I photographed weddings. I'd swallowed my panic and said no, but another couple had wanted to hire me for newborn photography, and while taking pictures of gaga-eyed parents and their kids skirted a little too close to photographing other people's happiness, the idea of working with tiny babies didn't make me want to gag.

My worry about disappointing Summer and the thrill of new possibilities were all I could think about as I wrapped up at work. I had grand plans to go home, reheat a plate of homemade lasagne, and put together a list of potential local business opportunities. Maybe I could make it my full-time job again within a few months. The idea had me chuckling under my breath. If someone had said to me ten weeks ago that I'd pick up my camera again so soon—and that I'd enjoy it—I'd have pointed at something over their shoulder and run the other way when they weren't looking.

I let myself out the door, looking forward to a quiet night in, and spotted Abbie waiting for me on the street outside the clinic.

"Crisis," she announced.

Hitching my handbag over my shoulder, I cocked my head. She didn't look panicked. "What kind of crisis?"

"Of the heart, obviously."

"Yours?"

She snorted. "Of course not. It's Jess. She ran into Luca and Natasha while shopping for groceries. Nightmare. They were forced to spend thirty excruciating seconds making small talk in front of the deli counter. Last thing she needed was a salami staring at her at a time like that."

I coughed and covered my mouth to hide a smile. "What can I do?"

"Girls' night." Abbie hefted the canvas bag she held in one hand. "I've got the essentials. Blue cheese. Red wine. Dark chocolate. Did you want to go home and change first?"

"Absolutely. I smell like wet dog."

Abbie leaned in, sniffed, and wrinkled her nose. "You're not wrong. We can swing past your place first. It's almost on the way."

Forty-five minutes later, we were making ourselves comfortable on the sofa in Jess's compact two-bed bungalow, a fixer-upper on an enormous block of land that she'd inherited from her grandmother three years earlier. Jess was a single schoolteacher with a single schoolteacher's salary, Abbie said, explaining away the condition of the place. Jess had been saving up for the renovations and was almost ready to start them when Luca had breezed back to the Bay with a new girlfriend, and Jess hadn't been up to thinking about the house since.

I reached for another handful of chips as Jess relived the horror that was the supermarket salami stand-off.

"I turned the corner, you know, from the dairy aisle to the deli section, and they were just *there*." She crumpled sideways onto the sofa, covering her face with her hands. "He looked so handsome, and she looked so ... so ... pretty. She was *kind* to me. Ugh."

"What a bitch," Abbie said, taking another square of chocolate.

"I know, right?" Jess sat up, leaned her head on the back of the sofa, and sighed. "No. That's not fair. She's bound to be a good person. Luca's not an idiot. Natasha must have done something right for him to want to bring her back here to live."

I took a sip of wine. "Did he really show up out of the blue one day with a new girlfriend? No offence, but that doesn't sound very kind to me. Sounds kind of cruel."

"He called first," Jess said. "We'd stayed in touch, you know. We weren't together, but we were still *friends*." She scowled into her wine. "He explained he'd met someone, and they were moving back, and of course, I pretended to be happy for him and enthusiastic about having him home again. I know he didn't want to hurt me." She made a sound in her throat. "This is my problem, not his. Not *theirs*. It's my stupid fault for not getting over him when I was supposed to. The same way he got over me."

"Was the break-up amicable?" I asked.

"Yes. Very. We could have written a book titled *How To Dump Your High School Sweetheart With No Hard Feelings*." Jess looked at Abbie, then me, then rolled her eyes. "Okay, here's the pathetic truth. I never thought it was a real-and-forever kind of break-up. He wanted to try city life. I didn't. He wanted to move away for work, and I wanted to support him without giving up my job here. But he was supposed to come to his senses and then come home to me. Not discover there are better women out there than small-town, plain, play-it-safe Jessica Jane Frost!" She dived headfirst into the cushions again.

"You're not plain!" Abbie squawked. "*You* are a fucking fox, sweetie. You've done a heroic job of keeping your shit together since Luca got back, and you've got the biggest heart of everyone I've ever known. Okay, you're not supposed to be with Luca. So what? He's not the last man on Earth, thank God. If he was *the one*, you'd be with him. You're not, so he's not. It's common sense."

Jess and I exchanged startled glances around the edge of her purple cushion before we burst into laughter.

"That's impressive logic, Abs," Jess said.

Abbie tossed her long blonde hair. "Thank you. I like to share my wisdom when I can."

Jess cuddled the cushion. "You have to be right. Luca can't be the one. If he was, he'd have come crawling back, or better, he never would have left in the first place. The problem is, we fit. On paper, we're perfect for each other. Luca was the most sensible and safest choice I ever made. If I can't make it work with him, I'll never make it work with anyone."

Abbie snorted. "Fuck sensible. Screw safe. Give me stupid sex with handsome strangers and a side of multiple orgasms, thank you very much."

I reached over and squeezed Jess's hand. "You'll find your guy when you least expect it."

Jess flashed me a grateful smile, then sipped her wine. "It'd be easier if Luca were a scumbag, and I hated his guts. And that reminds me, how are things going with your ex?"

I laughed. "It's definitely easier to move on when the guy who dumped you is a dickhead. Um, let me see. There are the flowers, of course. The text messages. The accidental meetings on the street and at the beach. I ignore it all, but he's still there. He keeps asking me to dinner, and I keep saying no, but it's less than two weeks until the wedding. It's only a matter of time before he gets more inventive."

"Should we be worried?" Abbie asked.

"Oh, no," I waved my hand away. "Tyler's not dangerous. He's *deluded*. I can handle him."

After taking a sip of her wine, Jess watched me sideways. "How are things going with Josh?"

Abbie shimmied, then tucked her feet up and turned to me, holding her glass in front of her lips to hide a smile. I didn't like the way her eyes sparkled, like she knew something.

"They're fine." I reached for a piece of cheese.

"Oh, come on!" Jess begged. "Distract me with something juicy. Everything I know about your arrangement has come second-hand from Abbie, and now that I have you here, I want all the details."

The images of Josh naked and sweaty that flashed through my mind came and went with no prompting from me, and when a flush started creeping into my cheeks, Jess screeched.

"I knew it! Spill."

I groaned and put my wine on the coffee table. "The sex is *so* good."

Abbie and Jess both squealed then, and I had to laugh.

"I'm so glad that boy is getting some," Abbie said. "He seems very, uh ... content."

"He really does," Jess agreed. "I bumped into him a few days ago, and the difference in him was almost shocking."

I shifted, feeling uncomfortable. "That might have more to do with him finally making plans to move to the city, don't you think? He feels lighter because he's decided to start over?"

"He's definitely happy about starting over," Abbie said, and my eyes narrowed. That wasn't exactly what I'd meant.

"Is it just sex?" Jess asked. "Not that that's a bad thing if the sex is good, but you two get along well, don't you?"

"Yeah, we do. It was Josh's idea to trade photography for all the wedding donations, and now I'll be doing a marketing campaign for the tourism council. I'm thinking about restarting my photography business, actually."

Jess grinned. "That's brilliant!"

"It is," Abbie agreed. "While you're at it, see if you can talk to the council about the horror show that was the Valentine's Day decorations this year."

"Ha! I think they want to play up the Valentine connection. Make this place a premier wedding destination. There'll be more pink around here, not less." At the horrified look on her face, I patted her arm. "I'll do my best to keep it classy."

"I appreciate that," Abbie replied.

"So, Josh has really made an impression on you, huh?" Jess went on.

"I suppose so."

Jess leaned her elbow on the back of the sofa and her head in her hand. "Emily. I just put my broken heart on a platter for you two, and you handed it back with one or two of the pieces stuck back together again. Plus, we're a bottle of wine in, and I'm about to open another. This is a time for *sharing*. Just say what you're thinking. That's what friends are for."

I played with the cracker in my hands, turning it and considering just how much of myself I wanted to give away. I didn't have a close relationship with my sister. I wasn't used to confiding in friends. Female relationships had been a mystery to me for most of my life, and I never did learn the rules of engagement the way other girls did in those formative years. More than that, I couldn't forget that these two particular friends had more loyalty to Josh than they'd ever have to me. Just how honest could I be?

On impulse, I risked it. It felt like something New Emily would do. Plus, saying what I thought out loud might take some of its power away, and I couldn't go around in circles anymore. It was driving me crazy.

I sighed and put the cracker down, then squared my shoulders. "I like him."

Abbie grinned. "Like him? Or *like*-like him?"

I rolled my eyes. "How old are you?"

"It's a valid question."

I rubbed my fingertips over my forehead. "Okay, fine. I *like*-like him. He's considerate and careful, and strong. He's insanely hot, and I've never had sex like this before. Oh my God, you guys. The *sex*."

Nothing could have wiped the goofy grins from Abbie and Jess's faces, and I had to laugh.

"But it doesn't matter what I feel," I went on. "He's leaving, remember? And I think that's for the best."

"What?" Abbie frowned at Jess, then back at me. "Why would that be best? I'm pretty sure he has feelings for you, too."

I shook my head. "Don't say that. Okay, he might like me, and I'm pretty sure he likes the sex, but he's not over Maggie."

They exchanged a look again, and I could almost see the history floating through the air between them. "Did he say that?" Abbie asked.

"Yes, actually. He said he didn't want to move on from Maggie because then she'd be gone. And as much as I like Josh, I can't be with him if he's still in love with someone else."

Jess considered me with patient eyes. "Em, he'll always love Maggie. We all will."

"I know! Oh, God, this isn't coming out right." I twisted my hands together. "I would never expect Josh to replace Maggie or forget her. I'd be honoured if he talked to me about her, but he's a closed book, and he can't move on if he's not ready to say goodbye to her, you know?" At their understanding nods, I went on. "I don't want to be the reason he stays in Valentine Bay, stuck between two lives. I won't be with a man who thinks he can have something part-time with me here and something else over there— that was the lesson I learned from Tyler, and I won't forget it—but being in the Bay causes Josh too much pain, and I want him to be happy."

Abbie nodded slowly. "We all want that. I'm not convinced Josh needs to leave town to be happy, though."

Jess sighed. "Josh sees the way life worked out for his dad and assumes the future will be the same for him." She smiled sadly at me. "We've never pushed him because we thought he just needed time, but the longer we left it, the more set in his ways he became. Perhaps we should have intervened earlier."

"I'm starting to think you might be right," Abbie mumbled, picking at the cluster of grapes in her hand.

"What was she like?" I asked. I'd been curious about Maggie, of course, but didn't want to ask Josh questions he might consider intrusive.

Similar grins appeared on Abbie and Jess's faces, and their expressions took on dreamy, faraway kinds of looks.

"She was tall, with wild dark curls and perfect olive skin," Abbie started. "And she had those long fingers. Do you remember, Jess?"

"Yep. Her hands looked made to play piano, but Maggie was outdoorsy. She was a runner and on all the rep teams for school sports. There wasn't a game she couldn't play."

"So, the exact opposite of me," I said, trying—and probably failing—to behave as though that didn't bother me. "What else?"

"After high school, she worked at the bar with Will," Abbie said. "She was smart enough that she could have gone to university if she'd wanted to, but it wasn't her thing. Both she and Josh were dreamers, and they didn't know what they wanted to do back then."

"They were planning to take off the year that she died," Jess murmured. "Head to the UK, travel and try to get work. She was so excited. It was as if they'd finally figured something out, and the adventure was about to begin."

"Really?" Abbie looked at Jess in surprise. "I didn't know that."

Jess nodded. "We were at dinner one night—Josh and Maggie, me and Luca—and they told us all about it. Couldn't have been more than a month or two before the accident."

We were silent for a minute, and then the wine made me brave enough to say something I'd been thinking. "Do you think Josh will ever be ready to let someone in again?"

"I hope so. Maggie would want that for him." Abbie frowned into her wine. "Is he *really* going to leave the Bay?"

I scrunched my face up, not knowing if I should be the one to answer but wanting to think out loud. Maybe that would help me sort out my own feelings.

"I think ... maybe? I'm going to help him find a rental and fill out the application forms, but I'm waiting for him to tell me he's ready to start looking. I don't think he's going to sneak out of here under the cover of darkness, but he seems pretty set on leaving one day soon. Perhaps he thinks a new environment will make it easier to connect with someone."

Abbie sighed and tipped her glass to her lips. "I've tiptoed around this because he refuses to talk about it, but I just *know* that sooner or later, he'll find a person who can open him up again. He doesn't have to leave to do that. There's as much chance she'll turn up here as anywhere else."

I shifted and put my cracker back on the plate while the other two watched me with speculative gazes.

Jess brought her knees to her chest and gave them a hug. "If he leaves, he says goodbye to a place, not a person. If he can't find a way to let Maggie go, it doesn't matter how far he travels. He's going to take Maggie with him."

I nibbled my lip. "Is that such a bad thing? It's what he wants."

Abbie shook her head. "He looks at his dad and thinks the right way to mourn someone is to spend a lifetime missing her. He can love and honour Maggie and still be open to loving someone new." Then she looked me directly in the eyes. "And if he doesn't learn that lesson soon, he's going to miss out on a chance at happiness, even if it's standing right in front of him."

22

JOSH

———

IT WAS EIGHT o'clock the next morning, and I was standing on the street outside Emily's apartment building when Tyler appeared around the corner. I crossed my arms and ignored him, but knowing he was watching set my teeth on edge. Five minutes passed, then ten, and by then, I'd had enough. I glared directly at him. He seemed startled at first, but then he smiled and waved like we were old friends. I shook my head, determined to forget about him, and from the corner of my eye saw him disappear.

I had to wonder what his deal was. Did he love Emily, or was his persistence about his ego, like she'd said? Then I decided it didn't matter. She didn't want to be with him, and that's all I needed to know.

Finally, the door opened, and Emily stepped out, dressed in her work uniform because she was expecting to go into the clinic. Her head jerked in a double-take when she saw me and the hot pink longboard I held in one arm, and her eyes narrowed. She glanced up and down the street—for what, I had no idea—but the trepidation on her face made me laugh.

"What's with the worry lines?"

"I'm *worried* that surfboard isn't yours."

I twisted it a little to show off the colour. "It's not."

Emily tucked her hair behind her ears. "I'd love to stay and find out whose it is, but I've got to get to work so—"

"You've got the day off."

"I've what?"

"I spoke to Summer yesterday and called in a favour. You're all mine today."

A small smile curved her lips. "Under other circumstances, that would sound like a good thing, but you're up to something." She looked at the board and away again.

"Today, you're getting your first surfing lesson."

She paled. "I'm *what*?"

My stomach plunged, but I pressed on. "You can't live in Valentine Bay and not know how to catch a wave. It's practically a rite of passage here. I bought you a board"—I picked up the bag at my feet—"and a wetsuit, though you don't need to wear it today if you don't want to."

She wrapped her arms around herself in a hug and stared at the ground.

"We'll start with paddling," I said, feeling more and more uncertain by the second. "Practice pop-ups on the sand. I'll show you how to read the water. It's basic stuff, really. You'll pick it up quickly."

She looked up the street again, and I seriously believed for a minute she was about to run away.

"Or … not," I said. "We don't have to do any of this. I just wanted to—"

"I can't swim!" she blurted out.

I paused for a second. "You can't?"

Her face was red. "No. I never learned."

I looked towards the end of her street, where the water waited for us. "I … feel stupid. I've never known anyone who couldn't swim."

"This is so embarrassing," she muttered.

"No. No! If anyone's embarrassed, it should be me. I just assumed, and I shouldn't have. Every kid around here signs up for Nippers with the local surf life-saving club as soon as we're old enough to be let out of sight. You can't hold us back."

Emily's face reddened further, and she kicked the ground, watching the toe of her shoe send up little rocks of gravel. "I never had lessons or a pool to practice in. Then I reached an age when I thought, why bother? Water frightens me."

The ocean was my second home, and one of the few places that brought me peace. It was my refuge after Maggie died. I tried to understand what Emily was telling me, but it was too foreign a concept. More than that, I wanted her to love the water as much as I did.

"So, let's save the surfing for now. We'll start with swimming. You have a swimsuit, right?"

Her mouth did that cute little quirk thing, and my cock jumped. For a moment, I thought about skipping

197

the swimming lesson in favour of a full day in bed with her, touching and tasting and teasing her with my tongue, but I wanted to leave her with something after I'd gone. Learning to love the water felt like the most precious gift I could give her.

"Yes, I have a swimsuit," she replied. "Several, in fact. Most with the tags still on."

"Perfect. Let's go get you changed and down to the ocean baths."

She groaned but turned around and dragged herself up the stairs to her apartment. I walked behind her, carrying the board.

"The baths?" she asked. "Everyone's going to see me."

"Nobody will be looking at you."

"Panicked people tend to draw attention to themselves. Panicked people in a body of water tend to draw crowds."

"Did I tell you I'm a trained lifeguard? I've volunteered every summer for the last four years."

I'd wanted to reassure her, but I only made things worse.

"Oh my God," she groaned. "This is going to be so embarrassing."

We stopped in the hallway while she looked for her keys. "Is it really that bad?" I asked. "Maybe it's not a good idea after all."

She pushed the door open for me, and we went inside. "No, I'm exaggerating. A little. I've always wanted to learn how to swim but never had the motivation. Now I do. As long as you don't let go of me, I'll be fine."

I set the board against the wall in the living room, put my arms around her waist, and drew her in for a kiss. "It's a big ask, but I'll do my best to keep my hands on you at all times."

———

I'd thought Emily naked was a sight I'd never forget, but Emily in a tiny white bikini had me grappling for words. She'd been covered up on the walk to the beach, wearing a dress and sandals and a big floppy hat, carrying her towel and sunscreen in a canvas bag slung over her shoulder, but when she dropped it all on the side of the pool, it was me who had to pick up my jaw. Her warm ivory skin was lightly bronzed from the sun, as evidenced by the tan marks across her shoulders. I wanted to run my mouth over every line. As she stood on the side of the pool, staring down at the water and rubbing her hands over her arms to soothe herself, I was reminded again of just how petite she was, and I felt overwhelmingly protective.

She crept closer to the edge, casting an eye over at the junior bath alongside us, where a toddler squealed and splashed under the watchful eyes of her grandparents.

"Forget it," I said, jumping into the water and pushing out a few paces. It wasn't deep at this end, the surface lapping at the base of my ribcage. Even Emily would be able to stand head and shoulders out of the water. "We start here. The tide is on its way out, the water's clean, and it's not even busy today. Look." I gestured at the near-empty pool around us. "No audience, see? Jump in."

Her eyes lifted out to the ocean beyond, and I could see her throat bob with a nervous swallow, and then she looked around at the few people swimming laps up and down the baths. She huffed out a sigh, sat down, and dangled her legs in the water, but that was as far as she got. I ran my eyes over her smooth legs, her flat stomach, her subtle curves.

"Right," I said gruffly, shifting a little to accommodate my dick. "Feeling okay?"

"Yes," she said. "The water's not too cold, at least."

"What is it about swimming that scares you?"

She grimaced, then stared out at the ocean again as she kicked her legs along the surface of the water. "When I was four, I went swimming in a friend's pool. Her older brother promised to hang on to me, so I agreed when he wanted to take me out to the deep end. He thought it would be funny to let me go there. I was probably only under for about three seconds, but it felt like forever. I didn't know if he was going to pick me back up, and I remember the terror of not being able to find the surface. After that, learning to swim didn't seem worth the risk of potentially drowning."

"Well … fuck. That's horrifying." For a fleeting moment, I felt guilty for forcing the issue, but then I was more convinced that learning to swim would be good for her. *I* could do this for her. "But didn't you ever wonder if learning to swim would make you feel better about that experience? Give you some sort of control? Conquer your fears and all that."

"There's an easier way to feel in control around water." She pretended to scowl at me. "You don't go in it."

I ducked my head under, standing again and running my hands through my hair to get it off my face. Then I moved towards Emily and stretched out my arms, inviting her in. "Then let's spend today trying to find something for you to love about swimming. I won't make you do anything you don't want to do. Let's just get a feel for the way the water works."

Emily and I stared at each other for the longest time, her eyes searching for something in mine. I tried to let her know she could trust me. When she closed her eyes, took a deep breath, and pushed herself into the water, I grinned, but she kept her back pressed up against the side of the pool. Taking two slow, careful steps towards her, I braced a hand on either side of her and bent my knees to bring my eyes level with hers. "I'm not going to let you go."

She licked her lips, her focus dropping to my mouth and then back up to meet my gaze again. Her eyes were a different shade of green now that they reflected the blue of the water and the sunlight all around. She moved her head in the tiniest of nods, so I took her hands and guided her out.

We went slowly, and I held her hands the entire time, walking backwards and leading her on as the water rose higher and higher. I could tell by the look on her face that when she felt wetness licking at her collarbone, she'd pushed herself past any pretence of comfort. That's when I fitted my hands under her arms and pulled her close.

She flung her arms around my neck and twisted her legs around my waist, and I nearly declared the lesson over as I balanced the sensations of her wet skin on mine, the cool saltwater swirling around us, and the hot pulse of her centre pressed against my stomach, just inches above my cock. A quiet whimper escaped her throat, and I kissed the base of her neck.

"Are you ready to go under?" I asked. "I'll go with you."

Her eyes widened, and I felt her heart beating faster. "And you promise not to let me go?"

"Here. Let's try this." I lifted her by the arse and swung her onto my back. "I'm going to dip under and swim a little way, and you just have to hold on tight. Okay?"

"I think so."

"All right. Here we go."

I bent my knees, taking us below the surface, then pushed ahead, flattening our bodies and propelling us forwards. Her arms tensed around my neck, and I stroked outwards with my arms to go a little further before I took us up again.

"How was that?" I asked over my shoulder.

She didn't loosen her arms, but there was a touch of surprise in her tone when she said, "It was… okay."

We did the same thing over and over until Emily was comfortable enough to loosen her grip and hang onto my shoulders and gently kick her legs as we swam up and down together. When we'd both had enough, I spun her around to my front again, and my throat tightened at the sight of her. Her short dark hair was slicked back, her cheeks flushed, and her breasts pressed against me, gently heaving with her excited breaths. The smile on her mouth lit up her entire face.

"So, what do you think about swimming now?"

"I don't think you could call that swimming," she replied, gripping my waist with her thighs but unwrapping her arms so she could run her fingers through her hair and wipe the water from her face. "More like taking me for a ride."

I touched my lips to her mouth, tasting the salt of the water and the flavour that was all Emily. "Rides are good," I murmured between kisses.

"Mm. No argument from me." She tightened her legs around me, pressing her pelvis into mine and moaning against my mouth as my cock hardened and twitched against her. I ran my hands up and down her back, kissing her with a growing desire.

"Let's get out of here," I said, my voice low beside her ear.

As I kissed my way down the side of her neck and over her shoulder, she replied, "Now. Please."

I carried her towards shallower water, and when we reached a depth where Emily could easily stand, she unwound her legs and walked beside me. I held one of her hands the entire time, and when we got to the edge of the pool, I wrapped my hands around her waist and lifted her up.

I stood there dripping wet, admiring Emily's perfect arse as she retrieved our towels, when I noticed Mrs Kitchener, a retired high school teacher who I'd had for

Year Nine geography, watching me with a satisfied look on her wrinkled face.

"Hi, Mrs Kitchener. Nice day today, isn't it?"

"Just glorious," she said, smiling at me, then Emily. "Oh, Josh. It's so lovely to see you happy. Some of us worried this day might never come, and now here you are. You make a good-looking couple. Such a pair. I daresay Maggie would agree. She was that kind of girl. She'd want nothing more than for you to be happy."

The accumulation of hours of joy in Emily's company incinerated in seconds, Mrs Kitchener, the grinning arsonist, having thrown the match. The blaze burned quickly, and when it died, all it left was ashes of guilt, shame, and rage.

"Emily's not my girlfriend," I said shortly. "You know that. Nobody could ever take Maggie's place in my life."

The smile slipped from Mrs Kitchener's face, and she looked uncertainly at Emily, then back at me. I kept my concentration on the old woman. I didn't want to know what Emily was feeling right now. Fuck, what a dickhead thing for me to say. The shame came crashing in a thousandfold.

"Yes, well." Mrs Kitchener took two steps back. "You both have a good day now. Enjoy the sunshine."

I turned away from her as she shuffled off, pulling on my shirt and scooping Emily's bag up off the ground, handing it to her without looking up.

"That must have been hard," Emily whispered.

I still didn't want to meet her eyes. "Just leave it."

"But I—"

"I said, leave it!"

"I'm sorry. I didn't mean—"

"Are you all right to get home on your own? I just realised I have to help my dad with something at the house, and he'll be waiting for me. We can catch up a bit later?"

"Uh, sure. Did you want to come around to my place for dinner?"

"Sounds good." I started to walk away.

"About seven?" she called after me.

"See you then," I answered over my shoulder.

I was an arsehole. Emily didn't deserve any of that, but I had to get out of there fast. I was no use to anyone. I would never get over Maggie. This town wouldn't let me, and everything outside of her was just pretend. Emily was just pretend.

A part of my life was missing, and I would never get it back. I couldn't afford to forget it, even for a second, because when I did, the reminder hurt a million times worse than leaving myself to drown in never-ending agony.

23

EMILY

_____

I WENT STRAIGHT home and showered, taking time to thoroughly rinse the salt from my hair. When I was dried, dressed, and presentable, I went to pick up groceries for dinner. After they were put away, I folded the pile of clean clothes that had collected on the armchair in my bedroom. I operated on autopilot, my hands completing the simple tasks without explicit instructions from my brain because it was too busy going over the details of my day with Josh. A day that had been perhaps one of the best of my life, spending hours laughing and playing *in the water* with a man who looked at me like I was something special and made me feel confident and complete in my own skin.

A day that ended with me staring at his retreating back, blinking back tears of humiliation and rejection.

I wanted to be understanding. I knew he was dealing with a type of pain I'd never experienced. But today, he was kind of an arsehole. Old Emily was scrambling for a way to smooth things over, anything to make Josh feel better. New Emily wanted to shout a little and call him a jerk to his face.

Then I wanted him to tear off my clothes and do bad things to me.

I let the dress I was holding fall into a heap on the bed, then I crashed into the pile of clean, sorted, and folded clothes, landing face down on the mattress.

I had feelings for Josh. Real, actual, feel-them-in-my-fingertips *feelings*. Today at the baths felt like a taste of what we could have together if things were different. If we'd met in another way, at another time.

Was it too late to fix what was broken inside him? Could we find a way to make this work?

I jumped to my feet and furiously sorted my clothes. *Stop it, Emily.* He doesn't *want* to make it work. He wants to run away and stoke his pain for the rest of his life.

And who was I to judge? I wasn't what you'd call a poster child for good romantic choices. I huffed out a little laugh. My track record was all the proof I needed that falling in love with Josh was a bad idea. I wouldn't know a bad boy from a good one if he bit me on the bum—or kissed me on the mouth. The best compass I had now was the promise I'd made to myself never to make the same mistakes again, and at the top of the list was choosing men who wanted something else in life. Something that didn't, or couldn't, include me.

Josh wanted a life out of the Bay, and I was building a future here. Could I picture that life with Josh by my side?

I scrubbed away my tears, adding the last pair of shorts to a neatly folded stack and starting on the T-shirts. Yes, I could see it so clearly. He was brooding and moody and introspective so much of the time, but when he let his guard down, we *fit*.

But in the end, those guards never stayed down for long before he built them back up and blocked me out again. There was a part of his life he didn't want to share with me, and as much as it hurt, I couldn't make-believe otherwise.

A life with Josh was an impossibility, and the sooner I accepted that, the less hurt I'd be when he left.

I'd pulled myself together by the time Josh was due to arrive for dinner, choosing a loose tee and short denim skirt for our casual night in. I had a surprise for him underneath, and any unhelpful thoughts about love and what-ifs were tucked away in the furthest recesses of my mind. After hours of torturing myself with pretty pictures of an unlikely future together, I'd decided to focus on the things that were real between us.

Sex and a fake wedding.

The realisation that those two things were all we really had hit home harder than it should have, but I chalked it up as just another reason I couldn't trust what I felt. I'd had more orgasms in the last ten days than I'd ever had in my life, not counting the ones I'd given myself. So, of course, I was out of sorts. I was hopped up on oxytocin or whatever.

Earlier that day, as I'd been floating—literally and figuratively—from the sensation of Josh's back and shoulder muscles rippling under my hands as he dove under the water and pulled me along with him, I'd thought of a way to repay him for wanting to teach me something new. When he'd shown up with that surfboard and a boyish grin on his face, I'd had very low expectations for the day, convinced I was going to either make a fool of myself or turn him off completely with my incompetence—or both. But he'd made me feel safe, and he'd clearly wanted it to be fun for me too, that I decided while we were in the pool that I was going to return the favour. And it wasn't with sex. Or not only that. Sure, the moment he first disappeared under the water and reappeared like some sort of Greek god, hair dripping and water trailing over the lines of his body in a way that drew my eye down, down, down, I'd thought of plenty of ways to thank him, but I wanted to do more than drive him wild with my mouth. I wanted to give him something thoughtful. I didn't have many skills beyond falling for the wrong men and taking pretty pictures, but I could make a mean lasagne.

When he knocked on the door right at seven o'clock, I'd tamped down my irritation at our best day ever being spoiled by a nosy old woman and Josh's bad mood. I didn't want to waste a minute of the time we had left together feeling bad about myself. I'd known what I was getting into when we started this, and I knew what I wanted at the end of it. Tyler out of my life and a new chance at happiness. Josh was just a stopover on the way from Point

A to Point B. Those were the rules we'd both agreed to, and that was all he could give me. It was unfair to change the terms of the agreement now. Unfairer still to do it without telling him.

He looked a little sheepish when I opened the door, but he had a bottle of red wine in his hand, and he was wearing a nice navy shirt. My heart softened at the look on his face.

"Come in," I said, taking the wine.

He moved just inside the doorway and ran a hand through his hair. "Look, about earlier. I'm sorry."

"It's fine." I took the wine to the kitchen, pulled out two glasses, and poured us both drinks.

"It's really not." He took a seat at the island. "I shouldn't have said what I did, the way I did. I was a jerk."

I sipped the wine, taking a moment to experience the flavour, then set the glass down with a clink. "I don't want to talk about it."

"You don't?"

"Do you?"

He tugged on one earlobe. "I guess not."

"Good." I rubbed my hands together. "I had an idea today for how I could pay you back for the swimming lesson."

His lips quirked. "Oh God, are you going to egg my house or something?"

"Ha! No, but you're on the right track. It involves food. I've lived on my own for a long time now, and cooking dinner for one every night gets boring. I'll feel better when you leave knowing you can cook at least one thing that'll fill you up, so I'm going to teach you how to make my feed-you-for-a-week lasagne. Unless ..."

His face was blank, and the heat of stupidity flashed from head to toe. Maybe Josh was a brilliant cook. I'd assumed he'd be hopeless—he was a twenty-eight-year-old man who lived a bachelor life with his widowed dad, after all—but maybe his hands could handle chef's knives and wooden spoons as well as they could soothe the sick and drive me mad with desire. I slumped and dropped my head to the side.

"Unless you're actually a whiz in the kitchen, and this was a dumb idea," I mumbled.

The shadow that flitted across his face came and went so quickly I might have imagined it, and then he smiled, stood, and came into the kitchen. Wrapping his arms around my waist, he kissed the tip of my nose. "I can burn a steak and bake a potato, so I'll gratefully accept your cooking lesson. Thank you for thinking of me and my stomach."

His face hovered over mine, so close that I couldn't see anything but his warm amber eyes. He leaned in and touched his lips to mine, tickling them gently, and I laid my hands on his arms, enjoying the delicate touch of his mouth, so sweet and tempting, and such a contrast to the needy, bruising kiss we shared in the pool earlier in the day. He pulled back and brushed the tip of his nose back and forth against mine, and I sank against him.

Burrowing his nose in my hair, he murmured against my ear, "I nearly came in my shorts when I saw you in that little white bikini today."

211

I felt a damp throb between my legs, then pressed my face against Josh's chest and giggled. "I nearly came in that little white bikini when you dove under the water, then rose back up, dripping water and flicking your hair like a model in some sort of cologne advertisement."

"That's it." He scooped my legs out from under me and started towards the bedroom. "I do not wear cologne."

I snuggled my face into his neck, inhaling the fragrance of his skin. "You don't need to. You smell good just the way you are."

"Not half as good as you taste."

Laying me on the bed, he stretched himself over me and kissed me on my mouth, my jaw, my neck, my collarbone. I moaned and twined my fingers in his hair, arching my back as he licked and kissed his way lower.

Yes, *this* was real, if nothing else.

He pulled up my shirt, and I threw my arms over my head so he could peel it off. I wasn't wearing a bra, and he moaned as one hand closed around my breast, teasing and pinching the nipple so hard I gasped. He enclosed the other nipple in his mouth, and the heat of his tongue set electricity shooting to my clit.

"I'm not wearing underwear either," I whispered. His head popped up, and I laughed at the surprise on his face, like a kid who got exactly what he asked for at Christmastime. He dipped his head again, this time barely stopping to press his lips to my ribcage, my stomach, my hips, before he pushed up the hem of my short denim skirt, groaning when he saw there was nothing between him and my pussy.

He ran a finger along the slick seam with a featherlight touch before dipping a fingertip inside me, and I shivered.

"Jesus. I'll never get over how wet you are for me. Every time."

He ran his hands over my thighs, to my knees, and then up again before tossing my legs over his shoulders and dropping his head between my thighs. The flick of his tongue on my clit sent a spasm of ecstasy through my body, and I moaned. "Oh, you're good at that."

Josh lapped up and down my slit with just the right pressure, rubbing his thumb over my sensitive nub in tight circles before thrusting his tongue inside me. "Yes," I gasped. "Yes! Just like that."

He devoured me in a way that felt hungry and selfish, and it made me hungry and selfish too, as I begged him not to stop, to keep going, to take me higher. He moaned against my clit, and the vibration jolted me into another stratosphere of pleasure as my orgasm hit me hard. I cried out his name as I fisted his hair and struggled to breathe.

When the tremors in my body subsided, he leaned back, unhooked my legs, and pushed himself off the bed. Finding a condom in his pants, I watched him roll it on, panting with impatience at the prospect of riding him to another orgasm. I waited for him to stretch himself over me again, but instead, he pulled me to a sitting position, hooked his hands under my arse, and picked me up. When he positioned my hips over his cock, and I felt it brush against my wet centre, I looked into his eyes and nodded. "Yes."

As he slid me down onto him, I inhaled sharply at his solid thickness, never breaking eye contact as we adjusted to the tightness of my body around his. I grazed his lips with mine, pressing my breasts against him, and enjoying the tingles of pleasure as my nipples rubbed against his chest.

He sat on the bed, taking me with him, and I wrapped my legs around his waist. Grinding my hips against his, the tip of his cock hit something magical deep inside while the base of him rubbed against my clit, generating the most glorious friction. He sucked on my earlobe and my neck, put a hand between us so he could rub my clit again, and we clung to each other like magnets as we rocked our hips and chased the finish together.

"I'm coming," I panted, digging my nails into his back and my teeth into his shoulder.

I cried out as my pussy clenched down on him, and I felt the pulse of his orgasm throbbing inside me.

"Fuck," he moaned, his huge arms engulfing my frame so tightly it almost hurt as our bodies ricocheted with bliss. There was no way we could get any closer than we were at that moment. Every inch of my skin was pressed against him, and I held on as hard as I could. I didn't want to let go. Not now, maybe not ever.

Josh's arms stayed wrapped around me, too, neither of us wanting to be the first to move. But I had to. I had to give up the fantasy.

Finally, I leaned back a little. "So, about that lasagne …"

He kissed me with an energy that would usually come

before sex, not after it, and then grinned. "Thank Christ, you read my mind. I'm starving."

Josh was a fast learner in the kitchen. Over a bottle of wine, we diced the vegetables and put the ragu on to simmer while I showed him the correct way to make a bechamel sauce, and then I pulled out two good-sized glass baking dishes.

"I always make enough for two large pans. One to eat the week I make it, the other for the freezer." I swept my gaze up and down his large frame. "Though looking at you, what lasts me a week might only last you a couple of days. Three tops."

He chuckled and was about to reply when his phone chimed. He pulled it out of his pocket, looked at the screen, then flicked the "silent" switch and placed it face down on the island. I gave him a quizzical look, which he pretended not to notice.

"So, how do we put this thing together?" he asked.

"Uh, well, we start with the—"

The phone vibrated, skittering over the stone top, and I frowned at it. "If you need to take a call or return a message, I don't mind. You can go to the other room if you need privacy."

He snatched up the phone and hid it in his pocket. "No, it's nothing important. I'll take care of it tomorrow."

I searched his face for something, anything, that would quiet the unease in my gut. Tyler used to pull this kind of thing and refusing to answer his phone when I was in the room was a red flag I'd chosen to ignore.

Josh brushed past me and stirred the sauce. Was he deliberately not meeting my eyes? What did he have to hide? But then his stomach grumbled, and I had to laugh. This was *Josh*, not Tyler. I had to stop projecting past hurts on future relationships, or I would never be able to trust anyone again.

"Start with a little sauce in the base of the dish, then layer pasta, ragu, and bechamel to the top of the dish. I like to sneak a little grated cheddar in there too, plus extra on top, of course. Here—use the ladle."

We each assembled a lasagne and popped them in the oven, and because I already had some in the freezer, I insisted that the one Josh had made should go home with him to share with Jack.

"Thank you," he said. "Though you'd be surprised how well we eat, given that half the town likes to feed us. Hardly a day goes by that someone doesn't invite us around for dinner or drop off a casserole."

"Well, all the more reason for you to know how to cook something yourself. You're not going to have neighbours dropping round with food for you in Sydney."

"No, I guess not."

He refilled our wine glasses while I cleared my laptop and some paperwork from the dining table. I'd set myself up there to do the photo editing for the images I was trading for wedding supplies and got carried away with my business planning. The mess took up half the space.

"Shall we eat?" I asked, starting back to the kitchen to collect plates and napkins for us, but Josh already had a forkful of lasagne dug out from the dish and was shoving it into his mouth. He looked guilty, then pained, as the hot sauce burned his tongue. Flapping a hand in front of his open mouth, he gasped for cooler air.

"You couldn't help yourself," I scolded, rolling my eyes, though I secretly loved that he couldn't wait to try my cooking.

I grabbed a bottle of cold water from the fridge and handed it to him, then pushed him towards the table. "Please don't do anything to damage your tongue. It's one of your best assets."

He cocked an eyebrow, still unable to speak, and I blushed and turned away.

"Now sit down, and I'll get you a plate."

24

JOSH

———————

THE LASAGNE WAS fantastic. So was the sex. Emily had the face of an angel, fucked like a bad girl, and knew how to cook. A woman like her was wasted on me, but I was too selfish to stop now. The days were ticking over, my time was running out, and I was going to get my fill of her.

After dinner, we were in the mood for something sweet, and I needed something cold to soothe my scalded tongue. Finding her freezer empty, I volunteered to visit the late-night supermarket, Quick Sticks, for ice-cream. It was due to close any minute, so after a quick debate arguing the merits of strawberry versus mint chocolate-chip, we compromised, and I promised to pick up both.

I couldn't get there fast enough. I didn't want to be away from Emily longer than I needed to be, and for the ten minutes it took to jog to Main Street, all I could think about was her whispering in my ear, "I'm not wearing underwear." My cock thickened, and I picked up the pace, throwing open the door to the store, grabbing two cartons of ice-cream from the freezer case, swiping my card and not waiting for a receipt, then racing out of there as though the hounds of Satan were on my heels.

Two minutes from her door, my phone buzzed in my pocket. For fuck's sake, real estate agents had the worst bloody timing. I pulled it out and listened to the voice message as I kept up a steady pace. One of the rental apartments I wanted to apply for had been snapped up already, and the agent wanted to put me down for another two he was trying to move. Jesus Christ, surely that was a conversation that could have waited until office hours.

I could tell Emily thought I was hiding something, and in a sense, I was, but nothing sinister. I'd decided not to involve her in that part of my life. I couldn't take any of her with me, not even a discussion about where I was going to live, or else what kind of new beginning would it be? I'd already promised myself to never make her lasagne. I could picture it now. Sitting under a bare bulb in my new place, crying into a plate of pasta because it reminded me of a girl who once made me come so hard, I thought I was doing to die.

Jesus, I was a mess.

I finally turned the corner to her block and pulled up short. Tyler stood there in grey trousers and a cuffed shirt that looked out of place in Valentine Bay, and he had his hand on the door to enter Emily's apartment building. I put my hand on his shoulder and pulled him back.

"What are you doing here?"

He glared and shrugged me off, looking up at the window to Emily's bedroom. "I thought you'd left."

"You've been out here watching?" The idea sickened me, and I wondered if I needed to use more direct means to get Tyler out of the picture. My hand fisted at my side as I imagined thumping the guy in his pretty face.

He punched the wall, and I stepped back in surprise. "You've only known each other a matter of weeks. We were together for years! This is a rebound fling that's gone too far. *I* can give her a good life. That's not your job."

Rage clouded my vision. "Emily and I are real, and being with her is not a job. It's a privilege."

Tyler scoffed and squinted up at the window again. "If I could just explain things to her—if she'd just answer her fucking phone—she'd understand why I need her so badly."

I clenched my jaw and scowled at him, and when he squared up to me, I stood taller, taking advantage of my extra height. It felt good to stare down my nose at him. The dickhead had a death wish.

"When you screw this up, I'll be waiting," he growled.

"Excuse me," I said between gritted teeth. Stepping around him and into the building, leaving him on the street outside, I didn't look back as I took the stairs two at a time, then opened Emily's door without knocking. She'd left it unlocked.

I opened my mouth to tell her I'd seen Tyler downstairs, but at the delicious grin on her face, her eyes bright on the ice-cream in my hands, I changed my mind. I didn't want that prick to ruin one moment I had with this woman. Closing the door behind me and making sure it was locked this time, I retrieved two spoons from the kitchen and walked over to her. She watched me with an amused curve to her mouth as I took her hand and led her to the bedroom.

"What are we doing?" she asked.

"For dessert tonight, I want ice-cream and Emily. Any objections?"

"Hm, let me think." She tapped her lips, then climbed onto the bed and sat on her heels. "Nope. No objections. You may proceed."

Tyler's comments echoed in my head. *This is nothing but a rebound that's gone too far.* I knew this wasn't real. I knew Emily deserved more than the shattered heart I had to offer. And I knew Tyler was trying to get a rise out of me. But something about what he said rang too true, and I didn't like it.

I pulled the curtains closed, joined her on the bed, and set about making her come as loudly as I could.

I'd never had sex with ice-cream before, but I was a fan. The taste of it on Emily's tongue, her lips, her breasts, and other places sent us both a little wild, and afterwards, we needed showers. Emily, ever the generous one, let me go first, but as I lathered myself, the bathroom door crept open and her pretty head popped around the corner.

"I couldn't wait," she said, shifting from foot to foot. "I'm all sticky. Is there room for one more?"

"Hell, yes."

She darted in, and at the sight of her lithe body glistening with sugar and freshly fucked hair, I was hard again in seconds.

"Does this guy ever take a break?" she asked, glancing at my cock as she squirted body wash into her palms and began rubbing them together.

"Not when you're in the room," I replied, soaping my arms and watching her slide the lather in her hands over her breasts and stomach.

"Hm." Emily faced me and ran her slick fingers over my sudsy chest, down my sides, and over my abs. When they circled my navel, they continued south until her hand was wrapped around my dick, and I groaned. Running my hands over her shoulders, I stroked her neck and arms. The water made our skin slick and slippery, and she moved her fist up and down my length, biting her lip as I got harder and thicker at her touch. Then she fell to her knees.

Holy fucking Christ.

I watched, stunned, as she flicked her tongue over the crown of my cock, and I waited for the tease, but she took me in deep, working the base of my dick with her hands, and I swore at the sensations. She grabbed one arse cheek and used the other hand to cup my balls, then lightly ran two fingers along the sensitive skin behind them. When she pushed me further into her, I was deep enough to feel the moan in the back of her throat. We both felt the throb of my impending orgasm on her tongue, and I tried to pull out, but she held on like a drowning woman and swallowed every drop.

Holy hell. Emily gave me a blow job so hot my knees buckled when I came.

We knelt there afterwards, hot water streaming over our bodies, and I cradled her face while I kissed her. I couldn't stop stroking her tongue with mine—long, lazy caresses and gentle tugs on her lips. Every taste of her skin fed my craving for her instead of satiating it.

"Can I stay over?" I asked.

I didn't know it was possible, but she kissed me even deeper. "Absolutely."

———

The next morning, I woke with the sun streaming into my eyes and Emily's head on my chest, an arm and leg thrown over me as she held on like a little koala. I kissed her head, inhaling the scent of vanilla shampoo in her hair. I could have lain like that forever, and the temptation to do just that was my cue to move.

Snuggling with Emily felt too easy. Too *right*. The girl was magic, and I needed to move to break her spell. There was nothing real here and, lost in the fog of some serious sexual voodoo, I'd started to forget the only things I knew for sure. They were things I'd held onto for four long years, words I'd never say out loud, and they'd kept my head above water when I felt like I was drowning. They'd have to be enough to pull me up and out again now.

I tried to shift Emily without waking her so I could go in search of pants and coffee, but she woke up, lazily looking up at me, and a slow smile spread across her face. "Hey, you."

"I'm sorry. I didn't mean to wake you."

She tightened her arm around me and pressed her lips to my chest. "I have to get up for work, anyway. Where are you rushing off to?"

"Coffee." I peeled myself away and snatched my jeans off the floor.

"Great. I'll have a cup too. Meet you in the kitchen?"

Emily banged around in the bathroom while I switched on the coffee machine and pulled two mugs from the cupboard. I'd poured for us both when she reappeared in her khaki work uniform.

Picking up her coffee and wrapping her fingers around the hot mug, she sipped carefully. "So, what have you got on today?"

There was a comfortable domesticity to this scene that made my coffee taste like pond water, and the itch between my shoulder blades became too insistent to ignore. I set down my cup and swiped my phone and wallet from the dining table, where I'd left them the night before.

"Oh!" Emily said, reaching for her handbag. It was enormous, almost as big as she was, and she kept it slung across the back of one of the dining chairs. She dug around and pulled out a scrap of paper, then handed it to me.

"Coral Hanks was at the clinic on Monday afternoon. Her cat, Reginald the Third, is almost eighteen years old, poor thing, and being kept alive with buckets of pills and duct tape. Anyway, Coral mentioned her yard was overgrown because her usual gardener retired six months ago, and she's had trouble finding someone to step in. I told her you might be able to help."

I knew why she'd done it, but I couldn't think rationally about the reasons. The reminder of my life with Maggie was ice in my belly. I met Emily's eyes and flashed my teeth in what I hoped looked like a grin as I tried not to overreact. "Why would you say that?"

A crease appeared between her eyebrows, and she wilted a little. "I remember you said how much you loved the landscaping work you used to do, and I thought you'd enjoy helping Mrs Hanks with her gardens."

I turned my back and shoved my things into my pockets. "Sorry. I don't have time."

"Oh, all right."

I dropped a quick kiss on her mouth on my way to the front door. "I'm busy at work the next couple of days, so I might not see you again until the bonfire on Friday night."

She clasped her hands together and stuck them between her knees. "Okay. Will I meet you there?" Before I could answer, my phone rang in my pocket, and her eyes flicked toward the sound. "Are you going to get that?"

I yanked out my phone and silenced the ringtone without checking the caller ID. Emily's eyes narrowed, and I shoved the phone out of sight again.

"I'll see you on Friday night," I said again, walking out into the hallway and pulling the door closed behind me.

If I could have stepped outside my body and punched myself in the face, I would have. Piece by piece, I was falling for Emily Jones, and every time I let another shard of my heart hit the ground at her feet, the process of picking it up and putting it back again felt harder and more necessary. Every reminder of the life I could have had—should have had—made guilt and grief rage in my veins.

Nothing lasted forever, and there were no guarantees, but I knew what the future held for me. I'd planned it out four years ago, and this was no time to veer off course. I was going to spend every breath I had proving to the universe I deserved to be here when Maggie wasn't.

Forgetting that promise so I could be happy with another woman was the most selfish thing I could do, and what kind of man would I be if I let that happen?

25

EMILY

I CLIMBED THE porch steps to Josh's front door, a heavy black garment bag hanging over one arm, the other hand holding the lead attached to Frannie, an old, rangy goat belonging to five-year-old Charlotte Potter. Dr Hobbes had asked me to take the old girl for a walk, and Josh was at work, but that was fine with me. I might not have come had he been home.

I rapped on the screen and stepped back, staring at my painted pink toenails poking out from the tops of my sandals. I was going to hand over the suit Kate had given me for the father of the groom, and then I was going to get out of there. I already knew Jack's feelings about Josh and me, and I wasn't in the mood to laugh off his "I told you so". And boy, Jack really had told me so.

My phone pinged, and juggling the bag and the goat, I pulled it out of my pocket. I couldn't help the way my

227

heart skipped when I saw Josh's name on the screen. It was the first time I'd heard from him since our awkward goodbye at my apartment the morning before. He had to work a few long days, so I tried not to take it personally, but it was more than that, and I knew it. I wasn't an idiot, and this wasn't my first rodeo. Josh was showing all the classic signs of a condition I called "man-scared," and I was bouncing back and forth between feeling empathetic, irritated, and paranoid.

Josh had been through a lot, more than most twenty-something men, and he had good reasons to be wary of commitment. Tyler had pulled the man-scared card too, but that was comparing apples with oranges. Josh feared loss. Tyler was terrified of growing old and boring, settling for less than he deserved and wondering if there were smarter, hotter, more willing women than me out there. He was a dishonest, self-absorbed coward, and he had very few redeeming qualities. It was easy to resent Tyler for putting me through what he did.

On the flip side, Josh was smart and kind and generous, and I could be myself around him. It wasn't his fault that, in the haze of our sexual chemistry, I'd forgotten the terms of our engagement. Still, there were a lot of things he kept to himself, not least of which was the way he felt about Maggie, and the recent unanswered calls and text messages that had set off neon warning signs in my head.

Swiping the notification on my phone to open Josh's text, my stomach whooshed at his message.

Josh: Can't wait until Friday night. I haven't stopped thinking of all the ways I can make up for three days away from you, and each one is dirtier than the last.

My fingers flew across the screen, tapping out a reply before Jack appeared at the door.

Me: I've had a few ideas too. I'll tell you mine if you tell me yours …

I flicked my phone to silent and returned it to my pocket. I could worry about textual foreplay later, when I wasn't in the middle of a conversation with my lover's father. I knocked again and watched Frannie sniff and nibble at the faded wood of the timber deck porch. The heat in my cheeks faded, my heart rate slowed to its normal rhythm, and I sighed. If only things were different.

I wished Josh could find a way to open up to me so I could help him heal. I wished he could find a way to move on from Maggie. Not forget her but find joy in what he still had. Maybe even take a chance on love again. I stopped short at thinking *take a chance on me*. It was hopeless. How could I hope to reach him when an entire town who had known him his whole life and loved him like a brother and son hadn't been able to help him move on?

The sounds of Jack moving around in the house reached me, and a moment later, he was swinging the screen door open for me.

"Josh isn't here, I'm afraid," he said, scratching his head and looking at the garment bag, then the goat.

"Oh, I know. I'm not here to see Josh. I came by to drop this off for you." I lifted the bag by the hanger. "Kate insisted that the father of the groom have a nice suit to wear to the wedding, and I offered to deliver it personally. She seemed to think the size would fit, but I'm sure you can swap it for another if it doesn't."

He waved away my concern. "I'm sure it's fine. Here, hand it over. You tie up Frannie there, and I'll try the suit on now. Make yourself at home in the living room, and I'll be out again in a minute. You can tell me what you think."

Jack's ready acceptance of the suit took me by surprise. I'd expected resistance, not an invitation to approve his wardrobe for the wedding. "Oh, sure. That's a good idea. Take your time."

I secured the goat's lead to the porch railing, then went inside and sat down on one end of the living room sofa. I looked around again, taking in more detail than I had the last time I'd been there. The faded fabrics, the worn carpet, the dark timber furniture that shone with a dull, aged glow. This house was a time capsule, and it made Josh's grip on Maggie more understandable. Whether Jack had meant to or not, he'd shown his son a very specific way to cope with loss, and it didn't involve moving on.

Jack reappeared in the archway between the living room and the hallway, tugging at the sleeves of a dark suit jacket and rolling his shoulders irritably. He looked at the floor, the wall, anywhere but at me, and I rose to my feet slowly, unable to hide the grin on my face.

Standing in front of him, I fixed his collar and tie, then straightened his pocket square. "Now I know where Josh gets his good looks."

Jack flushed. "Damn monkey suit. I don't wear 'em often."

"No, I can't imagine there's much call for formalwear around here."

He turned and looked at himself in the small mirror above the stand in the hallway, and I hovered behind his shoulder, beaming at him. There was a rosy tinge to his tanned cheeks.

"You think it fits?" he asked, brushing the lapels.

"Like a glove."

"That's good. I won't have to put myself through this again at Kate's place."

Then he shuffled off down the hallway, his bedroom door closing behind him with a click.

I chuckled quietly into my hands, finding myself a little teary over Jack's reaction to the suit. Perhaps everything would work out after all. Maybe not the way I wanted it to, but good enough in the end.

Pacing around the house, I took a closer look at things while I waited for Jack to come back. The coffee table was covered in stacks of old magazines, newspapers, and books. Photos of Josh when he was younger lined the mantel over a fireplace that looked like it hadn't been lit in years. There he was in school uniform and there in his Nippers gear.

In another, he was standing on the sand, the ocean at his back, with a longboard upright in one arm. Beside the picture of Jack and Kelly on their wedding day, the one he'd shown me on my first visit here, was a photograph of Josh dressed up for a school dance. I picked it up to get a better look and laughed. The girls were all in fancy dresses, but the boys had paired their formal shirts and suit jackets with bright board shorts and matching bow ties. Josh was at the end of the long line of teenagers, aged about eighteen, standing in someone's front yard. I recognised a few of the faces. Abbie and Will, Jess and Luca, Josh … and that must have been Maggie.

She was just as Abbie and Jess had described. Tall and thin and pretty. Her hair was piled in a mass of uncontrollable dark curls on her head, and she wore a figure-hugging black dress. Josh had an arm around her waist, and every person in the photo grinned at the camera in a way only teenagers could. They had not a care in the world, their entire futures stretched out in front of them. I replaced the frame, feeling a mix of wistful sadness for the kids in the picture and a stab of envy because, despite the tragedy, the friends in that picture were as good as family. They'd had each other then, and they had each other now. What I wouldn't trade for that.

I wandered back into the hallway to the table that was almost buckling with papers. One particular pile listed in a way that looked ready to dump a month's worth of mail on the floor, so I busied myself by straightening things up and leaning the stacks against the wall so they'd be less likely to take a tumble. Unfortunately, they were too far gone, and my interference made things worse, sending everything sliding over the side.

With a look up the hallway and no sign of Jack, I crouched down and quickly swept everything up, taking care not to look at any paper in particular ... until I scooped up a bunch of stapled pages with the logo of a real estate agency printed on the top. I didn't mean to read it, but the details jumped out at me and then I couldn't stop. It was a lease application for a property in Sydney, completed and signed by Joshua Ford.

I frowned and pulled more of the papers into a neat pile. Then I saw a second lease application for a property two suburbs over from the first. After that, there was a letter from the state ambulance service confirming receipt of a request for transfer. In a daze, I stared through the pieces of paper in my hands.

Why hadn't Josh told me he'd applied for places to live or that he'd already initiated a transfer with work? He was making plans and couldn't be bothered to let me know. No, more than that. Sudden understanding dried my mouth. He was deliberately keeping this all from me. After I'd told him I wanted to be there for him, and after he promised to let me help, Josh was beginning his next life without me.

Why did this hurt so much? I knew I didn't belong in his future, but I'd thought he'd let me support him the way he supported me.

Stop it, Emily! This isn't news. Josh's fresh start was never supposed to include you.

"Well, that's done then," Jack huffed as he came towards me from down the hall. "Thanks for dropping by with the suit. I— Emily? Something wrong?"

"What?" I cleared my throat and dropped the papers onto the table, smoothing my hair back from my face and smiling as best I could. "No, nothing. Everything's great."

The lines across his forehead deepened as he frowned first at me, then at the mail I'd dropped like it had burned my fingers. "Er, can I get you a cup of tea?" he asked. "Maryanne from two doors down dropped off a passionfruit syrup cake this morning, and Maz's food is always good. I might have already had a piece or three, but there's plenty left."

Jack hesitated, and he must have sensed I wanted to say no—that I wanted to run far and fast from this house and that conversation—but then he spun and stalked into the kitchen, and I heard him putting on the kettle. I rubbed my eyes and dragged my feet after him, pulling out a chair and sitting quietly at the table.

I knew what was coming, and it wasn't a piece of Maryanne Diaz's passionfruit syrup cake. Jack was about to serve me up a whopping slice of I-told-you-so pie.

He set a plate with a chunk of fluffy yellow cake in front of me. While the tea brewed, he set a small pitcher of milk and a sugar bowl in the centre of the table, each made of smoky grey glass that was so retro it had recently come back into style. When we both had steaming mugs in front of us, he sat across from me, and we concentrated on tweaking our tea with milk and sugar. A long stretch of time passed between his first sip and first words.

"I was as surprised as you to see that letter on the table there. That one, and the lease applications."

I blinked in surprise. "You were?"

Jack nodded and set down his cup. "For a couple of reasons, and perhaps not the reasons you think. First—and I think I mentioned this to you before—Josh isn't good at letting people in, even me. Maybe especially me." His mouth turned downwards at the ends, and he hid it with a gulp of tea. "So, the fact that he left those lying around where I could find 'em, well, it's out of character. I'm starting to wonder if it was intentional, like maybe I should bring it up."

Jack busied himself with a fork and his cake, and I mirrored him, not meeting his eyes when I said, "Maybe that's a good idea."

"But the other reason," he went on as if I hadn't spoken, "is I think Josh has taken a real shine to you. I haven't seen much of him the last week or so"—he kindly kept his eyes on his cake while I blushed— "but what I have seen is different." Jack lifted his gaze and met my eyes. "I like seeing my boy this way."

"What way is that?" I whispered, craving the answer as much as I feared it.

"He's happy."

I blew out a breath. "I'm not sure how to process that. I'm glad that he's happy, but he still wants to leave." I snorted. "In fact, it seems the happier he is with me, the more determined he is to get away. I know how that story goes."

Jack tilted his head. "How do you mean?"

I played with the cake, pushing crumbs around my plate. "I was three days away from marrying my ex when he turned the other way and bolted. The closer we got to commitment—the nearer we got to *happy*—the faster and further he needed to get away from me." I dropped my fork and pressed my hands between my knees. "I'm not the girl men make a life with. Not a whole life anyway."

"That's not true."

"Isn't it?" Tears burned my eyes, and I couldn't help the snap in my voice. The kindness on Jack's face didn't help any, and I just felt so ... so ... hopeless.

"No, this is about Josh. It isn't about you."

"You warned me."

Jack grimaced and sat back in his chair. "I'm sorry, Emily."

"Don't be. I should have listened. I should have known better than to get involved with him in the first place. I thought he'd told me all his secrets when he explained about Maggie and said he wanted to leave the Bay, but I wanted to help him, and he's keeping it all to himself. I told myself having a part of him was enough because our relationship wasn't for real or forever, but I can't help it. It still hurts. I thought I could handle keeping things casual, but I guess old habits die hard. I started hoping for something more."

Jack's fists were clenched on the table, then he scrubbed his face with open hands. I'd made him uncomfortable.

Feeling the burn of stupidity rush to my cheeks, I jumped to my feet and pecked his cheek quickly.

"Thanks for the cake and the chat. If you don't mind, could you not say anything to Josh about this? I'd be humiliated if he knew I was this messed up about everything, and it's not important. Once the wedding's done and Tyler's out of the picture, Josh can get on with his life and forget this ever happened. We both can."

I heard Jack get to his feet as I rushed to the front door, yanked Frannie's lead free from the porch rail, and took off down the street. I needed to get away and pull myself together. I *had* to gain control of my emotions before I saw Josh at the bonfire. My head was a mess, sure, but I could still finish what we started with my pride and my dignity intact. Josh wasn't a bad guy—not like Tyler—but our misguided arrangement had proved to me I had no self-preserving romantic instincts to speak of.

Whether or not he meant to, Josh invited a level of connection that had broken down all my walls, and now I felt like a fool. Tyler had made me feel the same way. Josh behaved as though he cared for me, but he had secrets, just like Tyler.

There were too many similarities for me to discount them all, and there I'd been, in the middle of both situations, daydreaming of a future with a person who had no interest in sharing it.

26

JOSH

AFTER WORK ON Friday afternoon, I went shopping.
Bonfires on the beach weren't the kind of parties that came
with a dress code, but this was a pre-wedding celebration.
A new shirt wouldn't look out of place. I went straight to a
store where I could ask a sales assistant with fashion sense
to help me pick out something that wouldn't make it look
like I was trying too hard, and together we settled on a
linen shirt in a navy print. I chose a new pair of shorts
while I was there, too.

With the detour for new clothes, as well as the extra
time it took to wash my hair and shave, I was running half
an hour late. By the time I got to the far-south end of the
Bay, the bonfire was blazing, and the party had already
started. The familiar sight of people dancing around the
flames and the smell of hazy wood smoke in the air had
me lengthening my stride.

The south end of the beach, with its permanent ring of blackened stones and collection of driftwood logs, was a favourite with the people of Valentine Bay, and not just rowdy teenagers getting tanked on their eighteenth birthdays. People of all ages put on parties there for anniversaries, graduations, birthdays, even weddings sometimes, and it was so popular, the local volunteer fire service had initiated a reservation process. In a practical sense, it helped them keep tabs on irresponsible burning, illegal drinking, and general bad behaviour, but those weren't the reasons they did it. Partygoers had managed the venue well enough among themselves until the notorious Blue Moon Barney twenty-two years earlier, when Burt Spies Senior and Maverick Tebeau showed up on the same night, and things got ugly. Burt wanted to host his wife's seventy-fifth birthday bash, Mav arrived ready to set up for a grad night party, and it ended with both of them face down in the sand, Burt with chipped dentures and Mav nursing a dislocated shoulder. Town legend had it that Burt would have won the night if the cops hadn't shown up.

The sight of flames spitting cinders into the sky and the music thumping on the smoky air buoyed my mood. The energy of nights like these might always make me think of Maggie, but there was enough history—years and years of it—to remind me of other people, other nights, other milestones. The good stuff. I was at home at the beach and never more than around a bonfire.

Isaac and Luca were the first people I saw as I approached, and they clapped me on the back as I joined them.

"Hey! Kidd!" Isaac tipped his chin and then shouted over the noise towards a table where Will had set up the bar. A banner had been strung up over it, secured by tall poles with silver and gold balloons and streamers attached to the tops. "Get the groom a beer!"

"Thanks, mate," I said, scanning the crowd for Emily. There were more people here than I'd been expecting. The usual crew, of course, plus a bunch of friends I'd known since kindergarten, but over there was Raelene from *Le Gâteaux D'Amour* on Main, talking to Kate from the boutique, and Dawn, of course. The blonde woman's grin was too smug for my liking. Noa, the Samoan head chef from The Stop, was here, fussing over the food, and so was Alix Miranda, our wedding florist, and Ava Thacker, who was four years older than me and used to live in the Bay, but who moved north to be closer to Pepperberry Hill, where she ran the executive day spa. "Serious turn out," I observed.

"Abbie wanted to go big," Will replied, joining us with a bunch of bottles balanced between his fingers. He passed them out, and I took a long draw, licking my lips in appreciation. Will's own craft ale. The man was a maestro with the hops.

"Well, she's done that," I said. "It looks like half the town is here."

"Almost," Isaac confirmed. "But I just overheard dear old Dot March telling Burt the Third she wants to get home early enough to finish reading the book for this month's VBFYRRRBC meeting. Give it an hour, and the oldies will have given up."

I nodded. Mrs March was the eighty-year-old president of the VBFYRRRBC, some kind of super-exclusive, invitation-only book club for senior readers in Valentine Bay. They got around town decked out in pastel pink logo-branded T-shirts, hats, and bumper stickers, but just like everyone else in town who wasn't a sworn-in member, I had no idea what all those letters stood for.

"Any sign of Tyler?" I asked.

"Not yet." Isaac patted his pocket, where I assumed his phone was stowed. "The guys on shift tonight are going to let me know if they catch him lurking around."

I tapped my beer bottle on his with a pleasant *click*. "I appreciate that. And has anyone seen Emily?"

Will jerked his head towards the other side of the fire. "Abbie and Jess have her sipping on a margarita bottle and dancing over that way."

"Oh, God," I groaned. "How drunk are they?"

Will chuckled. "It's early yet."

Luca took a swallow of his beer. "I suspect Jess, at least, got in a few pre-game glasses. Her hair's doing that crazy curly thing it does when she's half-shot."

"Poor girl had to face you with Tash tonight," Isaac ribbed him. "Can't blame her for the Dutch courage."

Luca covered his eyes with a hand. "Don't make me feel more like a dick than I already do."

"It'll be right." Isaac clapped him on the back. "You only have to tell her about the engagement and announce Logan's coming back to town. Nothing to it. Just get it done, man, like ripping off a bandaid."

Luca downed the rest of his beer in one long swallow. "Not tonight."

"No," I agreed. "Not tonight. Let's have one bonfire without drama. What do you say?"

Will's eyebrow quirked. "Got no idea what the fuck you're talking about," he deadpanned.

I smirked. "The fuck you don't. No *issues* with Abbie, got it?"

"Tell her that," he grumbled under his breath.

I gave myself a minute to calibrate the notes of music and talking and laughter, breathe in the smells of the bonfire and roasting marshmallows, process the dozens of familiar faces waving at me and smiling or swarming the bar table stacked with pre-mixed cocktails, craft beers in glass bottles, and platters of Noa's sensational food. This was going to be my last bonfire for a while, maybe ever, and I was going to get through it without screwing it up.

I'd given myself a pep talk about what kinds of conversations I'd have to navigate tonight. It'd be comments about Emily and me as a couple, and me moving on and finding happiness *finally*, but it was water off a duck's back tonight. Emily and I knew the truth about our relationship—Jesus, so did most of the town, though they'd conveniently decided to forget it—and I was perfectly capable of controlling how I responded to them. A polite smile. A nod of the head. Make an excuse to get away, then run. That had always been my M.O. and I wasn't sure when or why I'd forgotten that.

"Cheers, boys," I said, raising my bottle towards theirs. "I'll catch you later. I'm going to find Emily."

Isaac and Will smacked their bottles against mine as Luca said, "Ah, screw it. I'll come with you."

"Your funeral," I replied.

Luca and I strolled around the fire along the ocean's edge. The tide had already hit its high point and was on its way out, yet there was still plenty of soft, dry sand between the fire and the water. As I drew closer to the table with the drinks, I saw what was written on the banner rippling in the slight breeze. Someone has painted a bunch of hearts and kisses and scrawled "Josh & Emily!" over the top of them.

"Not the way we thought life would turn out, is it?" Luca said, glancing at the bonfire, then the banner, and away again.

I grunted under my breath. "Nowhere near."

"I know my marrying Tash will be hard on Jess, but I can't help it, you know? The Bay is my home, and Tash is ..." He sighed. "There are no words."

"You don't have to explain yourself to me, Rossetti. If this is what you want, I'm happy for you."

"Thanks. I appreciate that."

"And don't worry about Jess. We'll keep an eye on her, and she'll find someone else. You're not irreplaceable, you know."

"Fuck off." Luca shoved me hard enough that I skipped a few steps to the side, and I chuckled. "And you're forgetting something. You won't be here to keep an eye on her."

"Abbie will be here. Will and Isaac, too." I sipped my drink and tried to ignore the hitch in my chest. I hadn't given much thought to the things I was going to miss when I left the Bay. I'd never thought of leaving as bailing on my friends, but that's exactly what it felt like now. "And Logan, don't forget."

"Please stop reminding me." Luca looked at me sideways. "Jess will have Emily, too. Those three have grown pretty tight."

"Yeah," I muttered, imagining Abbie dragging Emily and Jess out to Friday night drinks, flirting with guys at the bar. Emily taking someone back to her place, to the bed I'd slept in with her next to me. Emily liking him enough for a second date. My abdominals tightened, and I had to force down my next slug of beer.

"Oh, shit," Luca said, coming to a dead stop and staring, jaw slack, at a group of girls dancing to the music.

The sun was well below the horizon now, the twilight tones of the sky throwing the party into early shadows. Arms waved in the air, hips gyrated, and heads flung from side to side, whipping hair about in a tangle of music-induced good times. The sounds of women scream-singing hurt my ears, and I squinted at the crowd, instantly recognising Emily at its edge. She wore the tight olive dress I'd seen her in on Valentine's Day at The Stop and she was swinging her body and falling over her feet. Then she laughed, and she looked so beautiful.

It took effort to tear my eyes from her, but when I did, I noticed Abbie was there, too, twirling and rocking to the beat. Jess was close by, moving a half-second behind the rhythm of the music, her hair a cloud of matted curls. In one hand, she held a bottled cocktail with a straw sticking out the neck, and under her other arm, swaying along with her, giggling and stumbling, with an identical bottle in her hand, was ... I had to look twice to be sure my eyes weren't playing tricks on me. Was that *Tash*?

"Hey, Frost," Luca said, walking up to the girls as though he were approaching a pack of wild horses—slowly, palms up, not quite making eye contact, taking care not to spook one in case it made the lot of them bolt. "Looks like you're having a good time."

He reached out a hand towards Tash, and she took it. "Babe!" she shouted in Luca's ear, making him wince. "Where you been? I'm just dancing with my girls here."

Luca pulled Tash towards him, and Jess let her go without a fight. They all kept dancing, Tash now tucked against Luca's chest, and Luca and I exchanged a wary look.

"Jess is a cool chick," Tash announced, waving at Jess, who took a sip of her drink and didn't seem to notice or care that her dance partner had been stolen.

"So are you, Tash!" Jess called back. "Luca has great taste in women." She snorted with laughter, then stumbled over her own feet but righted herself quickly and swung her hips.

Luca tried to smile, but he just looked ill. "All right. As happy as I am that you two are, uh, friends, I'm going to have to steal Tash for a second. Is that okay, Frost?"

Jess gestured grandly, never quite looking at anyone, especially not Luca and Tash. "Be my guest."

Luca leaned towards me. "I'm going to get Jess a bottle of water. Be back soon. You need anything?"

I shook my head, no longer concerned about the Luca-Jess-Tash triangle. I'd locked eyes with Emily, and I couldn't see anything else. Her eyes were wide with delight, her cheeks flushed from the fire, the dancing, and the margarita bottle she held in one fist. She laughed and then let herself be spun under Abbie's outstretched arms. When she came to a stop, she tucked her hair behind her ears and wandered over, stopping so close that her nipples brushed my chest.

"Hey, you," she said, tilting her head up to look at me.

I leaned in and pressed my lips against hers, meeting the tip of her tongue with mine and stroking it gently. She tasted like strawberry and tequila, so I went back for seconds. And thirds.

"Mm." She pulled away and rested her hands on my chest. "You can't kiss me like that in public."

I grazed my fingertips along her arms, loving that they erupted in goosebumps at my touch. "Why not?"

"Because it makes me want to do the types of things that get you arrested if they're done in public."

I kissed her shoulder, swirling my tongue over her skin, tasting the salt that was her mixed with the mist off the ocean, then moved my lips up her neck and jaw to her earlobe. I nibbled on it, then whispered, "Maybe we should go."

She smacked me, then latched onto my hand and dragged me closer to the fire. "No way. This is my first bonfire, and it's our pre-wedding party. I intend to be the last one standing."

Emily went straight to one of the driftwood logs around the fire, took a seat, and pulled me down next to her. I liked the feeling of her cuddling up beside me as she looped her arm into mine and dropped her head on my shoulder. We sat there for a little while, watching the party. People stopped by to wish us well before they left, and the crowd started to thin.

Burt the Third was the first. He stood over us, looking down with a secretive, satisfied smile on his face. "Good to see you two so happy together," he said, and Emily tensed up against me. I rubbed my thumb over the back of her hand. "Looking forward to the big day, too. Raelene says the cake is to die for."

Emily flicked a glance at me, then up at Burt. "Thanks, Mr Spies. We think it'll be a good day."

Burt bent closer. "That ex-fiancé of yours came sniffing around the bowls club the other day. I told him you two were most definitely in love. Couldn't get two people more perfect for each other. Sent him on his way with a bee in his bonnet, but I think he got the idea." He pressed a finger to the side of his long nose. "We'll fool that fellow and have him gone from here in no time."

Emily got to her feet and gave Burt a hug. "Thank you."

Burt patted Emily on the arm, shook my hand, and ambled away up the sand. I watched him go, and when I turned back to Emily, she was staring at me with an unreadable expression on her face.

"What?"

She grinned and squeezed my arm. "Nothing."

Over the next hour and a half, the party grew smaller and smaller until it was just a handful of us. Isaac, Luca and Tash, Will, Abbie, Jess, me and Emily, plus a few others who were still drinking or else too drunk to get themselves home. Someone switched up the playlist, and the music shifted from up-tempo to chilled. One by one, everyone gravitated to a seat around the fire, staring into the flames, sipping on water and starting the slow climb to sober, or else skolling another of Will's brews and settling in for a long, boozy night under the stars.

"This is nice," Emily whispered, settling her head on my shoulder.

I rested my lips against her hair. "It is."

Her body shuddered with a small laugh, and she pointed at Will and Abbie, who were facing off a few steps beyond the fire. "What's the problem there?"

I groaned. "Who knows? But it's never a bonfire without something going wrong between those two."

"Wrong?" Emily asked, tilting her head away from me as she watched Will and Abbie between the flames. "It looks like he's trying to hug her."

"Something about the beer and the beach and the nostalgia of the bonfire triggers their teenage angst. They've always had a weird relationship."

"Have they ever dated?"

I watched absently as Will tried to coax Abbie into a slow dance. "Not that I remember."

Will suddenly dropped his arms, and Abbie stalked away from him and towards us. She rolled her eyes at Emily just as Will cupped his hands around his mouth.

"Hey, Jones!" he shouted. "Kindly explain to your friend there that I want to dance with her!"

He called her Jones, and I couldn't breathe. There was no more oxygen left in my world.

27

EMILY

WILL CALLED ME Jones, and tingles of pleasure rushed from my toes to my cheeks.

"I'll see what I can do!" I shouted back with a laugh.

Abbie came and sat beside me, right up close, so I was squished between her and Josh. Across the way, Will gaped at us, looking lost and forlorn.

"Don't feel like dancing?" I asked her.

Abbie sucked noisily on the dregs of her bottled cocktail. "Not right now."

Josh got to his feet. "I'm going to talk to Will."

"Have at it, Ford," Abbie said with a flail of her arm. "The boy's a mess."

As Josh made his way around the fire, I was distracted by the way he walked over the sand, the sight of the shadows playing over his face and arms, the firm line of his jaw. My stomach did a pleasant little flip, and

I hated myself for thinking it, but this night was so close to perfect—if only he would stay and make it real.

"Are you having a good time?" Abbie asked, overbalancing a little as she swayed first towards, then away from me.

I looped my arm through hers and pulled her against me again. "I'm having the best time."

She grinned, and the fire danced in her golden-brown eyes. "I'm so happy, and I'm so glad you came to the Bay."

"You know what? Me too." I glanced over at Josh again, his head bowed as he talked to Will. "I don't even think I'd take back everything that happened with Tyler, knowing that it brought me here. I think it's been worth it."

"Aw, that's so sweet." Abbie snuggled her head into my neck, and I chuckled.

"Just the truth. I don't think I've ever thanked you for inviting me out for drinks that night. I was so nervous! I've never been good at making friends." I sighed and rubbed Abbie's arm. "I don't think you all realise how lucky you are. I would sell my soul for the type of friendships you have with each other."

"You don't need to sell your soul," Abbie mumbled. I wondered if she was falling asleep and took the glass bottle from her hand. It was empty anyway, and she gave it up without an argument.

"I almost did," I murmured. "I'd given up any idea of Emily Jones as a complete person without someone to love her, and I was ready to make whatever sacrifices I had to if it meant someone would want me forever."

251

Abbie made a sound in her throat, and her head got heavier on my shoulder. "Tyler's a tosser."

"Yeah." I stared at Josh, watched his lips move, his brow crease, his jaw clench. He was so beautiful. "You know what's funny? I went along with Josh's fake wedding plan because I thought I needed someone to save me from Tyler. He always called the shots, and I let him, so I didn't think I could get him to leave on my own. And now, I'm not so sure. Having Josh in my life has made me more *me* than I've been before. I feel stronger and more sure about things, including what I want and what I can handle. Does that make sense?"

"Sure," Abbie mumbled. "Josh gave you the confidence to be the real Emily Jones, and she's awesome."

"Thanks, Abs." I smiled, then blew out a breath. "How is it that loving Tyler made me less than I ever was, but loving Josh makes me more than I ever thought I could be?"

I heard the words after I said them, and Abbie was silent for so long that I prayed she'd fallen asleep, but then she raised her head, slowly, like her brain had turned to mush and she was worried it might fall out her ears. Her eyes were bloodshot, but they were sharp. "You love Josh?"

"I—"

"Hey!"

Will's shout stole our attention, and we jerked our heads up at the same time. Josh had his fists clenched at his sides, and Will was staggering back a couple of paces, looking at his friend in drunken disbelief.

Luca ran over from somewhere in the dark and put a hand on Josh's chest. "Easy, Ford. What's the problem?"

Josh's nostrils flared, but he said nothing.

And then Jess appeared, walking straight to Will and whispering in his ear. Isaac wasn't far behind, and he did the same with Josh. I didn't miss that Jess's gaze flickered to me, then Isaac's did the same. Abbie must have noticed it, too, because she got to her feet and went straight to Luca, Isaac, and Josh. Her arms were crossed, and her brow furrowed.

I wasn't sure what I should do. It didn't feel like my place to intrude—because, in that moment, I'd never felt more like an outsider looking in—but I also couldn't ignore the niggling voice telling me, *this is about you.*

Getting up and walking over—and trying hard to act like I had every right to do so—I stopped next to Josh and put a hand on his arm. His muscles were hard as stone, and he didn't acknowledge that I was there.

"Is everything all right?" I asked.

Nobody said anything, though they exchanged the kinds of looks that turned the anxious niggle in my head into a storm in my chest, spinning around my heart so fast I felt strangled. "Can someone please tell me what's going on?"

Josh grabbed my hand and spun us around, walking so fast he all but dragged me up the beach. We cleared the vicinity of the party, and he angled up toward the street. I let him lead me as far as the first streetlight, then I yanked my hand out of his and stopped, crossed my arms, and waited. He went three steps further without me, then turned and crossed his arms too, but his face was such a heartbreaking picture of pain and rage that I dropped mine instantly.

"What's going on?"

At first, I was certain he wasn't going to say anything at all, but he took a couple of deep, heavy breaths, then said between gritted teeth, "He called you Jones."

I didn't understand right away. "You mean Will? Yeah, he did. So?"

Josh scowled, then turned and stalked up the street.

"Wait! Explain this to me." I ran after him and pulled on his arm. I didn't have the strength to spin him around to face me, but he stopped and turned anyway. There were tears in his eyes.

"It's a thing we do. *We* do," he said. "Me, Will, Isaac, Luca, Logan, Abbie, Jess …"

The list wasn't finished, and the last name hung heavy in the air between us.

"Maggie," I said on an exhaled breath.

A single tear dropped down his face, and he turned his back to me, walking away again, slower this time.

It took me a minute to make my legs work, and then I had to run to get ahead of him. He froze when I did and looked down at me. Our eyes met, and my heart broke for him and for me. Maybe that explains why my brain short-circuited the way it did.

"Why didn't you tell me you've applied for a work transfer or that you've already got a list of places you might want to live?"

Josh opened his mouth, closed it again, and frowned. "Who told you that?"

"I went by your house to drop off a suit for Jack. I saw the papers on the hall table."

"It's nothing you need to worry about. I've got it under control."

"Does that explain all the phone calls and text messages you don't want to answer when I'm around?"

He nodded shortly, and I felt relief on top of the anger and the compassion. It wasn't another woman. "Why keep it from me? I told you I wanted to help you."

"I don't need your help."

I tried to ignore the sting, but it was like pretending I hadn't been slapped in the face.

"Why did you run out on me the other morning after I mentioned that Mrs Hanks needed help with her gardens?"

Josh shrugged and stuck his hands in his pockets.

"Was it because landscaping was something you used to do before Maggie's accident? Work you actually enjoyed?"

The muscles in his neck tightened, and that was enough confirmation for me.

"And deciding to leave the Bay now, after you've met me, when all you've ever done in the past is live at home, with your dad, and think about going ... That's just—what? Coincidence?"

"It's just time," he growled.

All the anger and frustration and hurt bubbled over into one high-pitched shout. "When will you stop running away?"

Josh's eyes widened a little. "You're running, too! For fuck's sake, that's how you got here in the first place!"

As soon as he said it, I knew with stunning clarity the difference between Josh and me, and what made his desperation to start again so unlike my own. "I've been running towards something," I whispered. "I'm *chasing* friends and family and real love. You have all that, and you're trying to run from it."

I took a calming breath and pulled the faux-engagement ring from my finger. Josh watched me do it, and then his focus lifted from my hands to somewhere above my head. I blinked back tears of my own, then took a step closer to him and waited until he met my eyes.

"When you offered to fake a wedding for me and help get rid of Tyler, I said yes for two reasons. One, I liked you, and I liked the idea of spending more time with you, and two, I thought I needed to be rescued." His jaw feathered, but he still refused to look at me. "I don't believe that anymore, and you know why? Being with you has healed something that was broken inside me. I've got enough confidence now to say I can do this on my own."

I reached out, pulled one hand from his pocket and opened it, then dropped the aquamarine ring into his palm. I closed his fingers around it, then let his arm drop. "I never wanted to replace Maggie in your life or in the hearts of the people here." My voice cracked. "I came to Valentine Bay to make a new life for myself, one that was *mine*, and I thought I'd found it."

I huffed out a humourless laugh. "As silly as it sounds, having drinks at The Stop with Abbie and Jess, swimming with you at the baths, Will calling me Jones just then … It all made me feel like I'd found somewhere I belonged. And now I think maybe those things meant more to me than they did to any of you."

And don't I feel like an idiot for not seeing that sooner? I wanted to cry for more reasons than what I was about to say to Josh.

"Emily," he started, but I flung up a hand to stop him.

"It doesn't matter because I know that whatever happens next, you don't need to save me. I can do that myself."

Josh tossed his head away, and I let him because what I had to say next was going to be hard enough without seeing the pain in his eyes.

"You're so busy trying to prove yourself, saving other people's lives in a job you don't like, denying yourself a future to make up for the fact that Maggie never had one, sitting on your hands while your world falls apart around you." I took a breath and said the thing I'd never be able to un-say. "I could love you, Josh, forever if you'd let me, but if there's someone out there you need to rescue, it's not me. It's you."

I stepped around him, taking off towards my apartment as quickly as I could. I was equal parts relieved and disappointed that he didn't follow me. Perhaps I'd said too much, pushed him harder on the subject than Abbie or Jess had ever dared, but I'd bitten my tongue for too long, and New Emily wasn't blind to red flags anymore. She deserved better, and she was going to have it. Valentine Bay and Joshua Ford had taught her that.

28

JOSH

I FOLDED THE last shirt in my wardrobe and added it to the garbage bag that held all my clothes. The rest of my room was almost completely packed into boxes. I had little to show for twenty-eight years of life on Earth, but I didn't have the bandwidth to feel pathetic. I was at maximum levels of self-loathing already.

There was a knock at the front door, followed by the sounds of my dad chatting to someone in hushed voices. I ignored it all. Dad knew I wasn't in the mood for visitors, and I trusted him to tell anyone stupid enough to come looking for me that I wasn't home. The muffled conversation lasted a few minutes, then I heard the door bang shut and someone walk down the porch steps. Nobody for me, then. Probably one of the neighbours with a casserole. It was a comfort to know Dad would always be fed, even after I'd moved out.

The light tap of his knuckles on the other side of my door surprised me, and then Dad let himself into my room. He looked around at the bags and boxes but said nothing about them. He hadn't said much at all about my leaving, and I didn't know what to make of it. He wasn't a talker, and neither was I, but I still expected him to say *something* about me finally leaving the Bay.

"I heard along the grapevine that the wedding's off," he said. Of all the things he could have started with, this was the last thing I wanted to hear.

I grunted something I hoped he'd take as confirmation as well as an indication that I didn't want to talk about it, but he went ahead and lowered himself onto the edge of my bed. I disappeared into the wardrobe and started throwing shoes into an empty box. Dad waited patiently, and I could only stall for so long. When I was done, he was sitting there, staring at his hands as he played with a small box.

"What's that?" I asked with a jerk of my chin.

He twisted the box in his fingers and ignored my question. "Well, I'm sorry things didn't work out with Emily. I've only talked to her a handful of times, but I got the impression she's a sweet kid."

I shrugged and started rummaging in a box I'd already packed twice. It was filled with old sporting trophies. I don't know why I'd kept them. "Yeah, she is."

"Did us a favour with that clock, in the end. Forgot how handy it was to have the correct time right there on the wall like that."

"It's a nice clock."

"That's what Maz said when she was here dropping off that passionfruit syrup cake the other day. She noticed the clock and said she liked it. I told her I did too, but it didn't match anything." Dad scratched his cheek. He could have done with a shave. "She's taking me shopping next week to buy a few new things for the house. Freshen things up, I think she called it."

I froze with my hands around a junior league soccer award. "Really?"

Dad pressed his lips together and nodded as if to himself, his gaze going inward. "It's about time."

My throat felt all stopped up, and my voice cracked when I said, "Sounds good."

"We'll see. Maz is the one who told me about the wedding."

He kept passing the little box back and forth between his hands. It was black and looked like a jewellery box big enough for a pair of earrings or a ring. I stuffed my hand in my pocket and curled my fingers around the ring Emily had returned to me two days ago. I didn't know what to do with it. I didn't want to take it with me when I went—I couldn't live with the constant reminder—but I didn't want to leave it behind either.

"That is, until Emily came by just now."

I glanced at the window as if I could see through the curtains to the porch and find her waiting there for me. "That was Emily?"

"Yep."

"Did she … Did she ask for me?"

"No, son. Sorry. She came to say goodbye and drop this off for you." He offered me the box.

I took it, my heart taking off like a racehorse at the gate. "What do you mean by *goodbye*?"

"That was another thing Maz mentioned, though I didn't believe it 'til I heard it with my own ears from Emily herself. She's moving on. Says Valentine Bay's not the fit she thought it was, and she's going to start again someplace else. She's already spoken to Dr Hobbes and everything, and she'll be out of here just as soon as she finds a place to go."

I sank down onto the bed next to Dad, dropping the box beside me, setting my elbows on my knees, and resting my head in my hands. I could never have imagined how badly I would mess this up. It was my fault Emily wanted to leave. I'd taken everything and everyone she loved about this town and torn it up in front of her eyes. She *did* fit. Everyone loved her, and I was too wrapped up in my own past to see just how effectively I'd been shitting all over her shot at a new future.

"It's a shame," Dad went on, shaking his head. "I said we'd miss her and to stay in touch. Not sure who else knows about her plans, but I suspect she'll try to keep it quiet. Slip out when nobody's looking."

I picked up the box again. "If Maz knows, it's probably common knowledge already."

"You might be right about that. I wonder if Abbie's spoken to Emily? Maybe she can change her mind.

Abbie always could talk fast enough to make your head spin, and likely all Emily needs is to know that there are people here who'd really like it if she stayed." Dad pushed himself upright, stopped in the doorway, and pointed at the box. "Emily wanted me to give that to you. She said she bought it a while ago and didn't know what else to do with it, but she understands if you don't want to take it with you. No hard feelings if you leave it behind." Nodding once, he closed the door behind him and left me alone.

I played with the box for a while, toying with the idea of not opening it at all. I could just leave it here or throw it away. Tuck it in one of these packing boxes and forget it ever existed. I couldn't think what good would come of prolonging our break-up, if that's what it was. We were never technically a couple.

I left the box on the bedside table and stowed my phone and keys in my pocket. I wasn't in the right head space to handle whatever gift Emily thought I deserved, so I'd give myself an hour or two to think about what to do with it. There was someone I needed to see, and I'd been putting it off for two days. I owed more people than Emily an apology for what happened at the bonfire, and while I wasn't looking forward to making it, this one would at least be a little easier to spit out. I hoped.

I found Will at The Stop. It was mid-afternoon on a Sunday, and the place was packed, but he saw me almost the moment I stepped inside the door. I tipped my chin at him, and he jerked his head towards the set of stairs that led up to the private dining area. I took them two at a time, slipped into the room, and started to pace.

The long function tables and high-backed chairs were stacked against the walls, so I had a lot of space to move. Tall, wide windows along one side looked out to the ocean, and it gave me something to focus on. The day was grey, overcast, and blowy. The first cool spell in weeks.

It didn't take long for Will to join me, coming into the room with two bottles of water in his hands and shutting the door behind him. He tossed me a drink, and I caught it, then pulled a chair out from one of the stacks and sat down, cracking the cap on his water, and taking a gulp. I pulled over a chair and sat across from him, then put my bottle on the floor at my feet.

"So," I started, rubbing the back of my neck. "About the other night—"

"I'm just going to say it because we both know it's true. You're a fucking mess over this girl."

I leaned back in the chair, stretched out my legs, and stared up at the white painted ceiling. "I'm sorry I snapped at you."

"Don't worry about it. I was drunk."

I scoffed. "I wasn't."

"I don't know why I called her Jones. It just came out. It felt—"

"Natural?"

Will ran a hand through his hair. "Well, yeah. I like Emily. Abbie and Jess have practically adopted her. It doesn't feel like she's only been in the Bay a couple of months."

It didn't feel like she'd been in my life for only a few weeks. "I know what you mean."

"None of that is about replacing Maggie. It's not possible, and none of us would dream of trying. There's room for both of them, and you have to know that. You're not stupid. Usually."

"I know it."

"So, what's the problem?"

I pressed my eyes shut, seeing Maggie's face behind my eyelids, then Emily's. I sat up and scrubbed my face. "Why is Maggie gone while I'm still here, huh? She was smart and funny and sweet. She had so much to give this world, could have been anything she wanted to be, and what was I doing? Digging fucking holes in the ground while she waited for me to figure out what we were going to do with *our* lives. I let her down. She was less than she could have been because of me, and I promised her, after she died, that I'd spend the rest of my life making up for it."

Will was quiet for a beat, twisting the bottle around in his hands. "What's that got to do with Emily?"

I cleared my throat. "Being with someone other than Maggie was never part of my plan, and Emily seems to think I'm sabotaging my future because Maggie never got a chance to have one of her own."

He nodded slowly, staring at the water in his hand. "Smart girl." Then he looked up at me, his brow creased. "Not that you've ever asked me, but if you did, and I was in a mood to be honest with you, I'd tell you that the best way you can do right by Maggie is to just be fucking happy.

Dig holes if that's what you enjoy doing. Stay in the Bay if that's where you feel at home." He paused and waited for me to meet his eyes. "Let yourself love someone again if that someone is as special as Emily."

I reached out, and Will shook my hand as we stood up. "Thanks, Kidd. You're right, I didn't ask you, but I'll think about it."

29

EMILY

———————

I MADE A reservation at one of the few restaurants I could find open on a Sunday night. Aptly named Meat Me There, it was a tiny place tucked away in a narrow lane off Main Street that served thick steaks with piles of fries and beer in glasses as big as buckets. Peanut shells littered the floor. Tyler was going to hate it.

I'd never been there, and neither Josh nor Abbie had ever mentioned it, so I assumed it was a safe enough restaurant to meet my ex. I wanted to get this over and done with as quickly as possible, preferably without an audience.

I'd arrived fifteen minutes before Tyler was due, so I'd be sitting at the table when he got there. Tyler was nothing if not a stickler for punctuality, but I wanted the upper hand tonight. Scanning the diners to make sure I didn't recognise anyone, I checked my phone one last time for missed calls or messages and swallowed the disappointment that I had none, then stashed it in my bag so I wouldn't be distracted for however long it took to get this mess with Tyler cleaned up.

Right on cue, he walked in the door at five minutes to the hour. At the sight of him, I clasped my hands together on the table to stop myself from rubbing my palms up and down the tops of my legs. The smile he gave me as he traversed the room was loaded with a cocky confidence that, truthfully, looked good on him. More than one head in the restaurant turned to get a better look, and it wasn't surprising that women fell for that face. It took time to understand that the twist to his lips wasn't a cute affectation but a mirror of his personality.

I didn't get up to greet him, but he came straight to me and put his lips to my cheek while I did my best not to flinch. When he'd pulled out a seat and was settled across from me, I spoke before he had a chance.

"There's something you should know."

Tyler stretched a hand across the table, inviting me to hold it, and I tucked mine under the table, hiding them in my lap. Unperturbed, his smile turned to something more sympathetic, his brow creasing with concern. "I know what you're going to say."

I'd been prepared for this. Once I'd called Dawn to tell her the wedding was off—for real, this time—it was only a matter of minutes before the rest of Valentine Bay knew, too. It made sense that Tyler would have overheard the news somewhere in the last two days. Still, he wasn't going to steal my thunder. "It's about the wedding. It's off."

Tyler pulled back his hand and nodded. I imagined this was the face he gave to clients when they finally admitted they had, indeed, committed the crime. "I heard."

"That's not all. Josh and I aren't a couple."

There was the nod again. Patient. Understanding. Condescending. "I know," he replied.

I gritted my teeth. I was not going to get angry. I was calm. I was collected. For the first time in my life, I had my shit together. "No, you don't understand. What I want to tell you is, Josh and I were never a couple. This whole relationship-engagement-wedding story was just that—a story."

More nodding. "I knew that, too."

"I— What? You're telling me you *knew* we were faking it?"

He chuckled quietly. My hands clenched under the table, and I heard my knuckles crack. "I'm a *lawyer*, sweetheart. I'm too smart for this shit. And the people in this town"—he looked around—"aren't exactly winning the intellectual Olympics. It wasn't hard to figure out."

I inhaled through my nose and carefully blew it past my lips. "How long have you known?"

"A while."

"How long, Tyler?"

He sighed and raised his hands. "Fine, not that long. A few days."

"And you didn't say anything because …?"

He raised an arm, clicked his fingers to get the attention of a server, and ordered us both glasses of pinot noir.

Good. Red wine would make more of a mess when I threw it in his face.

As the waiter moved off, Tyler rested his elbows on the table and leaned in closer. "I didn't say anything because I thought I was doing the kind thing by letting you believe you'd pulled one over on me. And the closer it got to the big day, the more I wondered just how far you were willing to go." He leaned back again, picking up his napkin and laying it on his lap with a flourish. "I'll admit, you surprised me. You almost had me believing you'd go through with it."

I choked back a strangled-sounding laugh and glanced around to check nobody was close enough to hear us. "And you'd have let me marry Josh even though you knew the truth?"

He ran a finger over one dark, manicured eyebrow, then the other. I knew what that meant. He was about to *make me an offer I couldn't refuse.* "I told you I wasn't leaving here until you had a ring on your finger, mine or *his*, and I meant it. I let it go on as long as I did so that I could be the one you turned to when it all fell apart. This is my chance to put your life back together, Em. *Our* life."

He reached out a hopeful hand again, but this time it held an open jewellery box. Inside, the engagement ring he'd given me almost a year ago winked at me.

"You know that position I wanted with Harold & Beechman?"

I blinked at him, then at the ring. That wasn't the question I'd expected him to ask. Harold & Beechman was a highly competitive Sydney law firm, and Tyler had been trying—and failing—for two years to land a job as one of its defence lawyers. Six weeks before he'd called off our wedding, we'd attended a fancy gala dinner, and I'd spent the entire time schmoozing Mr and Mrs Beechman on his behalf. They had been, surprisingly, a lovely middle-aged couple with four teenaged kids and a stunning art collection, and we'd bonded over a shared love of photography.

"Uh, yes?" I answered.

"They want me!" Tyler's eyes shone bright with desire—for a job, not for me. "They loved you, Em, and they can't wait to welcome me—us—into their corporate family."

I shook my head a little. "I don't understand."

"They offered me a job." Tyler's grin slipped a little.

"What does *that* have to with this?" I pointed at the ring.

His smile wilted even further, and the pieces started to come together.

"Nothing, really," he said, then he sighed. "I mean, they assumed the wedding went ahead in December, obviously, and I didn't correct them. Mrs Beechman wants to have us over for dinner just as soon as I start."

"Us?"

Tyler made a grab for my left hand, and I snatched it away. Finally, his face folded with frustration.

"Look. It turns out I was going about things all wrong the last two years. They didn't want a heartless shark on the team. They wanted someone they understood." He rolled his eyes. "They *like* that I'm married. Mr Beechman believes lawyers with families fight harder, win more often, get better results." He leaned in like we were in on a secret together. "If you ask me, he's pussy-whipped, and it's his old shrew of a wife doing the hiring and firing in that firm."

I was stunned enough to pause for a moment, mouth ajar, wondering if I understood what Tyler was trying to tell me. "But we're *not* married."

"But we could be." He chuckled, and the sound made the hair on the back of my neck stand up. "Come on, Emily. Your life's a fucking mess. Come home with me, and I'll put it back together. I need you, baby, and you need me. We need each other. What do you say?"

I stared at his hand. "What do I say?" I echoed in a whisper. Confidence unfurled in my chest like a flower opening to the sun. "What do I *say*? Tyler. You're a smart guy. You said so yourself. What does it say to *you* that I was willing to marry a stranger if it meant I never had to see you again?"

Tyler opened his mouth, then closed it.

"Do you see a broken woman sitting across from you right now? Does it look like I need your help putting my life back together?"

He blinked. "Ah, well—"

"There's only one reason I asked you to have dinner with me tonight, and it wasn't to beg you to take me back or ask you to explain why you've stuck around the Bay for as long as you have. It was to tell you—for the hundredth time, and in no uncertain terms—that you and me? We're over. I'm not taking you back, I'm not asking you to take me back, and if it's at all possible, I mean that more now than I did when I said the same thing at The Stop on Valentine's Day."

"But you need me, Emily."

"I don't, Tyler. I really don't. I went the wrong way about proving that to you."

"This isn't just about my career, if that's what you think. What about all the flowers I sent you? And the gifts? Surprising you when you walked home from work?" He cocked an eyebrow, leaned over the table, and murmured in what I assumed was an attempt at a bedroom voice. "The texts?"

I bit my lip to stop myself from laughing. Oh God, I was so glad I could laugh about this now, but Tyler mistook the gesture as an attempt to control my lust.

"See?" One side of his mouth curled up. "I can be romantic and reliable. Haven't I shown you that these last few weeks?"

I reached out and set my hand over his, and he smiled with satisfaction. It made my next words even sweeter. "I don't love you, Tyler."

His face fell, and I gave his hand a quick squeeze, then stood. But as I made to leave, he grabbed my wrist, and he didn't let go when I tried to pull away. I was vaguely aware of the sounds of chairs moving and people getting to their feet. Tyler's eyes darted around the room, but all I could see was him. He looked desperate.

"I've already quit the prosecutions department, and if I show up at this dinner without you on my arm *as my wife*,

I'll lose my job at Harold & Beechman, too. It doesn't even have to be real. Marry me now, and we'll get divorced in a year." His top lip curled into a sneer. "I know you're not above faking it."

I shook my arm again, harder this time, and Tyler released his grip. His vicious smirk melted under the heat of my glare. "I hope, one day, you find someone else, and whoever it is, you treat her better than you treated me. Here's a tip: women don't like it when you cheat on them. And if you tell her you can fuck her until she screams so loud she loses her mind, you better have the goods to back it up."

I walked away and didn't look back. Something settled into my bones, a knowing that it really was over this time. Tyler liked games, and I'd made a huge mistake trying to play him. In the end, the only way to hit him where it hurt was with good old-fashioned honesty. And damn, it felt good.

30

EMILY

———————

I WOKE UP on Monday morning, dreading the idea of having to go to work and answer questions from curious customers about what went wrong with Josh, only to find a voicemail on my phone from Summer Hobbes. It was quiet at the clinic today, so she was volunteering me for a day off. Relief turned my muscles to water, and I flung the bedcovers back over my head. She'd been understanding about my quitting, and with only a week's notice. I suspected the rumour mill had run on ahead of me, and Summer was well aware of the reasons behind my snap decision to leave the Bay. A day spent sleeping sounded good to me.

Phone still in hand, I sat up, pressed my lips together and contemplated the screen. It would have been nice to have someone to talk to about Tyler and Josh and what I was supposed to do next. Tapping through to my contacts list before I chickened out, I scrolled to my sister's number and tapped to dial. It rang … and rang … pulling my nerves as tight as the strings on a violin, so by the time it went to voicemail, I'd changed my mind and decided not to leave a message. I didn't want to bother her, anyway.

My thumb, behaving as though it had a mind of its own, hovered over Abbie's number, then Jess's. Both women had tried to call me after the party, but I hadn't been able to bring myself to talk to them. I'd never had best girlfriends and the bond I'd forged with them over the last few weeks meant the world to me, but I couldn't stop replaying the look on Josh's face the moment he thought I was taking a place in their lives meant for someone else. I tossed my phone across the bed and threw myself back against the pillows.

Out of all the things I'd said to Josh and the things he'd said and done to me, one realisation was clearer than everything else. I'd overestimated my place in Valentine Bay. New Emily had gone in too fast and too hard, assumed too much about how she fit in, and made a world-class idiot of herself. I wasn't surprised. I was as good at making friends as I was at choosing men to fall in love with, which was to say, I was terrible at both.

Just as I dozed off again, my phone pinged. I stuck my arm out from under the covers and groped around for it, then pulled it to me, where I hid under the sheets.

Abbie: Have you had enough alone time yet?

My heart fluttered, and I started tapping out a reply, then thought better of it, deleted everything, and switched off my phone instead. I closed my eyes and sank back into sleep.

Thumping on my front door woke me, and when I checked the time, it was already noon. I'd have happily slept the day away, but the pounding wouldn't stop. I rolled out of bed, still wrapped in my sheets, and shuffled to the front door, then cracked it open just enough to peek out and see who had disturbed my denial.

"Hey, hermit."

I resisted smiling. "Hey, Abbie."

She jerked her head to the side. "Jess is here, too."

Opening the door a little wider, just enough to confirm that Jess was standing in my hallway—in casual clothes, no less—I frowned. "Don't you guys have work or something?"

"Abbie's next class isn't until four, and I called in sick," Jess replied.

Abbie set a hand on the door and pushed her way in, sending me shambling back before she could knock me over. While Jess busied herself in the kitchen, flicking on the coffee machine and rummaging in the fridge, Abbie took hold of my shoulders, turned me around, and directed me back to my bedroom.

"Brush your teeth. Get dressed. Fix your hair. You've got fifteen minutes, then I'm coming in after you." She smacked me on the bum. "And you don't want that. Now, move it."

I did what she said, dragging my feet for reasons I still didn't want to think about but feeling slightly buoyed by the fact that both Abbie and Jess had skipped work to cheer me up. Either that or they were looking for gossip. My heart, lightened by their appearance, sank a little. After what happened over the weekend, the second scenario seemed like the likelier one.

Back in the kitchen, my hair tidy, my teeth clean, and dressed in denim cut-offs and a tight white tank with a loose navy knit over the top, I climbed onto a stool at the island and gratefully accepted the cup of coffee Jess offered.

"Thanks," I said, taking a sip.

"Now, hear me out. I know a lot happened on Friday night," Abbie said, and I lifted a single eyebrow at her understatement. She ignored it and continued. "But I'm offended that I had to hear about the wedding cancellation from Dawn. Really, Em, you should know better than that."

I set down my cup but held onto it to keep my hands from fidgeting. "Well, then, I should tell you this before you hear it from someone else, too. I've given my notice at the vet clinic, and I'm leaving the Bay."

Jess groaned while Abbie narrowed her eyes. "You are not," she said.

"I am."

Abbie parked one hand on her hip and squinted harder. "Why?"

I ran a hand through my hair, knowing and not caring that I'd messed it up, and I probably looked like I just got out of bed again. "I appreciate everything you guys have done for me, and I'm glad I came here and got to know you and all of that ... But I don't belong here."

Abbie and Jess exchanged a look, and I was almost sure I got the subtext of this one. Something along the lines of *what is this girl on about?*

"For a minute there, I thought maybe I could stay," I continued, "but as it turns out, I was wrong, and that's okay. I'm ready to start again somewhere else. We'll stay in touch. I'll follow you on Instagram."

"I'm not on Instagram," Jess replied.

"Facebook, then."

Abbie pointed a finger at me. "This is about Josh and what he said at the bonfire. The way he reacted when Will called you Jones."

I swallowed my sadness along with a big gulp of coffee, glanced first at Abbie, then at Jess, and ignored the pang in my gut as I went about the task of pushing them away. "No, that's not it. I realise now I was relying too much on you all and that if I'm ever going to find a way to be happy, I have to work on myself first. I got off on the wrong foot here with the whole fake engagement thing, trying to trick my way out of a relationship with Tyler. But the good news is, I fixed that already."

"Oh?" Jess replied, sipping her coffee and raising her eyebrows. "How's that?"

I tilted my head and watched her from the corner of my eye. "You're a terrible actor. What do you know?"

Abbie let out an exasperated sigh. "Fine. Take all the fun out of it. Dawn saw you having dinner with him last night at Meat Me There. She wasn't close enough to hear what you said, but after you left and Tyler ran out a few minutes later, she was smart enough to send Mav out to follow him."

"Dawn was there?" How had I missed her? She must have been in a bloody disguise or something. "No, forget that part. She did *what*?"

"It's true." Jess leaned her hip against the island. "Tyler was obviously upset, and Dawn was worried he was going to chase you down and do something dramatic like blast a boom box at you in the rain, but Maverick reported that he went straight to his hotel, came out fifteen minutes later with a suitcase, got in his car and left."

Abbie snorted a laugh. "I called Victor Nicholas at the front desk this morning, and he confirmed that Tyler checked out last night. So, whatever you said to him, it worked." Abbie grinned at the look on my face. "Don't be so surprised."

I closed my mouth with a snap. "I'm not. I'm relieved. And, okay, yes, maybe a little stunned." I dropped my head back and closed my eyes for a moment. "I should have done that weeks ago and avoided this whole mess."

Jess cocked her head. "I'm not sure you were ready a few weeks ago."

I straightened and lifted my coffee. "I know."

"And would you really want to undo any of what happened in the last month?" Abbie asked.

I frowned as I thought about it, shying back from thoughts of Josh as if they could scald me. "No, I don't suppose I would."

"Good to hear it," Abbie replied. She set her elbows on the island and leaned towards me. "So, about Josh—"

I jumped off my stool so fast, Abbie cut off what she was about to say. "I don't want to talk about it. He said some things, I said some things, and it's best we go our separate ways. Now, thank you for coming. I appreciate the visit, and it's always good to see you, but I have a lot of work to do." I spread my arms wide and herded them both towards the door. "I need to pack, find a new job somewhere, figure out where I'm going to live. Busy, busy, busy. But I'll call you before I go. I promise."

"Hold on a second," Abbie said, pushing my arms down and stalling in the doorway. "That's it? That's all we get?"

I closed my eyes, willed away the tears, then opened them again and stretched my lips wide in a smile as bright as I could make it. "You've been so good to me, and I'll never forget it, but I don't belong in Valentine Bay. I'm not trying to take anyone's place. I want something that's mine, for me, and I'm going to find it. Now, I'll talk to you later, all right? Have a nice day."

I closed the door on them before they could ask any more questions or try to tell me I was wrong. I couldn't afford to hope that Abbie and Jess were real enough friends to care if I stayed.

The heartbreak in Josh's eyes kept replaying in my mind, and I didn't know what to think about Valentine Bay anymore. Was there a place for me here? Three days ago, I would have said yes, but now, I couldn't let myself believe it.

31

JOSH

———

THREE DAYS PASSED, and I still couldn't bring myself to open the gift Emily had left for me. I carried it around in my pocket alongside her aquamarine ring, and my hands kept straying to them. At odd moments, I found myself staring at one or the other, twisting it in my fingers or gripping it tightly without remembering when I'd plucked it out. Almost every hour since Friday night, I'd picked up my phone to call her but couldn't find the words. I asked for extra hours at work and tried to distract myself that way, but the unease in my gut wouldn't let up. I'd resorted to communicating in grunts and scowls. Dad gave up trying to talk to me, Abbie stopped texting, and I hadn't heard from the boys in more than forty-eight hours.

I was a lost cause, and everyone knew it.

On the fourth day, about half an hour before sunrise, I lay in my bed, one hand behind my head, the jewellery box in the other, staring up into the dark. Emily was leaving the Bay. I'd be gone soon, too. In a few weeks—a month tops—it'd be as if our relationship had never existed, and everybody, Emily and me included, would go on with their lives. That had always been the plan. Why deviate from it now just because things had ended a little sooner than we had expected? The end had been inevitable from the start, so it shouldn't have come as a surprise. It wasn't supposed to hurt.

But it did, and I couldn't go on denying what that meant. I didn't want her to go, and fuck it, I didn't want to leave. Will had been right. It had taken me this long to admit to myself that I wanted to be with Emily. Three days wasted arguing with myself about what I really felt.

With realisation came a release, a weight lifted, a light switched on. I didn't know yet how I was supposed to convince Emily to take a chance on me—a real chance, with a real future at stake—but there was something I needed to do before I could even think about that. There was someone I needed to talk to.

I flung back the covers, pulled on yesterday's clothes, and crept out of the house. The sun was just rising, the sky was clear and purpling in the east, and I stuck my hands in my pockets as I walked. I couldn't put a name to what I felt. I was eager to get to where I was going, but that didn't seem right. My head told me to turn back, but there was no stopping my heart.

I went straight to the far north end of the bay, where the headland loomed over the rocks below it, crossed the sand

and stopped short of the rock pools. With the ocean lapping at my ankles, I stared out over the water, breathing in the salt, my fist tight around the box in my pocket, letting the greys and blues and greens of the heaving sea talk to me.

Her whispers never failed to reach something deep in my chest, and I listened for a long time until the sun cleared the horizon, my chest moved steadily, and the tide came in far enough that I was forced to take a few steps backwards. Retreating until I hit dry sand, I dropped to the ground, looped my arms around my knees, and took a deep breath.

"Hey," I said.

She didn't answer me, but I knew she wouldn't.

"I know I should have come before today. It's been a while."

No response but for a flutter behind my ribs.

"I met someone, but you probably already know that. Her name's Emily. I think you'd like her."

The ocean hummed.

"I love her, Mags." I pressed my thumb and forefinger to my eyes, and the lump in my throat felt studded with glass. "And I'm going to tell her."

A gentle set rolled in, then another. The water was calm today, and I relaxed into its rhythm. The sun rose higher, people came and went around me, and I sat, watching her. With every wave, Maggie came, and Maggie went, and I was okay. I was better than okay. I was … free.

There was the squeak of feet walking towards me, followed by the scent of coconut, and Abbie sat down on the sand next to me. "Hey, Ford."

"Hey, Ellison."

"She's pretty today."

I smiled out at the water. "She is."

"So, listen, I talked to Emily. Well, I tried to, at least. She's being stupid stubborn about all this, and it's your fault."

"I know."

"Don't try to— What?"

My lips quirked. I didn't get the upper hand on Abbie nearly enough, and I was in a mood to enjoy it. "I know. It's my fault she thinks she needs to leave."

"Damn right. And another thing—"

"She loves me."

"Holy shit, Ford. What have you been smoking?"

"Nothing. Why, what have you got?" She scowled, and I smiled a little wider. "She told me."

"Are you serious?"

I nodded, squinting out at the sea.

Abbie grunted and fiddled with the stack of bracelets on her arm. "Well, not that your ego needs to hear it again, but she told me too."

I turned so I could check her expression and make sure she wasn't kidding, but Abbie looked dead serious—and a little pissed.

"I warned you away from Emily, didn't I? Didn't I tell you she wasn't the type of girl you could use as a test case for re-entering the dating world?"

"I don't remember," I lied.

"Yes, you do, and this was supposed to be a short-term

thing. No strings attached. Expiration date stamped right there on the side."

"All true."

"So, what the hell happened, Ford?"

"I fell for her, too."

Abbie threw up her hands and collapsed back onto the sand with a gentle thud. "Then why are you both avoiding my calls and packing your bags? For a smart guy, you have impressive skills in the complete idiocy department." Under her breath, she mumbled, "And I'm questioning Emily's brain power at this stage, too."

Abbie glowered at the sky, but then her expression cleared, and she straightened, smug as the cat who caught the mouse. "I told you things would change. I said that one day, you'd think differently about dating again. Didn't I?"

"Oh my God, Ellison. Give it up."

"No way. Feels too good to be right."

"Well, you're wrong about one thing."

"What's that?"

"I'm not interested in *dating* Emily. It's gone beyond that."

Abbie looked out to the ocean, then her gaze flicked up to the headland that towered over the beach to the north, the fenced lookout at the top. I knew what she saw when she looked up there. The same thing I did. That was where we'd stood three days after Maggie's funeral and scattered her ashes into the ocean. Understanding flickered across Abbie's face. "What are you doing up this end of the beach?"

I gazed out over the water. "I came to talk to Maggie."

Abbie followed my line of sight, drew up her legs and wrapped her arms around them, then set her chin on her knees. "What did you say to her?"

"I told her I'm in love with Emily, and I plan to do something about it."

Abbie fell against me and dropped her head on my shoulder. I leaned my cheek against her hair. "I'm proud of you," she murmured, so quiet I almost didn't hear it, so I pretended I didn't. I couldn't think of the right words to say back. We sat like that for a while until she sighed and pulled away. Then she nodded at my hand. "What's that?"

Emily's gift was in my fist. Again. I turned it around. "I don't know yet. Emily left it at the house for me a few days ago."

Abbie's eyes looked ready to bug out of her head. "And you haven't opened it?"

I winced at the pitch of her voice. "Calm down. I'm waiting for the right moment."

Abbie eyed it with speculation, then show-whispered, "You think it's a bomb?"

"Ha!" Then I grimaced. "You might be right again."

Abbie gave the box one last, suspicious look, then poked me in the bicep. "So, what happens now? How do we fix this?"

"We?"

She snorted. "I tried to stay out of it. I did my best not to interfere, but look at the mess you've made of things. There's no way I'm letting you screw this up further."

"I don't know. I need more time to think about it, okay?"

Abbie climbed to her feet, brushing the sand from the back of her legs, and I did the same. "Don't think too long. Emily's not taking my calls or returning my texts. I'm half-scared she'll up and run in the middle of the night, and we'll never see her again." She put her hands on either side of my face and looked into my eyes. "I like her, and I want her to stay, so fix this, all right?"

"I will. I promise."

"Let me know if I can help?"

"Absolutely."

She wrapped her arms around me and squeezed tight, and I did the same. It felt good. Different, somehow. I couldn't sense pity in the way she held me, and it made me wonder. Had Abbie changed, or had I? How many times had I seen charity in someone's eyes when it wasn't there? Heard sadness in their voice when I shouldn't have? Treated friends with suspicion because I was too wrapped up in grief to take people's kindness at face value?

Abbie let go and started back up the beach while I stared down at the box in my hand. Impulsively, I opened it.

Inside was a ring. White gold, brushed finish, gleaming edges. Understated. Classic. Just my style. I pulled it out and ran my finger around the outside, twisted it to get a better look in the sunlight. Was this the ring Emily planned to put on my finger on our fake wedding day? I felt a swelling in my chest and had to bite back a smile at the vision of Emily in her sexy white dress. Then the curve of an inscription caught my eye. I turned the ring to make out the lettering, squinting as the sun bounced off the metal.

Day One, One Day.

I didn't know what Emily had intended it to mean, but I knew what I felt when I read it. I didn't want day one of my new life with Emily to remain a far-off date. A *one day* without a name. I wanted it to be today. Tomorrow. Yesterday. I wanted to tell her I loved her. I wanted to take her to bed and worship her, hold her all night and wake up with her the next morning. I wanted my home to be in her sheets, her heart, and her life. I slipped the ring back into the box and ran up the beach after Abbie.

"Ellison, wait up!"

She turned to watch me jogging towards her, a hand covering her eyes to block out the sun's glare. "What's up, Ford? Did you think of something else I got right and you got wrong? Make a list and take a number."

I stopped in front of her. "You wanted me to let you know if you could help me win Emily back."

She cocked her head. "Yeah. What have you got in mind?"

I couldn't fight the grin on my face. "Is it too late to get the wedding plans back on track for Saturday?"

She hid her face in her hands and shook her head. "No, Ford," she groaned. "Whatever you're thinking, think again. This sounds like a disaster."

I laughed. "I'm not putting on a wedding, but a party's still a party, right? I want Emily to know I'm serious about her, and I want to make sure everyone in Valentine Bay knows it, too. If everything works out, there'll be no doubt in Emily's mind that she belongs here with us. And with me."

Abbie peeked out from behind her fingers, then dropped her hands and grinned back at me. "Okay, you've got my attention. What do you need me to do?"

"First things first. You'll have to call Dawn."

32

EMILY

THUD, THUD, THUD.

I groaned, pressed pause on my trashy television show, set the bucket of ice-cream on the coffee table, then rolled off the sofa and dragged myself to the door.

Thud, thud, thud.

"I'm coming!"

Cracking the door just wide enough for me to peek out into the hallway, I scowled when I saw Abbie standing there, bright eyed and beaming and *happy*.

"So, you decide to answer the door today," she chirped.

"You've been banging for five minutes." I opened it a little wider and leaned my head against it. "What is it?"

"I want you to put yourself in the shower, then dress up in something nice." Her nose wrinkled as she swept her eyes over my outfit, grimacing at my T-shirt. I looked down at it and the artwork of stains. Pasta sauce on the left breast, chocolate ice-cream on the right. Made sense. I'd been wearing the thing for three days.

"Why? I'm not going anywhere," I replied.

"Yes, you are. There's a party."

"No way." I tried to shut the door on her, but she scooted in before I got a chance to lock her out.

"Here's the thing," she said, her face softening. "You know all the wonderful, generous, decent people who agreed to take care of the food and drinks and decorations for your wedding reception? Most of them had already begun planning for it, and you cancelling things with only a week's notice didn't give them time to find other clients. So, they all got together and decided to have the party anyway."

I blinked. She couldn't be saying what I thought she was saying. "You want me to go to my own cancelled wedding reception, having just split up with the groom?"

"Well … It's not exactly a wedding reception anymore."

She looked guilty, and my hackles rose. "What have you done?"

"It's a party for Josh."

My stomach heaved, and I had to swallow before I could speak. "Are you doing this to torture me? Everyone in the Bay thinks I've hurt Josh too badly for it to go unpunished, and you're planning some type of extreme, elaborate revenge plot?" I pictured myself walking into The Stop only to be hit with a bucket of fish guts balanced on the door, and half the town ready to coat me with glitter and feathers.

Abbie rolled her eyes. "Paranoid much? It's a *party*, and Josh wants you there."

That was even harder for me to believe. "Josh told you he wants me there? He said that to you in explicit language? 'Please ask Emily to come.' That's what he said to you?"

"Yes. Almost word for word, though I added a promise to bind, gag, and drag you there if you gave me too much trouble. Either way, he's expecting you."

I nibbled my lip. What reason could Josh have for wanting me to attend his farewell party? Perhaps he wanted to make sure there were no hard feelings between us before we went our separate ways. Maybe he'd opened the gift I'd given him, recoiled in horror, and wanted to give it back. More than likely, no matter his reasons now, he'd chicken out altogether and not even show, and I'd be left facing the music alone, then spend the rest of my life wondering what happened to him.

Abbie patted my cheek. "Party starts at two this afternoon, so you have plenty of time to fix yourself up. Wash your hair, wear something nice, and don't stress, okay? Two o'clock. If you're late, I'll come back here with Isaac, ropes, and duct tape. Got it?"

She left me standing there in the living room, staring into nothing and wondering if I was crazy enough to actually leave the house for the first time in a week, to go to a party with the people I'd been trying to avoid, to see the man I was in love with but who couldn't love me back.

The answer was yes. I was that crazy.

Three hours later, I stood on the street outside of The Salty Stop, staring at the door much the same way I had the first time Abbie invited me to meet her and Jess for drinks. Except this time, I'd left my second-best dress at home and worn my all-time favourite. What was I saving it for, anyway? And it wasn't like anyone around here was going to see me in it again after today. I'd be long gone before I had a reason to pull it out again. I smoothed the soft, deep red fabric over my stomach, checked the neckline, and took a deep breath. All I had to do was open the door, but my feet wouldn't move. I couldn't make myself go in, and for thirty seconds, I considered turning around and going straight home, but there was Abbie's abduction threat to think about. I wasn't sure if she'd been kidding.

I scanned around for a valid reason not to go in, but Main Street was unusually quiet for a Saturday afternoon. It felt like an eon since I'd been outside. Summer had kindly extended my personal leave for the week—and I did my best to appreciate her empathetic support rather than feel rejected by the fact that I was, apparently, not so critical to the function of her practice after all—and I'd been in hiding, living off dry toast and tap water and reheated lasagne. I'd discovered I could only eat *that* when distracted by bad television, otherwise it reminded me of how good Josh had been in the kitchen—and even better in my bed— and the pasta turned to garlic-flavoured glue in my mouth.

I put my hand to the door handle and reminded myself, again, that I'd assumed far too much about my place in Valentine Bay. This was Josh's party now, and I was a guest.

A last-minute one, at that. Emily Jones was no more than a footnote in *The Joshua Ford Story*. There was a comfort in that. I might be able to slip in and out of the party with nobody noticing me. Good chance nobody would even want to talk to me, given everything that had happened.

The familiar weight of rejection settled over my skin. I was without a family again. Perhaps it would always be that way, and I'd need to find a way to live with it.

Ugh. Old Emily was still alive and kicking, no matter how hard I'd tried to leave her behind. Perhaps the real me wasn't all Old Emily or all New Emily, but someone in the middle of the two.

Pushing the door open, I slipped into The Stop and froze.

It was quiet inside, and all the overhead lights were switched off, replaced with a million tiny string lights crossing the ceiling and walls and door frames. And there was no party. One lone person stood in the middle of the supernatural glow, and my stomach flipped at the sight of him.

Josh pushed his body away from where he had been leaning against the bar, took a small step towards me, and stopped. His hands were in his pockets, his shoulders tight, and he smiled at me crookedly. "I wasn't sure you'd come."

I looked around for the punch line of whatever joke this was supposed to be and answered absently. "Abbie threatened to abduct me if I didn't."

His lips tilted a little higher. "She might have done it, too."

"That's the impression she gave me." I fiddled with my hair, sweeping it behind my ears, then clasped my hands in front of me to stop the fidgeting. "I don't understand. Am I early? Late?"

"You're right on time."

Josh took another two steps closer, and I moved one back. He stopped.

"Emily. I'm sorry for behaving the way I did at the beach party and all those times before that. You were right. I was running away, and I have been for a long time. First, it was from memories that made me sad, then from a future that didn't include Maggie. Next, it was from the people who loved and cared about me, and the Bay altogether. In the end, I was running from you. I've been stuck in a loop, trying to get away, going around and around, never arriving anywhere. Never finding something, or someone, to run *to*."

Gripping my hands together to stop them from reaching out for him, my pulse raced fast and hard, like a freight train under my fingers. He was making me hope, but his words could still mean anything. He hadn't said what I needed to hear.

Josh took another step, and I let him, wanting the scent of his skin in my nose, the possibility of his touch within reach. Soon he was right there, and I had to crane my neck to meet his eyes.

"Until now," he murmured.

He pulled his hands out of his pockets and brushed the back of his fingers over my cheek. It was all I could do not to sigh and close my eyes, but I held his gaze. He needed to say it. I needed to hear it. His lips, the ones I wanted so badly to kiss me, smiled a little wider.

"You told me you could love me forever if I'd let you. Emily Jones, I want to love you back if you'll have me."

His mouth hovered temptingly close, and I couldn't help the way my body leaned in, the way I rose a little on my toes, but he didn't move to meet me, instead picking up my hand. I looked down, and he had a ring.

It was a plain white gold band, similar to the one I'd bought for Josh, and my thoughts moved through fog as I saw *that* ring shining dully on the fourth finger of his right hand. My eyes started to sting.

"I got you this," he said, holding up the smaller band. "And I had it engraved." He took the ring finger on my right hand and slid on the ring. "It says, *Day One, Today*." With the white gold around my finger, my eyes unable to look away from it, Josh cradled my head in his hands and tipped my face up to his. "I don't want to wait anymore. I'm ready if you are."

I wanted to say yes, but I was still afraid. I'd hoped before and been let down.

"What about …?"

His thumbs swept over my skin, and goosebumps erupted all over me. "It's okay. You can ask."

"What about Maggie?"

I waited for the shadow to move behind his eyes, for the inevitable retreat, but he stayed with me. "I've spent the last week thinking about her, talking with people who knew her—knew me when I was with her—and I had a chat with her, too, if you can believe it." I gave him the smallest nod I could manage, terrified I might ruin the moment. "And here's the thing I've truly been running from." His shoulders lifted, then dropped with a sigh. "I've been too ashamed to admit it, especially to myself, but I let go of Maggie a long time ago. I've been using grief as an excuse to not move forward, but it stopped being about Maggie and somewhere along the way, I made it all about a promise I couldn't bring myself to break. I've been stupid. Loving you isn't going back on my word. Loving you is doing right by it."

There were the words. I closed my eyes and answered them. "Yes," I said. "I'm ready."

Emotion tightened his voice when he said breathlessly, "Thank fuck." I only had a chance to chuckle for a second before his mouth was on mine, devouring me with a hunger I returned. I clutched the front of his shirt and yanked him closer to me as he slanted his head and delved deeper, our tongues stroking hungrily. It had been more than a week since I last tasted him, but it felt like an eternity. His hands roamed down my shoulders, over my arms, skimming the curve of my breasts, and my nipples stiffened into painful peaks. I pressed myself against him, the shape of his erection between us eliciting a small moan, and he smiled against my mouth, but I couldn't stop kissing him.

"Do you want to get out of here?" I mumbled, my lips moving over his jaw and neck, my fingers starting on the buttons of his shirt.

I felt the rumble of his laugh on my tongue and through my hands on his chest. "We have a party to go to, or did you forget?"

I drew back, my grip on his clothes tightening again. "You're still leaving?" I glanced over his shoulder, expecting the town to jump out from their hiding spots and yell, "Surprise! No happy ending for Emily after all!"

He grinned and took one hand, guiding me towards the stairs up to the private party rooms. "Not exactly."

The tight stairwell and the hallway at its top were lit up with more strings of tiny white lights. The doors to the function rooms were closed, and it was eerily quiet. "What's going on?" I whispered.

Josh put a hand on the door to our right, winked at me, and pushed. A chorus of a hundred voices greeted us.

"Surprise!"

33

EMILY

I STARTLED AS a crowd of faces beamed at me. The smiles were wider than I'd believe possible, cheeks were stretched to bursting, eager eyes glittered with merriment. And then I burst out laughing, which made everyone whoop and cheer. I pressed my hands to my hot cheeks, seeing for the first time the enormous banner slung across the far wall. It read, "Josh + Emily + Valentine Bay = Forever!" And underneath, smaller but clear: "Day One = Today."

Will appeared like magic, a drink in each hand. "Local IPA for the lucky guy," he announced, handing Josh a frothy glass. "And a pinot grigio for the beautiful lady."

I gratefully took the chilled white wine. Around us, people laughed and talked, their attention split between socialising and staring at Josh and me. I exhaled with relief as the music switched on, covering the hum of conversation. Will shook Josh's hand, and they exchanged a nod, then Will ruffled my hair and grinned. "Good to see you again, Jones."

I shot a quick look at Josh, but his smile didn't falter—if anything, there was a pleased twinkle in his eye—and a flush burned my cheeks. "Hi, Will. Thanks for the drink."

"You looked like you needed it." He shook his head with mock disappointment. "Can't believe you're giving this guy another chance."

"I'm a generous woman. Sometimes all a man needs is one more chance to get it right."

I glanced at Josh from the corner of my eye, remembering our first time with me pinned to the dining table, our second time with the sexts, and my promise to give him as many opportunities as he needed to make the times after those even better. He'd never needed that promise. From the second he put his lips on me, I was hooked. But he must have been thinking about it, too, because he wrapped an arm around my waist and pulled me closer, nuzzling into my neck and pressing the hard length of his cock against my side.

"I'll leave you both to wrangle the riffraff," Will said. "I've got drinks to pour and food to serve. Enjoy yourselves."

"Thanks for everything," Josh said.

Will dipped his chin. "Anytime." He gave me a kiss on the cheek and paused to speak quietly in my ear. "He's a good guy, and I'm glad he found you. And Jones? Call me Kidd."

I gave his arm a squeeze before he walked away, then looked around at the balloons and streamers and guests with wonder. "Did you organise all this?" I whispered to Josh just as I spied Dawn making her way over.

Josh nodded at the incoming party guest. "I had help."

Dawn folded me into her arms. "Oh, Emily! I'm so happy this all worked out for you, and I'm not going to lie. Everyone's thrilled we could use the party supplies we had ready to go for the wedding." She picked up my left hand to look at my finger. "No ring?" I offered her my other hand, with the plain gold band circling my finger. "Oh, well, that's nice, but what about that divine engagement ring? It was one of my favourites, you know. I'd hate for it to end up buried in a drawer somewhere—"

"It's here." Josh held up the aquamarine halo ring between two fingers. It was stunning, but I loved it for better reasons than that. Josh had said it reminded him of my eyes, and he bought it for me because he wanted to, not because he had to. "But I don't know if Emily wants to wear it." He smiled lopsidedly at me, an apology in his eyes. "I don't mind if you'd rather not."

I lifted my left hand and wiggled my fingers. "I want to."

He slipped the faux-engagement ring on my hand, and it felt good—it felt right—to have it in place again.

Once Dawn was done telling us how happy she was, we barely had time to take a breath before Jack wandered out from the crowd. A woman about his age, with fine lines around her eyes, a smooth straight nose, and long, dark hair, followed him, hovering a little behind his shoulder. I shot a questioning look at Josh, but he shrugged slightly.

"Hey, Dad," he said. "And Maz. It's good to see you. Thanks for coming."

Jack clapped a hand around Josh's cheek. "I'm proud of you, son," he said gruffly.

I did my best to resist my tears while Josh cleared his throat. "Thanks, Dad. I appreciate it."

"And Emily." Jack started forward, stopped, then tried again, taking me into an awkward one-arm hug. I put my arms around him and squeezed a little. "Glad to have you in the Bay and the family."

Now I was the one with something stuck in my throat. "Thanks, Jack."

Jack gestured to the woman beside him. "Not sure if you know my neighbour, Maryanne?"

I reached out to shake her hand. "We met once at the clinic. Lovebirds, wasn't it?"

Maryanne blushed and her eyes flickered to Jack and away so quickly, I wondered if I'd imagined it, but Jack flushed, too, and one glance at Josh was enough to tell me that he'd noticed the exchange as well. "Er, yes," Maryanne said. "They were in for a check-up last month. It's nice to see you again, Emily. You and Josh make a lovely couple."

Josh squeezed the hand he had resting on my hip. "Thank you," I said, looking up at him. "I think so, too."

As they moved away, Josh turned his back to the room, giving us the semblance of privacy. "Are they *dating*?"

I looked around his arm to where Jack held two drinks while Maz loaded up plates of food, then they took seats side by side next to one of the enormous windows. The table was otherwise empty—they had plenty of space—but they sat together. "It certainly seems that way."

"Right." Josh stole a look over his shoulder and watched his father for a moment. "Good for him," he said finally, then he took my empty glass. "I'll get you another one. Same again?"

"Yes, please."

His focus shifted to someone behind me, and he rolled his eyes. "Here comes trouble."

Abbie bounced over and threw her arms around my neck, squeezing me so tight I started to sputter. She let go and grinned. "Hey, Jones."

"Hey, Ellison," I answered, loving the thrill of calling her that as much as marvelling at how naturally it rolled off my tongue.

"I'm going to the bar," Josh said. "Do you need a drink?"

"Margarita," Abbie ordered. "Thanks."

When Josh was gone, Abbie grasped my hand and led me to a table in the corner, where Jess sat with her head propped on one hand, a half-finished cocktail in front of her.

"Oh, no. What's wrong?" I asked, taking the chair next to her.

Abbie sat on her other side and gave Jess a sympathetic smile before leaning in. "Luca told her this morning he's going to ask Natasha to marry him."

"Oh, Jess. I'm sorry." I reached over and rubbed her arm, swapping a helpless look with Abbie.

"That's not even all of it," Jess said, rolling her eyes towards the ceiling.

"It gets worse?" I asked.

Abbie tilted her head from side to side. "Eh."

"Oh my God!" Jess groaned. "Don't pretend like this isn't the most revolting news you've heard in years." She took a sip of her drink.

Abbie spared Jess an exasperated look. "Logan's coming back for the wedding," she explained.

Jess scoffed, choking on her cocktail. "He's coming back for *six weeks*. A wedding only takes a day. They've organised it this way just to annoy me."

"They have not," Abbie disagreed. "Stop being melodramatic. Luca and Logan are best mates, so *of course*, he's coming home for the wedding. He'll be the best man, obviously, and Luca will want him around for the planning. Plus, he's married, for Christ's sake! Logan's a proper grown-up, which is more than I can say for us. He'll be way past all that childish bullshit, I promise you."

I did my best to follow the conversation, but in the end, I had to ask. "What's the problem with Logan?"

Jess rolled her eyes as Abbie laughed. "Nothing! He's fantastic. He and Frost just … rub each other the wrong way."

Jess's eyebrows climbed higher and higher. "He spent every spare moment he had, from the minute we started kindergarten to the day he left for London, tormenting me."

"Logan's a bully?" I asked, confused.

Jess opened her mouth, but Abbie got in first. "*No*. Jess gives as good as she gets. They have a love-hate kind of relationship."

"Tolerate-hate might be more accurate," Jess mumbled around the cocktail glass at her lips.

"Whatever you want to call it, he'll be back soon." Abbie clapped her hands and smiled. "It'll be good to have the crew back together again."

"Yeah. I can't wait." Jess got to her feet, taking her empty glass with her. "I'm having one more. Anyone else?"

"We're good," I said, waving her away. "Josh is at the bar right now."

"I'm so sorry. I'm a terrible friend!" Jess wrapped her arms around my neck. "I'm so happy for you and Josh. You're lucky to have found each other, and I'm glad you're staying in the Bay. Welcome home, Jones."

"Thanks, Frost. Things are going to work out for you, too."

She straightened and scrunched her shoulders. "We'll see."

Josh returned with our drinks, and the rest of the afternoon passed in a blur of well wishes and congratulations. Isaac barrelled at us both, scooping me up in a hug and twirling me about wildly enough that I laughed until I lost my breath. I stumbled a little when he set me on my feet, but Josh was there to steady me. I could get used to the sensation of his hand on my back, his arm around my waist, his broad chest always close by.

"Careful, Greene," Josh pretended to grumble.

Isaac laughed. "She's tough." He punched me playfully on the shoulder and threw me a wink. "Going to fit right in around here."

I really liked this big, dark bear of a man.

Kate and Raelene sought us out for hugs of their own, and once the congratulations were out of the way, they raved about the images I'd emailed them earlier in the week.

"Thank you so much for all your work," Raelene said as I wondered if she was ever going to let go of my hand. "I posted a few on social media, and I've had people ask me about you. I gave your name to the head chef at Pepperberry Hill. Do you know it?" When I shook my head, she went on. "It's a family estate about half an hour north-west, with a vineyard and winery, and the most incredible restaurant. Jacob might be in touch in a few days. I hope that's okay?"

I thought about the resignation letter I'd already given to Summer and how I'd need to work double-time on my business if I had any hope of replacing my income. "Yes, that's fantastic. Thank you."

"My pleasure."

She gave me another kiss on the cheek, and Kate did the same, and finally, Josh and I had a moment to ourselves. He dragged me into a corner and watched the room from under a hooded brow.

"I can't wait another minute to get that dress off you," he said, his voice low and husky, and I felt a warm throb between my legs. "What would you say to sneaking out of here?"

"I say, yes. Please. A million times, yes."

He grinned, swept his eyes over the room one last time, and took my hand. Scooting around the walls to the door, he opened it just enough to slip out into the hallway, but I paused to look back, not caring if someone saw me and objected to us leaving. I didn't think they would—the party was too far gone for many people to still be sober enough to care if we stayed or left—but I needed to take it all in one last time. The balloons and the streamers. The half-eaten wedding cake and the shoes strewn around the floor while people danced barefoot. The empty wine glasses and wadded-up napkins, the music and the laughter and the friendly chaos. Abbie and Will flirting over the bar. Isaac twirling Jess under one arm on the dance floor. Luca and Natasha dancing beside them. Jack and Maz sipping coffee under the window and gossiping with Dawn.

And above it all, the banner on the wall with my name on it. I was home. These were my friends. I stepped into the hall and kissed the back of Josh's hand.

And this was my family.

34

JOSH

I ALMOST RAN up the street, pulling Emily along behind me. She laughed the whole way, so I didn't think about slowing down. I needed her out of that tiny red dress, in bed, and underneath me immediately. But she'd be keeping her heels on. My dick had been hard on and off for the last four hours, and the thought of waiting another minute to be inside her was unbearable. I growled at the delay, and Emily laughed louder. I stopped, spun around, and pretended to glare at her.

"What's so funny?"

She looked up at me, delight dancing across her face, and my heart nearly burst clear out of my chest. "You," she said.

I scrunched up my nose as I smiled and leaned in to kiss her—and missed. One minute she was right there underneath my mouth, and the next, she was flailing and falling.

"What the hell?" I exclaimed.

She landed on her arse first, then collapsed onto the ground, holding an ankle with one hand, her stomach with another, and gasping between laughs. "Oh my God. I think my knees buckled. You've got to dial down the gorgeous, Ford."

Hearing that name on her tongue did funny things to my stomach. Good things. Things I wanted to feel for the rest of my life.

I crouched down to check her. "I can't believe you've been practically running in those shoes for ten minutes, and you fall over standing still. Here, let me examine you." I put my fingers to her foot, felt my way over her ankle, and I couldn't stop there. I grazed my hands over her calves, around her knee. Up her thigh, higher and higher, teasing the edge of her panties before sliding one finger inside the fabric and sweeping it over her wet, warm seam.

"Oh, God," she moaned.

I pulled out, appeased to know she wanted me as much as I needed her, and pressed more firmly on her ankle. She hissed in a sharp breath.

"Any numbness or tingling?" I asked.

"No, just pain where you touched it."

"Good news, young lady. I think it's just a twist."

"Is that your professional opinion, Mr Ford?"

"It is." I slid an arm under her legs and the other around her waist, then lifted her as I got to my feet.

"And what's the bad news?"

"I'm going to have to carry you home, put you into bed,

take off all your clothes, and spend the rest of the night making you feel better."

She widened her eyes. "Are you sure you're a paramedic? That doesn't sound like any treatment for a sprained ankle that I've ever heard of."

"I'm beginning to think I'm wasted in the job," I replied, starting up the street. I couldn't get over the warmth of her body against mine, and I revelled in the opportunity to take care of her, protect her, love her in all the ways she deserved.

"Then what else are you going to do with your life?" she asked, sensing the serious undertone of our banter.

"I don't know yet, but I'm going to start by making you happy."

Emily snuggled in closer, and I tightened my arms around her. "My hero," she mumbled into my chest, then she giggled. "Do you know what this reminds me of?"

"The first time we met," I said immediately.

"You sure know how to knock a girl off her feet."

Inhaling the vanilla fragrance of her hair at every other step, we reached her building and I climbed the stairs to her apartment. She fished her keys out of her bag and handed them to me, so I had to balance her and unlock the door at the same time. As I crossed the threshold with Emily in my arms, I felt her tense a little. The moment wasn't lost on me either.

"Day one, today," I whispered, touching my lips to the tip of her nose.

"Day one, today," she echoed.

Dropping the keys on the table and kicking the door closed behind us, I carried her straight to the bedroom, laid her on the bed, and knelt over her, pulling the short sleeves of her red dress over her shoulders and down her arms. My lips were never far from her body as I peeled back the layers of fabric between her skin and mine, and as soon as another inch of her was revealed, I pressed my mouth to it. I sucked and nibbled and moaned as she trembled and writhed beneath me, but then she put her hands to my face, pushing me back just far enough that she could stare into my eyes. Hers were green pools of invitation, and I wanted to lose myself in them forever.

"Thank you," she said.

"For what?"

She shrugged a little. "For letting me love you and for loving me back."

Her kisses grew deeper, more needy, and I was only too happy to respond. I was going to spend the rest of the night showing Emily Jones just how much I loved her, but first, I had to share another secret. The last one I'd ever keep from her.

"I'm the one who has to thank you," I said.

Her lips quirked in a tiny smile. "For what?"

"For rescuing me."

She brushed her nose against mine. "I didn't do that. You rescued yourself."

I kissed her eyelids, her jaw, her neck, her mouth. "Maybe, in the end, we rescued each other."

ONE YEAR LATER

EMILY

"OKAY, MRS ATTARD," I said. "If you could do something to soothe the piglets a little, I should be able to get a few good frames in the last five minutes of our session."

Evelyn pulled a dirty old blanket from her bag of pet supplies and tucked it around the three little pigs arranged in the tiny timber barrel. They snuffed their noses into it and rolled happily around each other, and when she slipped them a couple of apple slices, I snapped them with my camera from as many angles as I could manage. When I was satisfied there'd be at least two or three images I could pull from the last set-up, I put the camera down and grinned.

"I think we're done! These are going to turn out great. Would you mind if I used some of these shots on my social feeds?"

"Oh, not at all." Evelyn started scooping up the pigs, easing collars over their necks and clipping on their leads. "I'm so glad Dr Hobbes suggested it. What a clever woman you are to do all of this."

"Thanks, Mrs A."

I looked around at the white walls of my photographic studio off Main Street, where samples of my work hung all around. I'd tried a lot of different things over the past year. There were plenty of pictures of newborns wrapped tight as beans and balanced in buckets. And there was a whole section devoted to food and wine, thanks to a dozen or so restaurants in the region who used me for promotional campaigns. Another wall was covered in my commercial and retail work for small businesses in and around the Bay. Pet photography was a relatively new feather in my cap, starting six weeks ago when Summer began suggesting to clients at her vet clinic that they come see me about taking pictures of their fur babies.

As I helped Evelyn wrangle the piglets and hang all the bags she'd brought with her over her shoulders, a little bell rang as the front door opened. I turned to greet my new customer but stalled and smiled as Josh slipped inside, eyeing the piglets and biting back a grin.

"Good afternoon, Mrs Attard," he said. "How did the shoot go?"

"Just wonderful," she exclaimed, beaming. "Emily here has a way with them." She scratched one of the little things under its chin. "Hamlet here loves her."

Josh choked back a laugh. "Hamlet?"

"Yes." Evelyn indicated one pig at a time as she gave their names. "Hamlet, Henry, and Hermione."

"*Ham*let. Really?"

"Yes." She looked confused now and a little annoyed. "Why? What's so funny?"

Josh cleared his throat, and I busied myself with some paperwork so she wouldn't catch me grinning. "Nothing. Great names, Mrs A."

"I'll have the images ready for you by the end of next week," I interrupted. "I'll let you know when you can pop in to collect the prints."

"Oh! I can't wait to see them. I'll see you then."

Josh and I watched through the glass walls of the studio front as Evelyn walked the piglets down the street. Once she was gone from sight, we burst into laughter.

"Oh my God," I said, wiping my eyes. "Hamlet. She really has no idea."

Josh wrapped his arms around my waist and lifted me up for a kiss. "Always knew you were a pig whisperer."

His mouth on mine was a warm, wet trip to heaven, and I wanted nothing more than to melt into him, but this close, I was all too aware of his damp shirt, his dirty hands, and the smell of sweat and grass on his skin.

"Ew! You're filthy."

He chuckled and burrowed his face into my neck. When I squirmed to get free, his arms tightened around me, and I felt him harden against my hip. "I thought you liked me filthy." I squealed and laughed as he ran his tongue around my earlobe, but then he put me on my feet. "Sorry. I just finished the job over on Hillcrest Drive and wanted to see you on my way home. We're still on for drinks with the crew at The Stop tonight, right?"

"Yes, but I won't be there until later. The tourism council hired me for three hours during the Valentine's Day festival tonight. I have to make my way around most of the town and photograph as much as I can."

He groaned. "I didn't think the place could get worse than it was last year, but it's pink on steroids. Thank God Will stood up to the decorating committee again. We need a place safe from all the insanity. Balls of steel on that man."

I laughed and patted his arm, then contemplated skipping the festivities altogether and spending all night in bed together. Josh's shoulders had grown harder and his body more mouth-watering over the past twelve months, what with all the manual labour he'd been doing. His time was split evenly now between part-time paramedic shifts, studying for his landscape architecture degree, and building an outdoor design business that would one day— we hoped—be his full-time job. He was more bronzed than I'd ever seen him, his hair longer and lighter, and I couldn't get enough of that grin on his face.

"Three hours, that's it," I promised. "I'll start around five and meet you at the bar just after eight. We'll have one, maybe two quick drinks and then … we're going home and taking things very, very slowly."

He dropped a kiss on my mouth and dug his fingers into my hips. "Maybe we skip the quick drinks and go straight to the slow parts."

"I'm up for that."

He dragged his mouth away from mine with a sigh. "No can do. We promised everyone we'd be there." He backed away, staring down at me with that crooked smile I could feel in my underwear. "I'll see you at The Stop at eight-thirty, and don't be late."

JOSH

I FIDGETED WITH the collar on my shirt, twisted the glass on the bar in front of me, rubbed my fingers over the shape of a small box in the pocket of my jeans, and checked the time. It was twenty minutes past eight. Emily would be here any minute. I took a sip of my beer and wiped my brow.

"Chill, Ford." Abbie nudged me with her shoulder. "Everything will be perfect. Our girl is head over heels for you."

"Does everyone know what to do?" I asked for the millionth time.

Abbie rolled her eyes and stood on the rung of her bar stool. She cupped her hands around her mouth and shouted, "Do we all know what to do?"

The fifty-odd people sitting around The Stop yelled back, "Yes!" and I waved them down, staring daggers at Abbie. "You want to ruin this before it even begins?"

"She just sent me a text, and she's at least five minutes away. It's under control."

I blew out a breath and ignored Abbie. Her confidence was grating on my nerves. Five minutes, that was all I had to wait.

I knew the moment Emily walked in because an unusual hush fell over the bar. Had I not been waiting for it, I probably wouldn't have noticed, and Emily didn't seem to sense anything odd. The conversation started up again, the band played on in the background, and she walked over to me. She must have gone home and changed because she was in her little black playsuit with the heels I liked. My favourite thing to see her in, and she knew it.

My eyes were glued to her as she hopped up onto the bar stool next to me. "You look gorgeous," I murmured in her ear.

"You like it?" Her eyes sparkled because she knew my answer.

"I like you in it."

Abbie stood again, this time to lean over the bar. "Hey! Babe! A glass of pinot grigio for Jones, here!"

Will, down at the other end of the bar, raised his hand to wave hello to Emily, then he spared an eye-roll for Abbie. She scrunched her nose up at him and winked.

"How are things out there tonight?" Abbie asked, sipping her cocktail and shuddering ostentatiously. "I've managed to avoid the most offensive parts of town."

Emily shrugged, and the apples of her cheeks turned pink. "It's not that bad. Kind of romantic, actually. Lots of happy people in love. Men winning stuffed animals for their girls. Flowers everywhere. The park is covered in fairy lights, and there's a jazz band playing. The food markets are unreal." She leaned in, and both Abbie and I bowed our heads towards hers. "I saw Noa out there manning a tapas stall for The Stop. Guess Will wanted in on the action after all."

We all looked over at Will and he grinned sheepishly, raising his hands.

There was a pause in the conversation, and I threw Abbie a look. She bounced off her chair immediately and announced, "I'll be back in a minute."

As she disappeared, I wondered if she could be more obvious.

Will handed Emily her wine, then darted away to serve other customers, and I raised my glass to hers. She clinked it gently.

"Do you remember Valentine's Day last year?" I asked.

She took a sip of her wine. "How could I forget it?"

"You know, the only reason I came that night was because I hoped you'd be here."

Her smile said she was pleased. "That's funny. I only came because I wanted to see you."

I looked surreptitiously over my shoulder. The place was slowly, carefully emptying out. Abbie darted around like a mother hen, directing traffic and clearing everyone out of the room.

"So, I thought that, in a way, Valentine's Day might be our anniversary."

Her grin got wider. "I like that idea."

"A year since this crazy ride started."

"A year since I fell in love with you," she corrected, and my chest tightened. I had to ask now, or my heart might actually explode.

"It wasn't much of a proposal, though, or an engagement. No wedding in the end."

Emily put a hand on my thigh. "I wouldn't change a thing. It got us here, didn't it?"

"I suppose it did." Will saluted me from behind the bar, then slipped through the back door, and I cleared my throat. "We sat right here, on these chairs."

"I suppose we did …" She looked around and noticed for the first time that the bar was empty. "Hey, where is everyone?"

"I held your hand and told one man you were mine, but I got it all backwards and didn't ask you first." I pulled the box from my pocket, and her head jerked to my hand, to my face, and back again around the bar. I tried not to smile at her confusion as I pushed off the stool and dropped to one knee. "Tonight is my chance to do things right." I cracked open the box to reveal an oval-cut diamond solitaire, and she gasped. It was similar to the aquamarine one she still wore on her finger, only larger and more *real*—not the gem, but the intention. "Emily Jones, will you marry me and let me be yours forever?"

She fell off her chair and onto the floor next to me, throwing her arms around my neck. "Yes! Yes! Yes!"

I exhaled with relief, then took her hand and removed

the plain white gold band on her left ring finger. I'd already made a promise to her a year ago, and in some ways, our *One Day, Today* was as much of a vow as we'd ever need to make to one another, but I wanted this woman as my wife, and I wanted her to know it. I wanted the world to know it.

I slipped the plain band onto her right hand, next to the aquamarine ring, and she laughed. "You have to stop giving me rings. I'll run out of fingers soon."

I kissed the place where I was about to add the diamond, then slipped it on. "Looks good."

She shifted her hand under the light, throwing sparkles into the air. "It does."

I stood, pulling us both to our feet, then cradled her head between my hands and kissed her. She latched onto my shirt, and we lost ourselves for a moment. I picked her up and set her on the bar, and she locked her ankles around my waist.

"Maybe we should take this home," she panted, then she looked around again and frowned. "Where the hell is everybody?"

I kissed her one last time, light and slow on her top lip, then the bottom, then picked her up and set her on her feet. Taking a hand, I led her up the stairs to the party rooms on the second floor and stopped outside the closed door.

"I hope you don't mind," I said, "but everyone wanted to celebrate."

I pushed open the door, and nearly a hundred voices screamed at us. Bodies and arms rushed in to capture us in hugs and cover us with kisses, and soon Emily was swept away by a knot of enthusiastic women exclaiming over her ring. I watched her go and just stood there, half-stunned, staring at the banner attached to the wall. In faded lettering, it read, "Josh + Emily + Valentine Bay = Forever!" And underneath, "Day One = Today." In clearer text, someone had scrawled, "Congratulations!"

As someone shoved a beer into my hand and I absently acknowledged the claps on my back, I searched Emily out, and our eyes met across the room. She laughed, and my stomach flipped. Fuck, she was beautiful.

"I love you," I mouthed at her.

"I love you," she said right back.

BONUS SCENE

———

Psst! There's a little more to Josh and Emily's story
(and it might involve surfing and babies).
Do you want to know what it is?

Use the QR code to sign up to the Samantha Leigh
LoveLeigh List and you'll get a link for the
Ready For You bonus scene delivered to your inbox!

UP NEXT: MEANT FOR YOU

Do you want to see the sparks fly when Jessica Frost faces Logan Reeve, her ex's best friend and childhood enemy? Here's what you're in for ...

He's my ex's best friend. The man I love to hate.
A total temptation who is totally off-limits.
And he's everywhere I turn.

My life's a disaster. My ex-boyfriend is getting married, my house is falling apart, and I haven't slept with anyone in ... Well, long enough that I'm not sure I remember where everything is supposed to go.

The last person I'd ever ask for help is my childhood enemy, Logan Reeve. He's smug. He's infuriating. He's gorgeous. And lately, he's caught me in one too many weak moments. A cocky carpenter who knows how to work a sledgehammer, Logan promises he can renovate my house before my parents sell it out from under me.

I can't deny it. Logan's got the skills I need to turn things around—in life and in the bedroom.

I'm craving some old-fashioned action, and Logan is always—irritatingly—*there*. As the tension takes us dangerously close to a line we shouldn't cross, we find ourselves flirting with forbidden territory. Flirting, flirting … until finally, we fall.

Why does it feel so good when it's so, so bad?

It won't last. Nobody can ever know. There's nothing real between us, right? Logan Reeve was never meant for me.

But one thing I know for sure. The man I can't have loves nothing more than proving me wrong.

Meant For You *is a first-person, dual POV contemporary romance with lots of steam and a satisfying happily ever after.*

ACKNOWLEDGEMENTS

Writing romance is all sorts of fun, and at the same time totally terrifying. I'm first and foremost a reader, so I have a long list of authors I adore. Putting this book out into the world feels a little like asking for a seat at the cool table, and I've never been good in social situations.

But if there's one thing I've learned so far, perhaps the most important lesson, it's that the romance community—the readers *and* the writers—are almost without exception kind and generous and welcoming to all, even new authors like me. Discovering there's pocket of the world that values happily ever afters above all else has made writing this book worth the hard times a thousand times over, no matter how many people end up reading my words.

Thank you to my husband for your endless patience. You've supported my hours in front of the screen and obsession with creating a life that fits, and if there was ever a real-life example of my dream book boyfriend, you're it. You are my everything. Always.

Shay, you are the sweetest, smartest, most generous writing partner a girl could ask for. Thank you for your support, your insights, and your endless patience. I don't know how this journey would go without you.

To the team who helped me put this book together: Dawn A, Kate, Dawn M, Gina, Brandi, and Savannah. Thank you for all your brilliant work, your willingness to answer my questions, and your support over the months it's taken me to get here.

And to Gina especially, thank you for every time you picked me up when I fell—and there have been a lot of stumbles along the way! I feel very fortunate to have found you.

Thank you to all those clever, generous, talented women bunkered down in that super-special corner of the internet where romance writers help each other for no other reason than they've been there, done that, and they want to pay it forward. It's my sincere hope that I'll be in your position one day, and I'll know enough to help someone who is finding their way, like I was not so long ago.

And finally, thank *you*, for taking a chance on this book and on me.

ABOUT THE AUTHOR

Samantha Leigh is an Australian author who writes steamy contemporary romance. Her first series is set in a fictional small beach-side town called Valentine Bay, and because she's the writer and it's within her power to do so, she filled the Bay with a disproportionate number of divine, dirty-talking surfers. It's a hard job, but someone has to do it, right?

Writing is Sam's happy place so it's hard to tear herself away from the keyboard, but when she's not playing matchmaker in imaginary worlds, she's reading books with all the feels and all the spice. In the tiny slices of time she has between all the word wrangling, Sam likes to hit her yoga mat, go for walks in the bush or on the beach, continue her search for the perfect poke bowl, drown herself in coffee and hot cacao, and binge-watch bad television.

samanthaleighbooks.com

Made in the USA
Las Vegas, NV
15 August 2023

76140163R00198